THE HOLIDAY WIFE

"About the divorce . . ." Maddie started, her voice trailing off as she realized she had no idea how she planned to finish the sentence. She had been Mrs. Maddie Davis for most of her adult life. She didn't want it to end. But she was going to have to give up the right to the name. She'd never really had it anyway. She had just been borrowing it.

"Yes?" Warner prompted.

"I don't know. I just wanted to say that . . . I guess it won't be any problem to get one, right?"

"It should be easy. The process seems pretty straightforward," he told her.

"And so, then what?" Maddie couldn't resist asking. "Are you planning to propose right away?"

"Maybe." When she looked at him disapprovingly, he added, "Probably. I'm thirty-three years old, Maddie. It's time I settled down."

"Fine," Maddie said soothingly. "I'm all for it. I just don't think you should rush into . . . anything."

"This, from the woman who is out the door the second a guy even says he likes you. You are not exactly the first person I'd go to for advice about relationships," Warner said.

"I'm not—" M_____ ying that I think you _____

"I've thought, _____

BOOK YOUR PLACE ON OUR WEBSITE AND MAKE THE ARABESQUE ROMANCE CONNECTION!

We've created a customized website just for our very special Arabesque readers, where you can get the inside scoop on everything that's going on with Arabesque romance novels.

When you come online, you'll have the exciting opportunity to:

- View covers of upcoming books

- Learn about our future publishing schedule (listed by publication month and author)

- Find out when your favorite authors will be visiting a city near you

- Search for and order backlist books

- Check out author bios and background information

- Send e-mail to your favorite authors

- Join us in weekly chats with authors, readers and other guests

- Get writing guidelines

- AND MUCH MORE!

Visit our website at
http://www.arabesquebooks.com

THE HOLIDAY WIFE

Roberta Gayle

ARABESQUE

BOOKS

BET Publications, LLC
http://www.bet.com
http://www.arabesquebooks.com

ARABESQUE BOOKS are published by

BET Publications, LLC
c/o BET BOOKS
One BET Plaza
1900 W Place NE
Washington, DC 20018-1211

All Kensington Titles, Imprints, and Distributed Lines are available at special quantity discounts for bulk purchases for sales promotions, premiums, fund-raising, and educational or institutional use. Special book excerpts or customized printings can also be created to fit specific needs. For details, write or phone the office of the Kensington special sales manager: Kensington Publishing Corp., 850 Third Avenue, New York, NY 10022, attn: Special Sales Department, Phone: 1-800-221-2647.

BET Books is a trademark of Black Entertainment Television, Inc. ARABESQUE, the ARABESQUE logo, and the BET BOOKS logo are trademarks and registered trademarks.

First Printing: October 2003

10 9 8 7 6 5 4 3 2 1

Printed in the United States of America

ACKNOWLEDGMENTS

I would like, as always, to thank my mother, Ollie Cohen, without whom I would be lost. She is my inspiration, and my proofreader, and when she drives me crazy, she does it in the nicest way.

Thank you, Mom.

LABOR DAY
WEEKEND

CHAPTER ONE

Cairo sizzled under the September sun. Maddie welcomed the heat after the long, cold year she had spent working at the British Museum in London, England. The dust didn't bother her too much, either. It was a minor inconvenience and it was well worth it to be back in Egypt again. She was working an hour from the great pyramids at Giza. She had a view of the Nile out of her apartment window. This was her dream. She would put up with a lot to be here.

She walked down the street, somewhat accustomed already to the strange odors of the food sold by the street vendors and to the bizarre street traffic, both vehicular and human. The men in their turbans and western suits cluttered streets peppered with the black chadors and more colorful hijabs of the women. She could almost ignore the mix of bicycles, limousines, motor scooters, tiny little economy cars, and small three-wheeled delivery trucks, but she didn't suppose she would ever completely get used to the sight of the women in their burkas.

This was a very cosmopolitan city, even with its ancient origins omnipresent in day-to-day life. One never forgot, in Cairo, the nearness of the river, the deserts, and the great archeological treasures. It was not only in the interest of promoting tourism that the billboards featured gorgeous photos of Giza at sunset, and the Bedouins in their romantic garb. It was the pride that the Egyptians took in their heritage that caused them to keep their past not only alive but also very much present in the city's architecture, and advertising. And in the academic world—Maddie's world—the ancients still walked. She traveled back in time, every day, to that long-ago culture. Then she awakened, to find herself in this modern city of Cairo in the twenty-first century. Still, contemporary Egyptian society felt a bit backward to Maddie because of the Moslem custom of hiding women's bodies, and their faces, under yards of black material and behind scarves. Despite that jarring note, or perhaps because of it, it was a sight she couldn't get enough of and Maddie almost regretted going inside to her musty office on a day like this.

But work called, and she eagerly ascended the steps of the university, and went into the building, picking up her mail from her little cubbyhole on her way past the scarred wooden countertop that formed the reception/administrative offices of the university's Department of Antiquities. When she reached her office, she unwound the hijab from around her face and head and hung it on its hook behind the door before she made her way to her desk.

Head scarf and all, she loved living in this city: primarily because of her position at the University of Cairo. She was fascinated by the cartonnage she'd been hired to translate. Trying to make sense out of the ancient papyrus was satisfying, if slow, work and Maddie was already certain that it was going to reveal more about the life and times of the man who had written it, or had it written, than she had even anticipated. In 200 B.C., when a merchant ship sailed, it had apparently been the custom for the ship's manifest to include not only the items that were stored in the ship's hold, but also a proposed rate of exchange for the goods. Reading about the cloth of cotton and silk, the tapestries and spices, the jewels and other treasures that were transported between the east and the west, Maddie pictured the merchant slowly sailing out to sea, and returning from his voyage, triumphant. She felt as though there were a bond between herself and the author of the document she was slowly deciphering. He wanted her to understand that world. She would happily spend the next year trying to oblige.

Maddie had been in Egypt for a little over two months, and she already felt pretty much at home. When she arrived, in July, Maddie suffered from a pretty severe case of culture shock. The Egyptian people were so different from the British, and her Egyptian colleagues were so different from the distinguished and austere gentlemen and women whom she worked with at the British Museum, that she sometimes wondered if she would ever establish herself as one of them.

It helped that she'd spent a summer at a dig here in the Valley of the Kings, in '95. Also, Cairo University had a long history of educating women while trying not to flout Moslem tradition concerning what women could and could not do, so the administration was not unsympathetic to the difficulties she faced in trying to adjust to her colleagues, her living quarters, and her status as an unmarried female foreigner, and they did their best to guide her. She was certainly more circumspect in her behavior here than she had been in London. She had to be. Her colleagues in England had all been academics of a certain class, and so they were uptight and sometimes pompous, but they accepted her, anyway, despite their disapproval of her flamboyant personality, because they appreciated her intellect, and her achievements. She might have been treated as a bit of an outsider, but at least, in London, she had understood the rules.

Fortunately, when Maddie felt frustrated, or just plain lonely, she could always retreat into her work. That was what she had come to Egypt for, and it was enough, more than enough, to make up for all of the minor annoyances she had to deal with as a woman, and as a foreigner. The only insoluble dilemma that she faced was the ceaseless barrage of inquiries from the government concerning her status at the university as a research assistant. At first, it had merely been a nuisance, but as the requests for verification of her credentials, salary, and employment continued to show up in her mailbox day after day, Maddie had grown frustrated with all the bureaucratic hoops that the Egyptian government seemed determined she had to jump through. She had received not only the usual tax and other resident-alien forms, but also detailed inquiries about her financial situation, with attendant forms— in triplicate—to be signed by her employers, as well as by officials at the American embassy. It seemed they questioned the authenticity of her visa, her fellowship, even her identity.

When she found the letter with the Pennsylvania postmark in the upper left-hand corner mixed in with the small pile of interoffice communiques, academic journals, and mail order catalogues, Maddie looked at the neatly typed return address with a feeling akin to nostalgia. After all of the official-looking missives she'd received from the Egyptian authorities, any mail that didn't come from a government office was a breath of fresh air. She was surprised to see that it was from Alton Emerson, who was an old friend of the family, as well as the family lawyer. Though he had never written to her before, the arrival of the letter didn't set off any mental alarms. Any news from home was a treat. He could have been writing about anything . . . probably to complain about her mother. Janet Delaney's exploits constantly got her into trouble. As the only truly rational member of her family, Maddie was usually the one everyone turned to when things got out of hand. If the lawyer was contacting her, chances were her mother had done something really outrageous this time. Still, she thought, as she inserted the letter opener into the envelope, news from home—no matter what it was about—was better than another request from the authorities for "further information" about the Fellowship that paid her salary.

"So, Mommy, what are you up to now?" she said aloud as she unfolded and flattened the slim piece of elegant, mist gray stationery. Whether it contained good news, or bad, any mail from anyone that wasn't a petty government bureaucrat had to be a welcome relief, Maddie thought. That was, until she actually read the letter.

"Ted, I really need your help with this," Maddie pleaded with her younger brother.

"I don't see what I can do, I'm sorry," Ted answered. The buzzing that came through the receiver of the ancient black rotary telephone made it difficult for her to be sure, but Maddie thought she heard sincere regret in his tone. "You know how Mom felt about Great-Aunt Becky" was his excuse.

"The black magic thing? She can't still be harping on that. Not now," Maddie exclaimed in disbelief.

"Why not?" Ted said. "If Mom was right and Great-Aunt Becky really was a witch, she can say whatever she wants to about her now. There's no danger." Maddie thought she heard a note of derision in his voice as he answered, but the connection wasn't exactly crystal clear. She couldn't be sure, and she preferred to think she imagined it. It was disrespectful for her brother to speak so flippantly about Rebecca Tanner's passing.

"I can't believe she's gone," Maddie said.

"Yeah, well . . ." He cleared his throat, and she could picture him, fiddling with the phone cord, as hopeless as ever when it came to expressing what he really felt.

"Mom would never speak ill of the dead," Maddie continued. "I thought she believed that the spirits of the dead could hear you or something."

"Maybe she does, but . . . you know Mom. She's never been normal about Aunt Becky. A little thing like the woman's death isn't going to stop her from saying whatever she feels. And she doesn't think it's over yet. She's still afraid of that old lady."

"Oh, come on, Ted. *You* don't believe that nonsense?" Maddie replied, exasperated.

"Hey, what do I know?" he retorted, but even through the static and hum of the transatlantic phone line, Maddie knew that he wasn't as unaffected as he pretended by the tragedy.

Maddie was still in shock. It didn't feel real to her. When she was home at Christmastime, her great-aunt seemed fine. They celebrated New Year's Eve together. Her friends thought she was nuts to spend the best party night of the year with an elderly woman, but Maddie told them, "There is no one wilder than my Great-Aunt Becky." The lady had more energy than her five teenage grandchildren.

Maddie wasn't sorry she had already missed the funeral. She preferred to remember Becky the way she was the last time she'd seen her; dressed in black chiffon, champagne in hand, telling stories about the men she might have married and the life she might have had—if she'd been born just a few decades later. If she knew her time was coming to an end, Great-Aunt Becky didn't give any indication of it that night. She said she loved the life she made for herself, but she also said she wished that she'd been just a tad more like her great-niece . . . independent and unfettered. Most importantly, she told her great-niece that she should never give in to the pressure that anyone put on her to conform.

"Never let anybody try to stop you from chasing your dreams," Great-Aunt Becky advised. "You've got a heck of an imagination, girl, and you've got a responsibility to live up to it."

"Were you at the services?" Maddie asked Ted.

"Everyone was. That's when Alton told us Rebecca requested that the whole family be present for the reading of the will," he answered. "Mom was not pleased."

Maddie knew that that condition was directed specifically at her. The rest of the family lived within a half hour's drive of the tiny town where she had grown up, and where her parents and Great-Aunt Becky still lived.

Had lived. Up until her death ten days ago.

She felt tears welling up again, and she quickly swiped at her eyes and nose with a tissue. She could cry later. Maddie needed to stay focused on the problem of her inheritance now. "Do you have any idea what she might have left me, or why?" she asked him, baffled.

"I don't have a clue," her brother answered. "And I don't think anyone else does either. Here, Mom wants to talk to you."

"No, Ted, I—" Maddie started to protest, but knew it was useless even before she heard her mother's voice.

"Hi, honey, how are you?" Janet Delaney asked blithely.

"Hi, Mom." She should have known better than to call Ted at her mother's place. She had only chosen to call him during the family's Sunday dinner because it was the one place she knew she could catch him at home, but as she listened to her mother, she realized it was a big mistake. Her second, actually. She *should* have known better than to call anyone in her immediate family. They were all completely under the influence of her mother and therefore susceptible to her looney ideas, such as her conviction that her aunt, Rebecca Tanner, was a witch.

"Are you there?" Janet's voice echoed over the transatlantic phone line.

"Yeah, Mom. I'm here," Maddie said.

Janet barely waited for the words to leave her mouth. "Honey, I saw a television show the other day about a woman who was stoned over there."

"Here? In Cairo?"

"I'm not sure. I think maybe it was in Riyadh."

"That's in Saudi Arabia, Mom. That's a whole other country."

"But they have the same thing there, don't they?

This was a girl who was raped and someone in her own family killed her."

"Mom, it's too hard to explain this to you over the phone. I promise no one is going to stone me. Certainly no one in the family."

"Oh, well, I guess we could talk about it later. But be careful, okay?"

"Definitely, I'll write," Maddie promised, and she meant it. It probably wouldn't make a bit of difference, but she'd try again to explain to her mother about the attitudes toward women here. As a Western woman in a metropolis like Cairo, she knew there was little chance that anyone would attack her. Those who disapproved of her tended to ignore her. Not that that wasn't annoying. They acted as if she didn't exist, as if they couldn't see or hear her. But that wasn't the kind of ill treatment that her mother was worried about. Her mother had been nervous when Maddie first accepted the offer from the University of Cairo, because Janet's perception of Middle Eastern countries was all tied up with the events of September 11th. The very word Moslem had become a source of unease to her, despite her admiration of many black activists of the sixties, including Malcolm X, who had accepted the religion.

"I heard somewhere that girls don't even go to school over there," Janet told her daughter, at the time.

"Women have been studying at Cairo University since early in the century, Mom," Maddie explained. The atrocities committed in the name of religion were political, and cultural, and that kind of blind fanaticism was not likely to touch her at all in the rarefied atmosphere of the university, she insisted. But her assurances had not made her mother feel any better. She made Maddie promise to call her every other week.

Maddie had befriended some of the Arab women who taught at the university, and they were much more forward-thinking than her mother could ever imagine. If Mom could have met and spoken with these women, Maddie was sure she would find she actually had a lot in common with them. They wore their hijab as much to declare their feminism as to demonstrate their solidarity with their religion. As one female professor said, her clothing concealed her femininity so that she could appear to her colleagues, her students, her superiors, and her peers as a human, instead of as a woman.

Maddie knew that eventually she could make her mother understand. There wasn't much that she and Janet agreed about, but a woman's right to express herself, and to worship freely, were two matters about which they were in complete accord. She just had to convince her mother that the Koran did not advocate the oppression women suffered in this culture. She would write soon, she vowed to herself. She didn't need Janet to worry needlessly about her safety. Maddie had had enough of that, over the years.

"I was afraid something like this would happen," Janet said.

"I promise I'll be fine, Mom," Maddie said, thinking Janet was still talking about the stoning.

Janet quickly disabused her of that notion. "Ted just told me that Alton wrote to you about Becky's will." Mom had always tried to persuade her that she shouldn't listen to anything Rebecca Tanner told her. "That woman is poison," Mom said, more than once. "I can guarantee you that her advice is not what's best for you. She just wants to get you on her side." Maddie learned at an early age not to report to her mother the conversations she had with her great-aunt. She only spoke about her visits with Becky enough so that her mother didn't think that the two of them had any secrets.

Even that didn't always work. For instance, there was the time when Janet accused Rebecca of being a witch right at church, in front of the whole congregation. That day she had discovered that Maddie had told her great-aunt that she had gotten her first period before she informed her own mother. On another occasion, Mom told everyone not to eat the brownies that her aunt had baked for the school fund-raiser. She implied that they might be laced with something. She meant hemlock, or witch hazel, or some other herb, but the school principal thought she was talking about marijuana or perhaps opium, and promptly confiscated the tin of chocolate brownies.

Maddie had spent years trying to convince her mother that her accusations were unfounded, but it didn't have any effect. Her mother was absolutely positive that Becky was using black magic to try to bewitch her daughter. And even death hadn't changed that.

"It's clear she was even more powerful than I thought. Here I was thinking you were safe now that she's gone. I was always terrified of the influence she had over you all these years and I can't believe that old woman has reached back out of her grave to put one of her spells on you. I was scared when she was alive and now . . . I'm even more frightened for you, honey."

Maddie reminded herself that, ridiculous as they were, Janet's fears were very real to her. Even if the basis for it was imagined.

"You really don't need to worry about me, Mom. Great-Aunt Becky wouldn't hurt a soul."

"I don't think you should have anything to do with anything of hers. You can't see it, but she's still trying to bewitch you even from the next plane of existence. I'm going to put some arsenic powder on her grave just as soon as I get the chance."

"Oh, Mom," Maddie groaned. "Please don't start with that mess now. Let the woman rest in peace. Please."

"Maddie, I know you don't believe me, but I'm just trying to help you. It's my job to protect my children."

"Protect me from what, Mom? Great-Aunt Becky loved me. She loved you, too, even though you hadn't said a kind word to her in twenty or thirty years." When Maddie was asked to the junior prom during her sophomore year in high school, it was her great aunt that she went to for advice, makeup, and a much needed boost to her confidence. Rebecca Tanner gave her a bracelet of rhinestone and onyx that night. Maddie still wore it when she needed luck. When Maddie's mother heard about the date, she was not nearly as helpful as Becky had been. She was more worried about what *that witch* might have told Maddie than she was in bolstering her daughter's faltering confidence. Maddie felt like crying. Again. But she kept her emotions in check as she continued, "Mom, look, I have to go now. I'll call again soon, okay?"

"All right, honey. Take care," Janet said, as if they had just finished one of their usual bimonthly conversations.

Maddie couldn't believe she'd actually expected her mother to be reasonable. Why had she ever thought her Great-Aunt Becky's death might have altered Janet's perception of the harmless old woman? *That* would have made sense. Whereas Janet Delaney didn't have a sensible bone in her body. And she never changed her mind once it was made up.

Finally, Maddie decided to contact the lawyer for the estate, Alton Emerson, directly. Unfortunately, he told her he couldn't help her. "It would be unethical for me to do anything more than facilitate the delivery of your inheritance to you," he said firmly. She should have expected something like that. Like everyone else in Richland, Alton knew Maddie and everyone else in her family personally. He was probably afraid of what her mother might do or say.

But he had a more convincing argument. "If I were to do anything further, it might be perceived as a conflict of interest," he tried to explain. "My client's family is already upset that you were left such an important portion of your Great-Aunt's estate, Maddie," he said. Which just worried her more.

What could Aunt Becky have left her? She was almost afraid to find out.

But Maddie was stuck. She would have relinquished any claim to her late aunt's possessions, except for the fact that Becky's own children had already been upset, as the lawyer had told her, by the bequest. Under the circumstances, it seemed downright rude to refuse the inheritance before the will had even been read. Her cousins already felt that whatever she had inherited should have been left to someone in the family.

Her cousins' resentment was nothing new. They had never liked her much. She suspected they were jealous of her relationship with their mother. But she couldn't possibly compound the hurt they'd already suffered by refusing to accept whatever it was that Becky left her. She was going to have to find a different solution.

Unfortunately, Maddie couldn't figure out what that might be.

She was left with only one person to turn to for help. Her husband, Warner Davis. There was a problem with that, though. She hadn't been in contact with him for almost a year. And she already owed him. She hadn't repaid him for the last two or three favors he had done for her yet. She just couldn't call him. It was way too embarrassing.

LABOR DAY

CHAPTER TWO

"Are you going to be our daddy?" Sabrina asked, gazing up at Warner adoringly. Her big brown eyes dominated her cherubic face, and she knew how to use them to good effect. She was so cute, he was tempted to say yes, just to make her happy, but Warner resisted the urge.

"You already have a daddy, Bri," he reminded the five-year-old, careful to keep his tone neutral. Admittedly, her father was an idiot, but he was still out there, somewhere, and he could come back at any time. As much as Warner loved these kids, he knew they'd drop him like a ton of hot bricks if their dad came home. Which was just as it should be.

"Kendra has two daddies," Sabrina declared, still smiling sweetly as she waited for him to give her the answer she wanted. "Please," she added, expectantly. He couldn't blame her for being so persistent. It had worked for her so many times before. He almost always did give in to the irresistible little girl.

"Ummm," he mumbled, completely thrown off balance by her question.

"They share her. You could share me with my other daddy," Bri explained simply. That "other" sent a shiver down his spine.

It served Radu right, though, he supposed. Warner couldn't understand how his best friend could have left this beautiful little girl and his equally wonderful eight-year-old son, let alone his wife, Samantha. Warner had been trying to fill in for the s.o.b. for almost six months, and he grew closer and closer to both mother and children with every passing week.

"I don't think your daddy would like that," Warner replied. Let Radu get the blame for this at least.

Samantha had shielded the kids from the worst of his abandonment. When they asked questions about where he was, or why he left, she made excuses for him. "It's for the children's benefit, not his," she told Warner whenever the subject came up. "They don't need to know what an inconsiderate bastard he is. Not yet, anyway. They'll figure it out when they're older."

Radu had left, offering no explanation for his departure beyond a short note to his wife saying he had to figure out what he wanted to do with his life, and he hadn't contacted anyone in his family, or his best friend, since.

"Maybe you could be my dad just till he comes back," Sabrina pressed. "He's been gone a long time." She loved her father, despite his absence, which was yet another reason why Warner was quickly coming to the point where he wanted to find his old buddy and beat him to a pulp.

"Well, uh—" Warner stammered. He suspected Samantha would have known just what to say, but he didn't have an answer. None, at least, that both satisfied his need to be honest with the little girl and fulfilled her mother's wish that she be protected from the truth. He needed a diversion. "How about some ice cream?" he asked.

"Okay," Bri agreed cheerfully, apparently content to let the matter drop. For the moment. He suspected this reprieve wouldn't last. The tiny little heartbreaker had her mother's determination, as well as Samantha's charm. Bri didn't give up easily when she wanted something.

They walked toward a nearby ice cream vendor, Sabrina swinging lightly from his arm, humming to herself, as he wondered if he should tell her mother about her request, as well as the rest of the conversation. *Nah,* Warner thought. *No point in bringing up the question . . . until it comes up naturally.* Surprisingly, the prospect was not an unattractive one. He was ready to talk to Samantha about stepping in for her children's father. He was almost sure.

Luckily, his diversion had worked. As Bri ate her ice cream cone, she told him about a movie she was hoping he would take her to see that was opening on the following weekend. He let her chatter wash over him, nodding occasionally, as they walked back through the park to find her mother.

It was a beautiful day. Warner could not remember a more perfect Labor Day Weekend. Quakertown Park was located in the center of Richland Township. Richland was probably built around it, just a small settlement at first, back in the eighteenth century when this part of eastern Pennsylvania was settled by the Quakers. Like many other rural townships in this region, Richland probably grew as the coal mines proliferated in this region, then prospered as the steel mills prospered in nearby cities such as Allentown. Now, the area was relatively crowded, though still mostly farmland. Richland was one of a string of small towns that dotted the countryside between bigger towns like Quakertown and Doylestown. He had moved here after graduate school because it was both beautiful and peaceful.

Once he moved, though, he found living in a small town offered something he hadn't expected, a sense of community and a spirit out of step with the century he lived in. Warner especially loved holidays. He found himself swept up in every celebration, happily overpowered by the palpable sense of fellowship among his neighbors and overwhelmed by the feeling he was part of the community, swept away by the excitement generated in the small township on the slightest excuse. The town of Richland had a Fair Day for every occasion from Groundhog Day to Christmas, all of which they celebrated as a community: black and white, upper class and lower, all joined together in their celebrations of life's simpler pleasures. The turnout for the events had increased since September 11, 2001.

Most of the town's population seemed to have turned out for the end-of-summer festivities in Quakertown Park. All around him, families picnicked and barbecued and played throughout the day. Warner lay on the blanket that Samantha brought and watched her children play with the other kids. He had moved the huge picnic basket and cooler—filled with everything from fried chicken to chocolate cake—off of the blanket, and had kicked his shoes off to stretch out, when she came over to join him. As he started to sit up, she motioned for him to lay back down.

"You look so comfortable. There's no need to get up for me," she said. "In fact, I'm going to get comfortable, too." She sat next to him, tucking her bare feet under her.

Samantha had every quality he admired in a woman. Warner respected her immensely for both her patience and her good humor in the face of her husband's betrayal. He could not find it within himself to be nearly so tolerant of his friend's horrifying behavior. She was handling the disastrous situation in which she found herself with incredible grace and dignity. To look at her, you'd never guess that she'd been abandoned eight months ago and had since had to completely revamp her life. She was so self-possessed. Despite being out of doors all day, running around with the children, she barely had a hair out of place. She sat and poured herself a glass of wine, took a sip, and sighed contentedly. He felt at peace when he was with her.

"Would you like some?" she asked, when she noticed that he was watching her.

"I'd better not. I just had some lemonade, and it's quite a hike to the bathroom."

Samantha smiled and settled down, leaning on one hand while she sipped daintily. Warner watched the ruby red liquid in her glass slip past her amber lips, and swallowed, his mouth suddenly dry as dust. She looked over the rim of her glass at him, and smiled again. He was pretty sure she knew what she did to him, though they had barely kissed.

Her husband—his best friend—had been gone for almost six months before he even thought to look at her as more than a friend who was hurting. Once he did start to think of her as a woman, Warner felt guilty whenever he caught himself admiring the curve of her throat, or her incredibly long legs. Finally, one day, she caught him staring but instead of getting upset, she brushed her hand against his cheek. It was pretty clear, from then on, that she was just waiting for him to make his move.

When he finally did kiss her, on the Fourth of July, it started out as just a friendly good-night kiss. They had been at the annual picnic, right here in Richland Park, just like today. After the food and games were put away, the kids and he had joined her on this same blanket, exhausted after all the food, and heat and excitement of the midsummer day. The four of them sprawled out next to each other, Bri and Eddy between him and Sam, talking quietly about swimming and soccer and starting the fourth grade. Sam was going back to work in the principal's office at the elementary school in the fall (only a week away now).

On that steamy July evening they had all waited patiently for the sun to set as more and more people came out to join the crowd and sat in lawn chairs or on blankets with their families and friends. Children chased each other and yelled, their anticipation growing as the blue of the sky darkened from pastel to indigo, and the moon appeared. Finally, when the sky became a black curtain, and the stars pinholes of light peeking through, the fireworks began.

Everyone oohed and aahed, flinched and cheered, and the children grew still as the light show above their heads grew more colorful, and more intricate. The fiery creations became more and more elaborate, until the fireworks culminated in a final crescendo of booming cannons and exploding stars.

The cheers and applause died down slowly after that last spectacular display and men and women slowly packed up and gathered their offspring for the weary ride home. Warner could walk to his place from the park, but he stayed to help Samantha get her two little ones home. He felt almost like a part of the family. When they reached her door, he said good night and the kids ran inside. She said, "Thanks for today," and the next thing he knew he was leaning down to kiss her as if it were the most natural thing in the world. Then, when his lips met hers, he felt as though he had come home.

It was a gentle kiss, a loving kiss. He felt it flow through him, and pool down somewhere in the vicinity of his toes. They explored each other's mouths gently, her hand on his cheek, his resting lightly on her waist. It had gone no further than that. A simple, sensual, intimate gesture. But it changed everything.

Since then, they had kissed again, more than once, but it continued to be a rarity, a simple gesture they reserved for those moments when words were not enough to express their pleasure in each other's company. At least, for him. He couldn't seem to bring himself to ask her how she felt. He didn't know how. And it didn't seem necessary.

"So, how are your classes looking?" Sam asked.

"Fine. The students seem interested, so far."

"How long does that usually last?" she asked cynically.

"If I do my job right, some of them, well, a few of them, will stay that way."

"How do you teach art? Don't the students basically have to have talent to start with?" Sam inquired.

"Usually my students have a little, at least. I don't teach talent, I teach discipline."

"That doesn't sound like nearly as much fun," she commented.

"I like it. It's a mixture of honest criticism and gentle encouragement. The truly talented ones will benefit from the former as well as the latter."

"On television, the professor demolishes most of the students with his or her comments about their work," Sam said.

"I try not to demolish anyone," Warner said dryly. "Of course, I do have to prepare my students for the real world. I can't coddle them. But a lot of the students, once their initial nervousness wears off, will appreciate my comments."

"Sure they will," she said teasingly.

"The elementary school opens this week, right?" he asked.

"Yup," Samantha replied, sobering.

"The kids seem pretty excited," Warner said. "I remember hating the end of summer vacation and going back to school."

"I don't hold out much hope that the kids will have that back-to-school enthusiasm for more than half a day," she confessed.

"You might be underestimating them," he remarked.

"I doubt it. That seems to be the basic pattern, every year. These aren't college students. They're second and fourth graders. They can't wait to go and see their friends again—until they get their first homework assignment, and then they spend their days trying to catch colds and anything else they can think of to stay home."

"I don't think it's much different for my students," Warner said. "I'm not sure, but it seems like they're always in a hurry to finish their classes and get to their after-school activities. I must admit, I'm in the same mode this term. I can't wait to get home after school, either." He smiled suggestively at her, and Sam laughed.

"Did you have enough to eat?" she asked.

"Yes, thanks. Everything was delicious. Especially the cake," Warner replied.

"Cake?" Eddy echoed, as if in a trance.

"Can I have some more, please?" Bri asked.

"You already had two pieces," her mother said.

"So?" Bri responded. Clearly, to the eight-year-old, her mother's answer was a non sequitur. Warner understood thoroughly.

It worried him sometimes how in tune his thoughts were with the children's. He had always thought of himself as a grown-up, unlike a lot of the men he knew. He didn't have a trace of a Peter Pan complex. The oldest son of a single mother of three, he learned to cook and clean the house and take care of his younger siblings at an early age. He had been too busy taking care of his brother and sister to be their best friend. Now they lived far away, and while he talked to them pretty regularly, he still felt more like their advisor than their peer. He hadn't had time to be very childlike, even as a child. So it surprised him, now, to find himself in accord with Sabrina, rather than with her mother.

"Tomorrow," Sam said. "You've had enough sugar for one day."

"But, Mom," the little girl wailed, "Eddy had three pieces."

"At least," Eddy said unhelpfully.

"It's almost eight-thirty," Sam argued, but Warner could already tell that she was going to lose this battle. Her heart wasn't in it.

"It's vacation," Bri pointed out. "I don't have to go to bed for a long time."

"I don't want you bouncing off the walls at bedtime, though," Sam tried to explain.

"I won't. I promise," Bri vowed. "I'll go straight to bed without even getting a bedtime story or anything if I can have some cake now."

"Fine." Samantha gave in. "I hope you remember

that you said that later, because I'm going to hold you to the deal."

Sam sat up and reached into the picnic basket for the remaining half of her homemade chocolate layer cake.

"I'll do it," Warner offered, reaching for the cake dish in her hand.

Samantha pushed his hand away. "Forget it, buster. You started this."

"Me? What did I do?" Warner protested. She gave him a wry look of accusation, which he pretended not to notice. "See if I try to pay you a compliment again any time soon," he said, pretending to pout.

"You can't have your cake and eat it, too," Sam said with relish.

"Well, if I can't have it, I'll just eat it," Warner said. "Cut me a slice, too, will you?"

She handed him the slice she had just cut and he realized that her daughter was already making inroads on her portion. This wedge of cake had been meant for him from the moment Sam cut into the luscious layer cake.

"His is bigger than mine," Bri whined. The fact that the bottom half of her face was covered with chocolate frosting and her mouth was full did not seem to affect her greediness.

"Because you ate half of yours already," Warner said childishly. "See?" He took a large bite, reducing his own slice of cake to the same size as hers.

Sam leaned close to him to say softly in his ear, "You are not providing a very good example for my impressionable children at the moment."

"Sorry," Warner said sheepishly.

*   *   *

When Warner took Sam and the children home that night, they kissed again. It was another searing kiss that left him wanting more.

"Do you know what you do to me?" he asked, his forehead against hers as they stood in front of her door, like teenagers on a first date. He felt a little like he had as a teenager, aroused, elated, and without a clue as to what came next.

"The same thing you do to me," Sam said breathlessly.

How do you feel about it? he almost asked, but caught himself in time. He still wasn't ready for that conversation, and he suspected she was just as reluctant as he was to name the thing between them. Her husband had been gone for less than a year. For that matter, his wife was off in a different time zone. Which wasn't the same thing at all. Maddie wasn't a real wife. Still, he couldn't imagine Samantha dating a married man. It wouldn't be suitable. Especially not with her two small children in the picture. They couldn't make this into more than it was. Not yet. She needed more time.

"Do you want to come for dinner next Friday?" she asked. "I promised the kids pizza to celebrate the end of the first week of school. I know I'll just end up eating it with them if it's just us, but if you're here, I'll cook us some grown-up food instead. If you want?" The attempt to make her invitation sound like just another casual evening at home with her husband's best friend was a failure. They both knew it was more than that. But since he was, technically, a married man, Warner was happy to play along.

"Sure," he agreed. "I'll bring some wine."

"That's grown-up," she said, smiling.

"That's the idea," he affirmed. He was happy to

follow her lead and keep the tone of the conversation light. "No kids' stuff for us. We're way past all that."

"I've got the gray hair to prove it," she replied wryly.

"Where?" he asked. "Let me see."

"You better not," Sam replied. "I pay Elmira Hutchins a lot of money to hide it."

"It's a good thing, too, or I couldn't afford to be seen out in public with an old lady like you," he teased. Sam was forty, seven years older than he was, and she made a point of reminding him of the fact regularly. But if she thought that he was going to let that stand between them, she was mistaken.

"Shut up," she ordered now, but without heat.

"Make me," he taunted her.

She suddenly wrapped one long arm around his neck and pulled his head down so his eyes were level with her. "You think I won't," she challenged.

He gave her a quick kiss and twisted out of her grasp. "I think you'd try," he said. "And I don't want to have to sit on you in front of your children, so I'm going to get out of here before you start something you can't finish."

"Go ahead, run away. You may have a few inches, and a few years, on me, but I could still whip you, if I wanted to," Samantha retorted.

"Uh-huh," he said sardonically.

"I just don't want to."

"Good," Warner said. "Methuselah," he threw over his shoulder, as he jogged down the stairs.

Part of him wished that they were both completely free, and could stop this little dance that they were doing around each other. On the other hand, they were friends largely because it was safe. They'd been brought together by all the excess baggage that they carried. If Sam hadn't married his best friend, he never would have met her. If he hadn't been married to Maddie, he wouldn't have spent so much time with the two of them. He probably would have been out dating, or at least hanging out with his single friends. Maybe he would have been married already. He had always wanted a family.

He used to envy Radu his wife and children. Now that his best friend was out of the picture, Warner might very well end up getting them.

He wouldn't have wished for this to happen to any of them, but since it had, it seemed maybe it was meant to be. He could imagine himself playing with the children every day, and tucking them into bed every night, and beyond that he could imagine himself waiting up for Bri after her first date and teaching Eddy to drive a car. Images like those, and other equally vivid pictures, formed in his mind at the oddest times. He pictured himself with Samantha, sitting together on her ivory love seat in five years, or ten, or twenty. The only thing Warner couldn't seem to picture was a wedding.

Maybe, he thought, *If Radu doesn't show up, and Maddie does . . . I can make something of this relationship.* Even though his wasn't a real marriage, he still felt disloyal to Maddie whenever he got involved with any other woman. Especially if she seemed like the kind of woman that he might want to marry. It was ridiculous, he knew, but he couldn't help it. He was a married man. He and Maddie had made vows in front of God and the county clerk, and even though they had never intended to live as man and wife once they graduated from graduate school, he still felt guilty when he broke those vows. It was hell on relationships. Just when he'd start to get close to a woman, his conscience would kick in. It overrode his baser impulses, despite his absolute certainty that Maddie did not expect him to be faithful to her at all.

They were two separate people, living divergent lives. He was sure she dated as much as or more than he did, since she told him so on her visits home to Richland. There was no reason for him to feel like he was betraying her. They had made no commitment to each other, nor had they promised to be faithful for even one day, let alone forever. It had never been a real marriage.

They lived together for two years in grad school and then they drifted apart as they began their careers. The separation was total after she began her work in earnest. If he hadn't moved to Richland, they probably wouldn't have seen each other at all in the last ten years. All of her short visits home for the holidays, added up, came to a total of under a year. That was enough time to keep their friendship strong, but it was not nearly enough to maintain a relationship like a marriage—even if they'd been trying to do so.

Maddie wasn't exactly wifely, anyway. She was loving, and beautiful, and elusive, and he'd always cared about her, but Warner was a pragmatist. He knew that they were not destined to be together. This wasn't one of those happily-ever-after types of stories. Theirs was a true marriage of convenience— and not in the romantic novel sense of the word. They married in order to defray their expenses and pool their financial resources while in graduate school, and they stayed married because . . . well, because there hadn't been a good reason to go to the trouble of getting a divorce before now. He might occasionally have flirted with the idea of falling in love, but Warner figured that any relationship that wasn't strong enough to survive the twinges of his overactive conscience wasn't worth pursuing anyway. He hadn't lost anything.

His feelings for Samantha had changed all that. If he was free, then he could pursue a relationship with her. That was what he wanted. At least, he was pretty sure that was what he wanted.

CHAPTER THREE

Mohammed Abdullah Ali dipped the last little tip of his flat bread in the *tsatsiki* sauce and polished it off, with a contented smack of his lips. Maddie watched him, revolted, although the Egyptian custom of eating loudly in order to show appreciation for the blessing of food didn't usually bother her. It was just him. Mohammed. She suspected she was repulsed by his lip smacking, and his other self-satisfied noises, because it was so . . . him.

He was her nemesis. He hovered nearby, gloating over errors he imagined she made in the work she was doing on the ancient scroll she'd been hired to translate. He smirked at the gaffes she made when she spoke his language. The worst incident had occurred when her boss was entertaining a wizened old man a week ago, and she put her foot in it by speaking to the ancient Imam, not realizing that his position did not permit him to speak directly to a woman. Mohammed couldn't hide his delight at her blunder that time.

He thought he should have gotten her job, and, while he was outwardly polite and respectful—

even obsequious at times—his jealousy made him almost impossible to bear.

Maddie might have been able to bring herself to feel sorry for him, if he had been just a tiny bit less obnoxious. She understood, and could sympathize with his situation, but Mohammed still got under her skin. What with her aunt's death and all the complications it had caused, her emotions were too close to the surface for her to deal with him right now. Maddie had even been tempted to ask him to eat somewhere else today. As much as she despised him, though, she pitied him more, and she couldn't bring herself to humiliate him by banishing him from the office they were supposed to share. Instead, she tried to ignore him as he sat at his desk, finishing his meal.

He made that difficult, though. "I understand from our superiors that another inquiry has been received from the visa office. That's too bad for you." He pursed his lips, shaking his head in commiseration. Maddie was not surprised that he knew that she'd heard from the Egyptian equivalent of the United States Immigration and Naturalization Bureau. He seemed to be aware of every little move she made. She continued to concentrate on her reading as he went on. "I don't know why they are . . . hounding you? Hounding? Is that the correct word?"

"It is," Maddie affirmed, without looking up. She was not in the mood to listen to any of his false expressions of sympathy.

"It is a shame that they do not simply accept your presence here as an American. You, at least, are not like those who come here to milk our poor country of its oil, or seek to incite our poor women to rebel against our culture." He nodded toward the *hijab* that she always kept on a hook on the

back of the door. Tempted as Maddie was to tell
him to be quiet and leave her alone, she couldn't
bring herself to do it.

There was nothing new in his comments. She
should have been used to his gloating by now. He
seemed to enjoy speculating about why the government might be opposed to her employment at
the university. In fact, it was one of Mohammed's
favorite subjects for discussion. But Maddie was
struck, suddenly, by a certain quality to his sneer. It
was a glimmer of something unpleasant in his eyes,
the kind of deep-seated satisfaction that one might
feel because he had information that his enemy
lacked.

"I'm no threat to anyone," Maddie insisted, as
she had so many times before. But this time she
watched Mohammed's face. Was that a flicker of
superiority she glimpsed in his eyes before he
dipped his head? "Why won't they leave me alone
to do my job in peace?"

"Tsk, tsk," he clucked at her. "What could they
think?" he asked.

She was sure, then, that he was withholding information. Information she needed. It was suddenly as clear as crystal that he knew something
about why the visa department was harassing her.
She was certain of it.

"Mohammed, you would tell me if you knew
why they were doing all of this, wouldn't you?" she
asked, in her best *I'm just a poor ignorant worm of a
woman who needs a man to explain the most obvious
things to me* tone.

"I, um, of course," he stammered. "I don't know
why . . ." His voice trailed off as her eyes met his.
"They might, I don't know why, but they might suspect you of . . . something, I suppose."

"What?" Maddie asked, holding his gaze, refusing to let him off the hook until he told her what-ever it was that he knew. "What could they possibly think about me that could lead to all this harass-ment?"

"Well, you are an American, and the relations between our countries are rather tenuous at this time—with everything that's going on in the world."

"So you're saying they think I could be what? Dangerous? Subversive?"

"Dangerous!" he snorted. But it was unconvincing.

"Just because I'm American? What do they think I am? A spy?" She laughed, but he didn't join in, not right away. That was when she knew.

"You've got to be kidding me!" she exclaimed. Mohammed smiled weakly, without answering her.

"Me? But I'm a linguist!" Maddie exclaimed in disbelief.

"You could be something other than what you say. It would not be the first time," he said, shrugging.

"I guess that's true," Maddie said doubtfully. "But—"

He stopped her. "I don't know anything. I'm just guessing."

"I understand," Maddie answered, her brain working hard to assimilate this intriguing tidbit of information. "So, they could think I'm working for the government? The U.S. government?"

"You are in a position to influence people, here at the university, and also to gather information about our most respected scholars. Your country has used this method before, in Indonesia and South America. They could have sent you here to get close to the intellectuals who shape young minds and ideals."

"I suppose . . ." Maddie drawled. "It's not completely ridiculous. But I've been here for a month. By now they must have figured out I don't exactly have what it takes to be some kind of covert operative. I hardly ever leave this office. The only people I talk to all day are you and the janitor."

"So, perhaps I am wrong," Mohammed answered, his tone hopeful. Maddie did not feel reassured. He just wanted to throw her off the track. She was convinced her assistant knew what he was talking about. His theory explained so much.

The trip home was long and exhausting. Her flight from Cairo to London was uneventful, but the changeover to the last leg of her trip involved a harrowing taxi ride from Heathrow to Gatwick, where she just barely made the connecting flight to New York. Maddie would have taken a stopover in London or New York, but she wanted to get back to Pennsylvania and settle the matter of her aunt's will, which felt as though it hung over her like a big black cloud, weighing on her.

She took the Greyhound bus from Newark, hoping an hour and a half on the slow-moving vehicle would give her stomach, and her nerves, time to settle. Unfortunately, Maddie felt too anxious about going home to relax. It was going to be a circus. Living with her family was nerve-racking at the best of times and the whole business with the will was only going to make matters worse. She knew her mother well enough to know that Janet was not going to drop the subject of her giving up her inheritance without a fight. Great-Aunt Becky had been a witch and her mother as much as told her that she would therefore regard any object that had been bequeathed to her daughter as cursed.

Maddie felt there was one tiny ray of hope. Becky might have left her something small that she could hide from Mom. She had no qualms about lying to the woman. Her mother was, after all, also the woman who made her promise to carry garlic in her purse throughout her teen years. Maddie had been lying to her mother ever since. For one thing, that was the only way she could visit home and still maintain peace in her family.

After traveling five thousand miles, Maddie couldn't seem to bring herself to take the last ten miles of the journey. When her bus arrived in Allentown, she got off and called a taxi, but instead of giving the driver her parents' address in Richland, she had him take her to her friend Patsy's restaurant on Seventh Street. Maddie felt she needed sustenance before she faced her mother. Sustenance in the form of comfort food. Patsy served the best Philly cheese steak in Pennsylvania at her family-style restaurant, Mama Jean's Kitchen.

Patsy Jones looked just the same. She was only five feet two, but she was 125 pounds of pure energy. Her round brown face was a welcome sight, with its big brown eyes and warm, genuine smile. She still had the space between her two front teeth, and the untamed head of frizzy hair that she fought to control, or rather, subdue, all through high school, though she had cut it a little shorter than it had been.

Her old friend was clearly happy to see her. She hugged Maddie and fussed over her as she served her a sandwich dripping with cheese and butter.

"Mmm, I missed this most of all," Maddie said, smacking her lips as she contemplated biting into the golden hero filled with grilled chicken, onions, and savory cheese sauce, thick with mushrooms. For her, Patsy substituted chicken for beef.

"You missed my food more than me?" Patsy asked, pouting.

"You can't be jealous of your own food," Maddie told her. "Or if you are, then you'll just have to stop being such an amazing cook."

"Can't do it, baby girl. It's who I am," Patsy proclaimed.

"So stop moaning and bring me some of those luscious sweet potato fries," Maddie ordered.

Patsy brought her a large plate of the delectable red-gold potato strips and sat down next to her at the table. "So where did you go this time?" she asked.

"Egypt," Maddie said, after she swallowed. "It was amazing."

"I wish I had your life," Patsy said enviously, but Maddie knew she didn't really mean it. In their junior year of high school, Patsy, Maddie, and their other best friend, Jennifer Li, had all mapped out their futures for an assignment for psych class. Jenny wanted to be a lawyer, and she was currently working on becoming a partner at one of the top entertainment law firms in New York City. Maddie, at seventeen, had not had a clue as to what career she wanted to pursue, but had planned to travel all over the world—which her work as a linguist had eventually allowed her to do. Patsy wanted to marry her boyfriend Chuck and open a restaurant. Chuck was ancient history, but otherwise Patsy had achieved her goals. In fact, all three women had followed their dreams.

By all reports, Jennifer was moving steadily up the corporate ladder, and when Maddie had visited her during a trip home a couple of years ago, Jenny happily acted as hostess and tour guide to *her* city for her old buddy. It had been a week of cosmopolitan pleasures: living in Jen's luxurious penthouse apartment in the center of Manhattan, attending the theater on Broadway, dining in restaurants that featured exotic cuisines from all over the globe, and clubbing in the hippest, hottest joints.

Of course, Maddie loved the life she had chosen for herself, rootless as she was, but Patsy had, in some ways, been the most successful of them all. She didn't marry her childhood sweetheart, but after a year of college she dropped out to marry the love of her life, Eddie, and the two of them opened their restaurant. She also had four kids, all of whom were bright, healthy, and—to Maddie's slightly jaundiced eye—adorable. No matter what she might say, Maddie knew Patsy wouldn't have traded a minute of her life for Maddie's, or even Jenny's. Which, Maddie thought, was just as it should be.

"It's an incredible place. You know I was there as a research assistant back in college, and I've been trying to get back ever since."

"I know," Patsy said, nodding. "I mean, I remember."

"I'm working on a translation of a document from a grave site, at the University of Cairo, which is interesting, and I even got out to Giza a couple of times, but it's not as much fun to live and work there as a grown-up as it was to visit as a college student."

"It never is, is it?" Patsy said philosophically.

"No, I'm not complaining about having to pay my own bills this time around," Maddie told her. "This isn't just the usual stuff. The government is driving me crazy. They seem to think I've got some ulterior motive for working at the university, and they keep asking me for proof that I am what I say I am and not some kind of spy or something. I don't know how to prove a negative. I'm obviously not a spy, but . . . denying it isn't going to help. If I were a spy, I'd have to deny it."

"You're kidding!" Patsy exclaimed.

"No, I'm serious. But I can't believe it either."

Patsy looked properly sympathetic. She shook her head, and pursed her lips; then her expression brightened as she pointed out, optimistically, "Well, girl, it sounds like you needed this vacation."

"A vacation? Yes. This? I'm not so sure. A trip to Hawaii, or the Bahamas, sure, but not a trip home to bury my favorite aunt." Patsy shot her a re-proachful look and Maddie quickly added, "I'm happy to be here, and see you and . . . everybody, but I am not looking forward to dealing with my mother and this situation with Great-Aunt Becky's will. I assume you've heard about that." It was a very small town, and Patsy was some kind of distant cousin to their family lawyer, Alton Emerson.

Her friend nodded. "It's not going to be pretty," Patsy predicted. She knew all about Janet Delaney's problems with Becky. Pretty much everyone in town knew that the two women didn't get along . . . and why they didn't. Many had witnessed the scenes that Janet made in church, or at events like the spring auction at Ely Whittaker's when Maddie's mother tried to have her aunt thrown out.

"I don't know what Great-Aunt Becky was think-ing," Maddie said ruefully. "She had to know how Mom would react to this."

"Well, maybe she figured Janet would let it rest, once she was actually dead," Patty said reasonably.

"I doubt it," Maddie answered, darkly. "She knew my mother better than that."

"Then I guess she really wanted you to have whatever it was she left you," Patsy concluded.

"I guess so," Maddie agreed. "But whatever it is,

I can tell you right now, it couldn't possibly be worth it."

While she finished her meal, Patsy gave her the update on the family, and their mutual friends, and by the time she ate her last french fry, Maddie was feeling somewhat more ready to face the trials to come. Gratefully, she gave her old friend a big hug and a kiss before heading for her mother's house.

Home was home. The two-story house with the blue shutters stood just as it always had at the corner of Old Bethpage Road and Pine Ridge Avenue. Walking through the front door was like walking into a time warp. Every stick of furniture was exactly the same, in the exact spot that it had been sitting in for years, and the photos on the walls, lovingly dusted every week, were the ones she'd grown up with, although a few had been added of the grandchildren.

Like the house, neither Mom nor Dad had changed a bit. Mom's ponytail was still a brown so deep it was almost black, and Maddie would have been willing to swear that Dad's salt-and-pepper cap of soft nappy curls still retained the same ratio of black to white. The only evidence that any time had passed at all was that Ted's dreadlocks were getting grayer, and, of course, Teddy's children had grown since she had seen them last. Lorraine, Teddy's eight-year-old daughter, was at least two inches taller, and Billy, her ten-year-old nephew, had feet bigger than Maddie's.

They were all waiting to meet her when she walked into the house, and they surrounded her, taking her bags and hugging and kissing her together and then one at a time. Her family was nothing if not demonstrative. For all her nervousness about coming back to this nuthouse, it felt good to see their faces and feel their arms around her.

"It smells good in here. Is that what I think it is?"

"Of course. All your favorites, ribs, kale, and macaroni and cheese, of course," her mother said, beaming.

"Thanks, Mom." She hugged Janet from behind, as her mother started toward the kitchen. Sometimes Janet Delaney was almost like a real mom.

"Go sit down at the table, you're later than we thought you'd be," she ordered.

Maddie couldn't tell her she'd just eaten. Besides, she knew she would manage to force down some portion of the dishes her mother had made especially for her.

Her father held the seat out for her. "Why didn't you call me from the bus station? I would have come to pick you up."

"I know. I just thought I'd save you the trouble. What have you been up to?" Maddie asked as he took his seat.

"Your father was out back in the garage all day, tinkering with that junk heap he calls a car," her mother answered for him as she came out of the kitchen with the serving dishes.

"I don't tinker and it's not a junker. I'm restoring a classic," Joseph Delaney retorted.

"What is Egypt like, Aunt Maddie?" Lorraine asked eagerly. Maddie's niece always liked to hear the stories of her travels.

"Cairo is an amazing place. The city is built right on the Nile. You've heard of it, right? It's just beautiful. Someday maybe you can go and see for yourself. If you do, you have to go to Giza. I think the

pyramids there may be the most incredible struc-
tures that man ever built."

"Some people say maybe aliens built them,"
Billy commented.

"It's possible, but I like to think we did it all by
ourselves," Maddie answered. "Just because we
can't figure out how they did it without the ma-
chines we use today doesn't mean it couldn't be
done. And if anyone did do it, I can believe it was
the ancient Egyptians. Greece may be the cradle of
our civilization, but this was a civilization that was
much older, and it certainly influenced the Greeks.
Much of what European culture considers its own
came from Northern Africa, including surgery and
geometry, and lots of other things. Even a lot of
our language. Hippocrates, the father of modern
medicine, was from that continent. The library at
Alexandria was the greatest ever built. That's our
heritage. That's one of the reasons I love Egypt.
That history, ancient as it is, it seems to come alive
there. It's so easy to imagine the past when you're
looking out of a window at the Nile River."

Her niece listened enraptured, but Maddie's
nephew was too restless to concentrate on what
she was saying. Luckily, she knew how to fix that.
"And the mummies keep me on my toes, of course,"
she added, lowering her voice.

Billy snapped to attention. "Mummies?" he repeated, intrigued.

"You did know they came from Egypt, didn't
you?" Maddie asked.

"There's no such thing," Lorraine scoffed.

"Well, I don't know about that," Maddie retorted.
"I haven't actually seen one myself, but then . . .
I've never been there at night."

"Where?" Billy asked, openmouthed.

"The pyramids," Maddie said, in hushed, reverent tones. "They used to mummify the dead before they buried them, and they also used to bury live people with them, like servants, and even their pets."

"They buried their pets!" Lorraine exclaimed, disgusted.

"To keep the dead company in the afterlife," Maddie explained.

"They buried them alive? With mummies?" her nephew repeated, both repulsed and awed by this revelation.

"Mm-hmm. I've heard that some of the night watchmen have heard some strange noises in there. Moaning, and even muffled screams."

"Did anyone ever see one?" Lorraine asked, curious despite herself.

"Well—" Maddie began, but her brother interrupted, halting her.

"Excuse me, but this isn't proper conversation for the dinner table," Teddy said severely. "It is almost dark out, and I don't want to have nightmares tonight." The look he gave her was more than a little bit annoyed. She remembered that glare from their childhood.

"Aw, Daddy," Billy whined.

"Just fifteen more minutes," Lorraine pleaded. As Teddy started to shake his head, Maddie jumped in. "I'll tell you all about it when I see you Sunday, after church," she promised both children.

This time it was her mother's turn to glare at her. "Do you think that's an appropriate time for blasphemy, Maddie?"

"It's not blasphemy. It's someone else's *culture*," Maddie pointed out. "Besides, there's plenty of gruesome stuff in the Bible."

"Hush!" Janet ordered. "This is definitely not a proper conversation for the dinner table."

"Fine." Maddie subsided. It wasn't worth it. She had to pick her battles carefully.

As she expected, the evening did not go by without a more serious skirmish. Her mother was determined to discuss the subject of her great-aunt's will. "A gift is supposed to be a blessing, even if it's something small or simple, a card, or a paperweight, or a scarf. But you've got to remember that that woman didn't even believe in God."

Maddie knew the subject of Rebecca Tanner's atheism would come up eventually. This was, supposedly anyway, what had started the feud between the two women. If Maddie remembered correctly, the whole mess started when a family friend, a woman that her mother and her great-aunt both cared about, lost a baby. Janet took solace from the idea that the child was in heaven, but Becky had not had any such comfort and, grief-stricken, she could not keep her opinion to herself. She came right out and asked Janet not to keep saying that God had a plan, or that the baby or her parents were better off, or any of the other platitudes that were common in stressful situations such as that one.

Rebecca Tanner and her niece had—until that time—coexisted, as family must. Although they could not have been said to have had a peaceful relationship since they were both extremely strong-willed women, they had, for years, maintained a kind of Swiss neutrality between bouts. But after that, Janet could not let it go. Her rancor grew over the months that followed until she finally labeled Becky a witch a couple of years later. She would have kept her daughter from ever seeing her aunt, but for once Maddie's father stepped into the fray, insisting that Maddie be allowed to visit the woman to whom she was so attached. He did impose one condition on her. She wasn't allowed to discuss religion with the old woman. Since Great-Aunt Becky had no interest in organized religion, Joseph Delaney's terms were easy to comply with, and Maddie spent as much time with her great-aunt as she could reasonably manage without starting a war at home.

When her mother went into the kitchen to get the dessert, Maddie appealed to her father. "You understand that I have to accept my inheritance, right? Can't you talk to her?"

"Rebecca is past caring at this point," he said. "Your mother isn't. I think you could show some consideration for her wishes."

Maddie sputtered, openmouthed, at the man sitting at the head of the dining room table. "I— but— What?"

"You heard me," he said, with a wry twist to his mouth.

"Do you honestly expect me to reject her last request? What's happened to you?"

"I am just saying you should think about it," he answered. Maddie couldn't believe he was serious. As if he read her mind, he added, "Seriously." It was probably her expression that made him say it, but whatever the reason for his insistence, his intention was perfectly clear. He really wanted her to think about giving up her inheritance, whatever it might be.

Maddie couldn't get over it. Her entire family was completely out of control—not just her mother, but her father and brother, too. Not to mention her sister-in-law and the children. They all needed a reality check.

Unfortunately, she wouldn't be the one to give it to them. Not at a time like this, over an event like this. Whatever her mother said, her aunt's bequest *was* a blessing. It was a gift of love. Maddie knew, without knowing exactly what her aunt had left her, that her inheritance was somehow important, especially to the old woman who had gone to the lengths of requiring Maddie to be at the reading of her last will and testament. This was Rebecca Tanner's last attempt to reach out to her great-niece. Maddie couldn't ignore that, and she didn't think she would be able to turn down her legacy, either.

The next morning, she awakened early, still on Cairo time. But not earlier than her mother. It figured that her first day home would happen to be the day her mom salted the house. Once a month or so, Janet carried out the arcane tradition. She sprinkled salt in the four corners of each room of the house, in order to ward off evil spirits and ill health. Whether her mother chose to follow this custom in tribute to her African ancestors, or from the Native Americans who had married them after they were brought to this country, Maddie didn't know. Native Americans believed, as did many other primitive cultures, that ill health was caused by the invasion of evil spirits into the body, but that wasn't conclusive evidence that Janet's devotion to "salting the house" originated with them. Maddie was inclined to believe it was an African superstition—perhaps even African-American—because the only other people whom she knew of who practiced the ritual were African-American characters in books.

She never actually met anyone who shared her mother's beliefs. Janet said she learned from her grandmother, mother, and aunts. Great-Aunt Becky always said, though, that she never heard of anyone in their family doing any of the bizarre things that her niece did, and Maddie was inclined to believe her because she was, by far, the more rational of the two women. She wouldn't have put it past her mother to adopt the ritual after reading about it in a book. It was the kind of thing that would appeal to Janet Delaney.

When they were teenagers, Maddie and her brother had done anything and everything they could think of to avoid the house on salting days. Now Teddy seemed to take it in stride, and his daughter even came over to help—following her grandmother around with a box of sea salt gripped tightly in her tiny little hand, and mimicking every move that Janet made.

Maddie fled.

CHAPTER FOUR

Maddie looked absolutely beautiful. Her heart-shaped face glowed and a healthy tan had darkened her amaretto skin to a chocolatey brown tinged with gold. Her dark eyes sparkled, and her full lips turned up at the corners, even during those few odd moments when she wasn't smiling. The rest of the time, her wide smile showed off small white teeth, shining like pearls. Warner noticed with approval that she had let her hair grow. It hung in curling tendrils around her face and down her back to her shoulder blades. After all the soul searching he had done recently, Warner was surprised that the sight of her was so welcome, but it didn't change the fact that it was great to see her again. She was the same. Exactly the same. She greeted him with a long, close embrace, talking all the time.

"It is so good to be with someone normal. I've only been home two days, and my mother has already tried to talk me into letting her read my tarot cards. I wish you could have seen us last night. Her crew came over to have coffee and dessert, and do their weekly paranormal research. She called it group meditation, but what it was was an honest-to-goodness séance—holding hands, in a circle, in the dark, with black candles burning at midnight and everything.

"Of course, the question that was burning in her mind was, what did her aunt leave me and why? It's making her nuts, not knowing what the old bird was up to. I want to know, too, of course, but Janet is just dying of curiosity. *She actually called a psychic.* The woman's a fruitcake, but usually she does manage to control urges that cost fifty bucks for five minutes. It was almost worth the trip home to see her like this. It's fun to see someone driving her nuts, for a change. Usually she's in the driver's seat and I'm the one who's going around the bend. Anyway, we'll all know soon enough, I guess."

She took a breath and he bent to kiss her hello, just as she said, "You look great, honey," and found her mouth slightly open, moist and warm. It sent a surprising chill down his spine. It must have been all that kissing he'd been doing with Sam that made him so aware of how warm and soft Maddie's lips had been. Warner felt he should apologize, but looking down at her smiling face, he realized she hadn't noticed anything wrong with the kiss.

She went on. "What have you been doing with yourself?"

"The usual. Work," Warner replied, almost stuttering. "It's a new school year, but I'm teaching a number of returning students, so it's not as harrowing as it could be."

"Remember when you first started teaching college and you had to teach all those freshmen, year after year? I didn't think you'd ever get past those introductory courses."

"I remember," he said. Warner felt awkward and

self-conscious but Maddie didn't seem to notice. Things had changed between them, but not for her. She didn't know anything about it. Maddie had no way of knowing that he planned to alter their arrangement. She probably figured they could go on forever the way they had been.

Apparently, he had satisfied her curiosity about what he was up to, because she started up again about her family. "You won't believe this! Teddy was at the séance. With his wife. I always liked Jordana before. She seemed really cool. Apparently, she's been dragged into my mother's delusions along with the rest of the family. She got a baby-sitter! She wouldn't leave the kids with a sitter to go to the city with me last time I was home, and she got one for my mom's ridiculous group. You should have seen it. Dad, Teddy, Jordana, Mrs. White, Ellen Fuller, and Dana Bronson, all gathered around the coffee table. It was a joke."

Maddie finally seemed to be finished. She looked up at him, awaiting his response.

"It sounds like a . . . unique experience," Warner said.

She seemed so young to him, so much younger than him, and so much younger than Samantha. There was barely a year's difference in their ages, so it wasn't that. It was something else. She hadn't changed in twelve years, and he doubted she ever would. After all, she wasn't exactly the type to settle down. She was free-spirited, uninhibited, and thoroughly herself.

"Okay, so I know that I'm being judgmental, and it's not fair. I never have a problem with other people's superstitions. Jeez, you should see what the workmen do in the pyramids. I meet so many strange people in my line of work, you'd think that having a mother like mine would be something I'd be grateful for. I mean, she did teach me every possible superstition in America. But it's not the same, you know."

He nodded, murmuring noncommittally, "Mm-hmm."

"I know I should just live and let live. I do know that. But my mom pushes all my buttons. She's so irrational. It's ridiculous, but I keep wanting to shake her. This is the twenty-first century, for goodness' sake. She's been fooling around with this voodoo for thirty years or so. She's got to realize by now that it's all just a big crock."

"So what do you say to other people when they do this kind of thing?" he asked, curious.

"I don't say anything. I nod and I keep my mouth shut. They really believe in it. At Giza, at sunset, all through the summer, they have this light show, you know. I went this summer, because I wanted to see it again. It's amazing. The pyramids look . . . otherworldly. You can believe almost anything the tour guides tell you. And it's understandable that people who live in the shadow of something like that believe in aliens, and ghosts, and all kinds of witchcraft. But this isn't Giza, this is Haycock Township. We're not talking about graves that are centuries old. We're talking about a house with cedar shingles, and a stone foundation that is barely fifty years old. The idea that a spirit, or a demon, or any other paranormal entity would even be interested in our house, or our family, is ludicrous. I'm sorry, but it's true."

"All right, all right. I wasn't suggesting—"

She ignored the interruption. "What would you do if your mother started doing this kind of thing? Not that she ever would. I mean, your mom is completely cool, but . . . what if she . . . I don't know, had an out-of-body experience at yoga class, and suddenly came home one day and started trying to commune with the spirits?"

Warner shook his head. "I can't picture it."

"Neither can I, honestly. But I'm just saying that if she did start acting strange and paranoid and delusional, you wouldn't just ignore it. Everyone acts as if my mother is acting perfectly fine. Especially my father. And now it's like the whole family has fallen for it. Teddy, Jordana. And the kids can't help themselves. They have to believe what the adults tell them. So they're stuck with all this craziness for now. Until they hit junior high, or high school at least. Just like I was." She paused to take a breath, and he waited, knowing she hadn't completely wound down yet. "I feel so bad for the kids. That's when it was hardest, when I was younger and I completely believed in her, and then I found out she didn't have a clue."

"But, Maddie, maybe that won't happen to them," he said reasonably.

"Maybe not. I hope not. But I think it will. You don't know what it's like to be raised in that atmosphere. You don't question it. You don't have any reason to question it. Then suddenly one day, you meet someone who doesn't think that animals can talk, and they ask you why you do. There's no defense. You're totally at the mercy of the other kids. And the worst part is, she doesn't understand what she's done to you. What she's turned you into. A walking, talking joke."

"It couldn't have been that bad," he said.

"It's worse. What I don't get is how Teddy can let it go on. He and Jordana are normally such loving, perceptive parents."

"Teddy is a good dad. Neither he nor Jordana would let anyone hurt those children," Warner insisted.

"I guess you're right," Maddie said. "She's not their mother. They've got relatively normal, sane parents. They'll be all right. I'll try to stop worrying, or at least talking about it. This is boring for you, I know. You've heard all the stories about Janet a million times. I just needed to vent a little."

A little, Warner thought, but he refrained from saying it aloud. He didn't need Maddie to turn on him. Especially not now.

Besides, he didn't want to hurt her. He never wanted to do that.

Examining her as she spoke, he thought it had to be her airy manner, her carefree attitude, that made her seem so much less earthbound than ordinary people. But he knew there was more to her than the persona she liked to present to the world at large. Maddie wasn't a frivolous woman; she was a respected scholar with an impressive intellect, who was ambitious, serious, and insightful. She just didn't want anyone to know it, for some reason he had never been able to figure out.

"Is something wrong?" Maddie asked. "You're very quiet. Not that I ever let you get a word in anyway, but you seem distracted today."

"I am, a little," Warner admitted. "There are things we need to discuss."

"Oh?" She looked up at him expectantly, her wide brown eyes curious. "Like what?" At that moment, she reminded him forcibly of little Sabrina.

That was it. That was why she seemed so childlike. It was those eyes, that guileless expression. Her open, eager, trusting face made her look so young.

Warner knew for a fact that Maddie had a mind like a steel trap. She was inexhaustible when it came to her research, devouring information like a Monday-night quarterback guzzled beer. But to look at her, one would never guess at her IQ or her ambition. They were hidden behind those innocent eyes, that exuberant smile. There wasn't a grown-up bone in her body.

Maddie worked hard to keep it that way. She said she had missed her teenage years, living with a mother who acted more like an adolescent than any of her friends.

She wanted to spend the years from twenty to forty making up for it. She was halfway through, and the plan seemed to be working for her. She looked fantastic: healthy and happy. Which made this the perfect time to bring up his dilemma. And to ask her to help him out with it.

"This arrangement of ours, this . . . marriage . . ." His voice trailed off as she laughed. "Right. I keep forgetting about that," she said, smiling. "What's up?"

"I . . . We—" Warner didn't know how to explain. "I think we need to make some changes," he finally managed to say.

"Oh, sure." Maddy waved a hand in the air, unconcerned. "Whatever you say, hubby." She was still grinning.

He didn't have the heart to just hit her with it. For all her nonchalance, Warner knew she counted on him, at least in part because of their bogus relationship. If those bonds were broken, she'd be adrift. It wasn't that Maddie couldn't take care of herself. She had been doing that for years. But he still couldn't just pull the rug out from under her without any warning at all. He needed to ease into this transition. She needed some kind of anchor. Whether she knew it or not.

"Is that all?" she asked.

"Yeah, well, we can hammer out the details later," he answered.

"So, let me tell you about Teddy—" she began. "He's getting to be as bad as my dad. He let Lorraine come over to help salt the house today." He must have looked confused, because Maddie explained, "It's salting day. That's when you go around the house, sprinkling some kind of salty solution in the corners of all the rooms, and other key spots. I don't even want to think about what might be *in* the solution. Supposedly, the ritual holds off the evil spirits, or something. Anyway, Teddy was just as horrified by it as I was when we were kids, and now he's sending his seven-year-old daughter over to be indoctrinated by our mother. I can't believe he's forgotten how mortifying it was to find out other people didn't do all that crazy stuff."

"Maybe he hasn't forgotten," Warner interjected. "Maybe he's mellowed. That was twenty-five years ago."

"Yeah, but—" Maddie shook her head in disbelief. "I don't know what's happened to him. He used to be pretty normal. It was bad enough that my dad humored her all those years. If Teddy starts, she'll never change."

"Haven't you figured out yet that people don't change? Not basically. Not who they are."

"That stuff she does isn't who she is. Janet went to college, for Pete's sake. She's got a bachelor's degree in sociology. She was a radio operator in the navy. She's an intelligent, modern woman with one foot stuck in a superstitious era filled with this outdated nonsense. She has to realize that eventually. But she won't if people keep going along with her."

"I think you're underestimating your mother," Warner said, shaking his head. "You said it yourself. She's smart, she's educated, and she's very sure of herself. If she were going to reevaluate her belief system, I think you'd have seen some sign of it before now."

"You may be right, but I can't give up hope. Not yet," Maddie said, sighing. "As long as I hold on to the vague hope, there's always a chance she'll come around."

"Who are you trying to convince? Me or you?" Warner asked.

She shot an annoyed glance at him and shrugged. "No one. It doesn't matter to me. I'm only going to be here long enough to deal with Great-Aunt Becky's will. Then I am out of here and my entire family can continue to spiral down into the abyss if they choose."

"So, how long do you think you'll be here?" Warner inquired, not sure what he hoped Maddie would say. The longer her visit, the more time he would have to ease into a discussion of their divorce. However, this might be a problem he should tackle head-on, like ripping off a Band-Aid in one clean swoop.

"I don't know. The reading of the will is on Monday. So I could be booking my return flight the day after, but I'm probably going to stay longer, at least another week, I think. It was a pretty long flight, and I don't feel like getting in an airplane again after one short weekend. Besides, I might as well visit a few people I didn't get to see last time I was home. Becky's death has made me see things a little differently. I mean, I didn't expect it. I thought I had plenty of time to tell her everything I needed to, but then *poof*, she's gone. On the plane here I thought about all of the older people I know, and, well, I made a list." She dug around in the bottom of her voluminous pocketbook as she continued.

"I don't want them to die without talking to them."

Maddie pulled a wrinkled piece of notepaper from the depths of the huge purse and thrust it at him. "I guess it's silly really." He looked at her list of Richland's senior citizens and nodded. "Any one of us could get hit by a bus tomorrow," she remarked.

"True," Warner agreed.

"I'm feeling very aware of my mortality these days. That always happens to people when someone close to them dies unexpectedly, don't you think?" Maddie obviously didn't require any answer from him as she continued to babble as they walked together into the living room and as she settled into one corner of his big leather couch. She didn't stop, or even pause, for a response from him. She just chattered away.

Warner only half listened to what she was saying as he watched her animated face. Maddie had kicked off her sandals and curled her legs under her and was fidgeting with the jade whale that he kept on the coffee table. He murmured, "Mm-hm" occasionally when she paused to take a breath. The steady stream of words flowed around him as he catalogued the things about her that he remembered, and the tiny changes that had occurred since he'd seen her last. She always wore the same pair of antique gold earrings nestled against her amaretto skin. Her black eyebrows arched more than he remembered above those incredibly round, dark eyes. He couldn't detect a single wrinkle anywhere on her face, although he thought he spotted a gray strand or two in the dark curtain of her hair.

But, overall, he felt as if they could have been in her dorm room in college, where he'd first gotten the brilliant idea that they should get married.

Back then, it had seemed like the solution to all of their problems. The University of Pennsylvania had offered married graduate students very affordable housing a few short blocks away from campus. The old saying that two can live as cheaply as one had struck him forcibly then. If they lived together, they paid half as much rent each as they would in the dorms. On top of that, he knew of at least two adjunct professors who had been offered better time slots in their departments because they were married and, presumably, needed more time at home. The tax benefits were also quite clear.

He thought it out, carefully weighing the advantages, and then suggested it to Maddie—and she agreed. After that, it was a relatively simple process to actually tie the knot. Since then, they'd never regretted their decision. He still didn't. It was just time to move on. Now, he had Samantha and her children to consider. There was also his feeling for all of them. And even if Samantha didn't turn out to be the right woman for him, Warner knew that he was ready to start a family of his own. He couldn't do that if he stayed married to Maddie.

CHAPTER FIVE

Warner had a dazed look on his face. It was not exactly the expression of a deer caught in the headlights of an oncoming car, but it was close enough. Maddie felt responsible, which was only fair, since it was her fault that his house, which was usually so quiet and peaceful, was now full of guests eating chips and dip, drinking beer and hot cider laced with rum and cinnamon, helping her cook up a pot of chili, and listening to music that was not exactly his usual soft, cool jazz. Occasionally, someone started to dance, and a few other people always seemed to follow suit.

These bursts of activity were not exclusively confined to the younger crowd, either. Her parents and their friends the Wheatleys were among the more energetic of the older folks. Not to mention Vanessa Andrews, who was over eighty years old and still appeared to enjoy dancing the lindy with her daughter and son-in-law, who took turns partnering with her.

The impromptu party was actually quite a success. It started out as one of those *come on over and we'll catch up on the last year* kinds of gatherings, and ended up being a bit of a do. At least, that was what her father called it, when he and her mother showed up, having been informed by a number of their friends and neighbors that their daughter had dropped by asking all sorts of strange questions. Apparently, the little visits that Maddie had paid to some of the older members of the community—friends and acquaintances of a certain age, whom she'd suddenly decided she wanted to see one more time, just in case—had disturbed a few people.

She thought she had been so subtle. They thought, based on the tenor of the conversations she'd had with them, that she was dying.

Warner had warned her. He said that she couldn't go around hugging and kissing all of those old folks, many of whom she hadn't spoken to in years, without starting the local gossips to chatting. She laughed at him. So what if she'd stopped her high school drama teacher in the street and dragged him into Kate's Pizza for a cup of coffee? She told the man she felt nostalgiac for her high school days. Why shouldn't he believe that?

Janet and Joseph showed up not long after her best friend from the third grade, Timmy Edgeway. Married and divorced twice, he was invited tonight by his latest lover, Maddie's archenemy from the fourth grade, Edith Jameson. Edith and she had buried the hatchet, and Edith and Timmy were talking away in a corner of the living room.

Warner, who had come home from work expecting to find her cowed, subdued, and apologetic after the night before, had been somewhat surprised, to say the least, to find Maddie throwing a party. A party where her mother was reading people's tarot cards in Maddie's room, while her father watched *Monday Night Football* with some of the guys in Warner's bedroom, and a couple of teenagers Maddie didn't even know were necking in the alcove in the upstairs hallway.

"I didn't mean for it to happen," she explained, for the fourth time, when they were alone in the kitchen for a minute. Each time she tried to explain what had happened, the conversation kept getting interrupted, so Maddie talked fast. "I just called Patsy, and said I was going to feed her, for a change, even though my cooking doesn't compare to hers. She mentioned I should call Lydia, who just moved back here after living in San Francisco for the last few years, so I did. Just to say hello. Of course, I had to say I would love to meet her new husband, whether I wanted to or not, and when I mentioned that Patsy suggested I call, when I called to invite her over to dinner, she mistakenly thought that I was inviting her and John to get together with Patsy and me, here, for dinner. From there, it kind of . . . snowballed."

"I see," said Warner, clearly not seeing at all.

"I'm trying to say, is it okay if I invite a few people over for my famous chili? And if it's not, then I want to take this opportunity to say that I am really, really sorry. I didn't set out to invite all of these people here. It just kind of happened."

"Uh-huh," he said, as if in agreement, but Maddie was pretty sure her explanation hadn't really registered. It was the best she could do, though.

"Okay, so . . . I'm going to go talk to them," she said, backing out of the kitchen. "The chili should simmer for another half hour anyway."

Patsy didn't arrive until ten o'clock, because she had to supervise her staff at the café through the dinner rush, she said. Maddie had saved some chili and chips for her, which had not been an easy task.

Most of the guests had left when the kitchen closed, except for a few of her closer friends, with whom she'd been catching up, hearing about what had been happening in their lives and telling them about her work in Egypt, her troubles with the government there, and Abdullah. Warner seemed happier now. He appeared to have forgiven Maddie for inviting everyone in town over to his house without a word to him.

"Hot rum and cider? Or beer?" she asked, as she served her oldest and best friend a steaming hot bowl of her tomatoey vegetarian chili.

"Beer, with chili, I think," Patsy said, tucking into the spicy dish with gusto. "Mmm, I love eating other people's cooking."

Maddie brought her a beer, and poured it into a glass stein she had chilled in the freezer, feeling like she had truly mastered the art of hostessing. Even her mother and father seemed to be having a good time, although Mom kept giving her meaningful looks every time Warner started talking to another woman. She had always thought that her daughter was too cavalier toward her husband. Joseph and Janet knew all about the marriage, and why Maddie had agreed to the arrangement, but ever since first meeting Warner ten years ago, her mother had nagged her continually about wasting this chance at happiness. "You're throwing away a perfectly good opportunity for a happy marriage to a good man," she always said. "And what's really sad is that you don't even know it."

Maddie was in too good a mood to have that conversation with her mother again tonight. She'd been avoiding her for most of the evening. Between Warner and the reading of Great-Aunt Becky's will on Tuesday, Janet had plenty to say to her, and Maddie thanked God that her father was there to divert Janet from her quarry. Mom's motives in coming over did not stop with checking on the rumors of Maddie's impending demise. She wanted to talk about Becky. Her daughter had no intention of allowing her to throw a pall over this evening. She was having a good time.

"Tell me more about this job you're doing in Egypt," Patsy said. "It's a translation of a shopping list, or something, right?"

"Or something," Maddie said. "It's a ship's manifest, basically. But it's more romantic than it sounds. It lists the goods that the merchant wants to trade, and what he hopes to get for them, as well as some of the crew members, and I think I may have found a notation about their share of the profits, which would have been their salaries, for those that weren't his slaves."

"So why did I think they didn't read and write stuff like that back then?" Patsy asked.

"Most societies weren't exactly literate—not that there's anything wrong with a good strong oral tradition—but in Egypt it's thought a lot of people recognized a number of hieroglyphs, which are sort of picture words. So there would have been a higher rate of what we call literacy, even among the masses, back then. Europe wasn't nearly as advanced as Northern Africa, in that area."

"Oooh," someone said. "Your ethnocentricism is showing."

"All right, all right, I know I'm a little biased. But I can't help it. It's something we weren't taught in school, twenty years ago, so it all feels like really revolutionary stuff to me. These are just dusty old papyri, crumbling when they hit the air. They're history. I feel like what I do is going to actually change the way we think about the world."

"So, what about men?" asked Jamie Ford, one of

Maddie's teammates from her high school soccer days. "Any Indiana Jones types in Egypt these days?"

"Well, I haven't gotten to know too many people yet," Maddie said. "Outside of work. And I don't date men where I work. Not that I'm giving up much, from what I can tell. The one man I've gotten to know pretty well is my assistant, and I don't know if he's typical of the Egyptian male, but if he is, I'm going to have a very dry year."

"What's wrong with him?" Patsy asked.

"You name it," Maddie answered. "He's a pig. He thinks he should have my job, presumably because he's so much smarter, and better, and masculine than me. On top of which, he is a really tiny guy. I think I may weigh more than he does."

"I hate that in a man," Patsy said. "So? Any other prospects?" Like most happily married women, she loved talking about her single friends' exploits. She said hearing about their dates satisfied some sick biological need to remember what it felt like to be ecstatic about some new love interest one day, and to hate the entire opposite sex the next. "Marriage," she reported, "kills all of your romantic hopes and dreams, whereas dating shoots 'em down, raises 'em up, and shoots 'em down again. Like a roller coaster."

"Sorry, Pats. The pickings are slim, these days. I'm not the man magnet I used to be." Maddie waggled her eyebrows at her friend.

"Oh, well," Patsy said, philosophically. "Good food, cold beer, and a lesson in ancient Egyptian literature is about all I was really hoping for from this evening."

"What about the women?" Janet suddenly asked. "You said that the university accepts them, right?"

"Yeah, Cairo University has allowed women to enroll since around 1918 or so. Women scholars have made a name for themselves, too. Although they're expected to follow a very rigid code of conduct even now, so I can't imagine what it was like for them fifty years ago."

"I never picture women in college in the Middle East," Lydia said. "I guess I bought all the stereotypes of them cloistered in some smoking kitchen in the back of the house while the men sit around debating about religion and politics."

"I've never been to Cairo," her husband, John, said. "I love to travel, and I've visited a lot of Europe, even some of the northern European countries, as well as Japan and India and Bali, and so on. I have always wanted to go to Africa, but I guess I never really thought about visiting the Mideast, and now, I don't know. It doesn't seem safe."

"I agree," Janet said, joining the little group.

"Mom, please," Maddie replied, hoping to head off a lecture. "Let's not get into this now."

"It's just that next year would be better. The clash between Saturn and Pluto in 2001 and 2002 left a lot of damage in that part of the world. When Saturn moved into Uranus, we might have seen some healing, but our president wasn't helpful and since Saturn entered Cancer in June, there's been even more talk about terrorists, and antiterrorists, and such. We've entered the shadow side of Cancer, and I don't know what the effect will be for Americans in the Mideast."

"Janet, this isn't the time," Dad said, and Maddie threw him a look of gratitude. "I think Egypt sounds like an interesting country, Maddie."

"It is," Maddie assured him. "People in that part of the world worry about the same things we do, making it through the workday, feeding their kids, just like us. And Egypt has survived worse than this. It's an ancient culture. I really think you'd like it. Both of you."

"I don't think I'm going to make it to Egypt, honey. I haven't even seen the Pacific Ocean, yet, and I always planned to take a trip out there. Maybe now that I've retired, your mom and I will go," Joseph said.

"You definitely should go, Mr. Delaney," Lydia said.

"Call me Joe," he suggested.

"Okay, Joe," she agreed, with just the slightest hesitation. "We drove to and from California, and it was an amazing trip. Maybe you can do it in a motor home or something, and really see the country."

"That's something I've always wanted to do," Warner said.

"Me too," Maddie added. "I've been all over the world, but I haven't seen a lot of this country."

"Not far enough away?" Patsy said, under her breath, so that only Maddie could hear her. She shot her old friend a warning look.

"It's getting late, I guess it's about time we were going," her father said. Maddie didn't know if he was leaving because he had heard Patsy's barbed comment. If he did, and he took it as a criticism of some kind, she could have told him that it was aimed at her, not him. Patsy teased her about running halfway around the world to avoid her parents, but it wasn't their parenting skills she was lampooning, but Maddie's inability to stay in one place for more than a year at a time. It wasn't their problem, it was hers. They were great parents, even if Mom was a little kooky and Dad was . . . well, Dad.

"Drive carefully," she told her father, as she saw him and her mom to the door. "And thanks for coming." She almost felt like hugging them both, but she just gave them each a quick peck on each cheek, European style.

"It was fun," Joseph Delaney said.

Mom nodded. "I'm glad we did this. Warner looked good, I thought."

"Me too," Maddie said automatically, but, although Warner did look good, as always, she wasn't sure it was true that she was glad they'd come to her party. As she walked back to the dining room after her parents left, she thought about it for a few seconds. All she came up with was, it was a nice change of pace to see them outside of their usual roles, as party-goers instead of parents. It surprised her how well they fit in with her friends, though it shouldn't have, since they had a wide and diverse circle of friends themselves. Mostly, she was grateful that they hadn't embarrassed her, the way they used to when she was younger.

When she walked back into the living room, her friends were reminiscing about some of Janet Delaney's wilder moments.

"That time with the brownies," Lydia was saying. She glanced up when Maddie came back into the room, and smiled, including her in the conversation. "I thought Principal Downey was going to have a coronary."

"I think he took them so he could eat them himself," Patsy joked.

"Hash brownies. Your mom is like the original conspiracy theorist," Jamie said, which Maddie found strangely annoying. She caught Warner's eye and knew instantly that he was thinking that she and her mother were more alike than she liked to admit. He'd said it often enough. And on the subject of conspiracy theories, she and Janet Delaney did seem to have some similar ideas. Maddie frowned at him.

"Remember the car she used to drive, the Beetle with the eyes painted all over it?" Jamie continued.

"Yeah, I learned to drive in that car," Maddie reluctantly admitted. "I'll never forget the look on the face of the testing guy at the DMV when I drove up to him in that thing."

That got Lydia going on the time her mother had gotten permission to do a cleansing ritual in the gym because Teddy's basketball team kept losing. "They did win the championship that year, though," Jamie pointed out, redeeming herself for the hash brownie remark.

Maddie didn't know why she suddenly felt like she should, perhaps, defend her mother. She had made fun of Janet herself, plenty of times, with these same women. They were teenagers, then, but . . . what had changed, really? Her mother was still driving her nuts with this stuff. For example, her obsession with what Becky might have bequeathed to her, and whether it would bring Maddie bad luck, was just like the garlic thing. It just wasn't rational. Great-Aunt Becky could have left her a million dollars, and her mother would think of a way to call it bad luck. She was going to want Maddie to refuse whatever it was that Rebecca Tanner left her.

The girls finally left the subject of her mother, and moved on to their jobs. Patsy, of course, was a fount of wisdom, since she'd never worked for anyone but herself.

"Why don't you tell your boss to screw himself?" she asked Lydia, after listening to her talk about the man's ridiculous ego.

Maddie, and everyone else, laughed. After they tried, unsuccessfully, to explain to Patsy that if you wanted to keep your job, you put up with your boss's idiocy, they talked about several other work-related issues, like trying to find affordable day care—which segued into a minor debate about the Republican party—as well as more specific problems. Maddie told everyone about her visa problems, and the Egyptian government's apparent conviction that she was an American spy.

"That would explain a lot about you," Jamie said. She was a home girl, who had only left Richland briefly to attend college in New Hampshire and then come right back again to marry and settle down. She ran a dairy farm a few miles away from that owned by her parents.

"What would?" Maddie asked, confused.

"The spy thing. I mean, you travel all over the world, and you're unattached. Maybe it's because you're in government work," she teased.

"Oh, right," Maddie said, laughing.

"I don't think Maddie's cut out for the CIA," Warner said. "She keeps losing her passport. I've had to verify her identity in two different countries. Not to mention that time she wandered onto the naval base in Italy and nearly started an international incident."

"You don't understand," Maddie tried to explain. "When I go somewhere I'm not supposed to go, past those little signs that say Do Not Enter in four or five different languages, I usually pretend I'm not an American, because its always the Americans who break the rules, so the security guards are nicer to people who speak Spanish. When they caught me in Naples, I thought I'd use the same trick, but it turned out that it doesn't work so well on a military installation. If I'd known they were marines, I would have told them I was an American right off the bat."

"Did they arrest you?" Jamie asked, wide-eyed.

"Nah, one of the guards was a Puerto Rican from Brooklyn. He knew right away that I was faking the Spanish. They just gave me a hard time so I wouldn't come back onto the base anymore. It worked, too."

As she and Warner cleaned up after the last guest had left, Maddie thought back over the events of the night. Everyone was tactful enough not to bring up the reason she had come home in the first place, and that evening had been the first since she'd learned Great-Aunt Becky was gone that she hadn't spent missing the lady and worrying about the reading of the will. She went to sleep smiling, thinking about how much Becky would have loved the party.

CHAPTER SIX

It turned out that, as Maddie's legal husband, Warner was invited to the reading of Becky's will as a matter of form. He didn't think he should be there, since it was clearly only for the immediate family, which he wasn't, even if by law he was considered a member. The Delaneys and the Tanners were both pretty interesting clans. It made sense that they would be. The matriarch in each was, or had been, a strong and unusual woman from a line of strong women.

Rebecca Tanner had been a real character. Warner completely understood Maddie's affinity for the woman. Even with the difference in their ages, they had been, very much, two of a kind. Both were outspoken and unconcerned with how they might appear to the people around them. They seemed a little bit flaky, but they were as smart as they were strong-willed, and each, best of all, had a very big heart.

Janet Delaney was an original, too, which was not at all surprising according to people who had known her mother, Elizabeth Tanner. Janet's mother,

Maddie's grandmother, had been the equal of her sister, Rebecca, if a tad more conventional. She was a mainstay of the community throughout her life, and was remembered by the older residents of Richland, whom Warner had talked to about her, for her kindness, her indomitable spirit, and for organizing a boycott of segregated businesses in a demonstration of solidarity with those boycotting the buses. It seemed Janet's and Maddie's personalities were the product of this earlier generation of women.

Warner would have been proud to have been part of the tribe—if his marriage to Maddie had been real. But he didn't feel he had the right to intrude on this very private, and intimate, family gathering. He couldn't say no, however, when Maddie begged him to attend.

"I need someone there who will be on my side. Please." As usual, he crumbled like a piece of burnt toast. Warner rarely refused her anything, especially when she was as desperate as she was at the moment. So he agreed to meet her at the lawyer's office on Tuesday afternoon.

Alton Emerson was a very distinguished and kindly-looking old gentleman. Warner hadn't actually spoken to him before, but he'd seen the man at church, and he'd voted for him when he ran for a seat on the town council. Mr. Emerson always seemed to him to be an intelligent and compassionate man, and his behavior when they arrived at his office for the reading of the will reinforced Warner's impression of him as a throwback to an earlier era, one of old-world gentility. He was businesslike but subdued on this sad occasion. He greeted the family members by name, and he introduced himself to Warner with a warm handshake.

"It's nice to meet you, son. Although I wish it could have happened under more pleasant circumstances."

"Thank you, sir."

"I think everyone is here. Will you all be seated?" Emerson asked, once they had all arrived and been ushered into a room dominated by a long, highly polished oak table, which looked as antique, and nearly as elegant, as the old gentleman himself.

They sat around the table, as directed. The lawyer, rather than sitting at the head of the table, moved to a cabinet on the wall, and opened it to reveal a television, which he turned on. Everyone watched as Rebecca's image appeared on the screen, her smiling face bright-eyed and joyful, caught and frozen forever just as they remembered her.

"I, Rebecca Tanner, being of sound mind and body, do hereby bequeath my worldly goods to my beloved family," the videotaped will began. Tears welled up in Maddie's eyes, and looking around the ornate table, Warner saw that the others also appeared to be moved. Even Janet seemed somewhat affected.

"I decided to record this will so there will be no mistake about what I want for all of you, which is for you to live as long and as happily as I have. I love you all. It is easy for me to say this to you because you are the light of my life. My children and their children have been everything to me. I am sorry that I ever have to leave you." There was a sniffle or two, and a sob escaped her daughter, Rachel. Maddie, beside Warner, was trying to maintain her composure.

"I don't think I am going anywhere for a long, long time, but my old friend Alton insists that I update my will every year or two. This is the first time I've recorded it, and I like it. I feel like I'm talking to you, and I like that you can see me and hear me, and my words, rather than some flowery writing on a legal document."

This was not a woman who feared death, but this was also, clearly, a woman who loved life. She talked about the items she wanted to leave to her children, grandchildren, nieces, and nephews. Warner only half listened. Maddie was holding his hand under the table, and her grip on him tightened as Rebecca said, "To my niece Janet, I leave the cameo she used to love when she was a little girl. I hope that by the time this will is read, we will have made peace." Like everyone else, Warner couldn't resist looking toward Maddie's mother. Janet was clearly touched by the woman's words, though she pursed her lips and tried not to let it show. "If she wants, she can have all my brooms, too. Just kidding." She giggled, and Maddie smiled, though some of the other family members sitting at the table shifted uncomfortably in their seats.

"And, now, Maddie . . ." Everyone's eyes were riveted on the television screen. "My children don't want this old house, or need it. I would leave it to them to sell or whatever, but I think you can make better use of it. I know you don't think you are going to come back to live in Haycock Township, but, at the moment, this is still your home. You grew up here, and your family is here, and this is where you will always be welcome. So I'm leaving my house to you. Now, you'll have a home of your own, right here in your Richland, PA."

Maddie's grip on his hand had loosened as she stared, gaping, at Rebecca's image on the TV.

Her great-aunt wasn't finished. "You don't think you need a home base, I know, but I disagree. I'm an old, bossy woman who has no right to say this to you, but, much as I understand, I just can't agree.

You can live here, or not. That's up to you. I just ask one thing. Please don't sell my house. Not until you've given it some time to grow on you. It's a big old barn, but it's been well loved, and pretty well taken care of, even if I have kind of run out of steam lately. With a little work, it can be your home base, without tying you down. I know how much you value your independence. The house is paid for, and the taxes aren't high, so it shouldn't be a burden. And I think you could love the old place as much as I did, if you give it a chance. You might want to try living here for a while." She paused. "Damon, don' be mad. You know I had to do this. I did try to warn you, and your sister. I love you and Rachel very much, but you don't need my house, you have lovely homes of your own. I love you, all of you."

When the recorded message ended, there was complete silence. Everyone looked from the lawyer to Maddie, who stared back at them, equally stunned. "Her house?" Maddie said.

Rebecca's children, Rachel and Damon, were clearly dismayed by the news. "Why would she leave our house to you?" Rachel asked.

Warner almost blurted out, *You just saw the video-tape! You know as much as we do, you dolt.* He managed to control the urge, just barely.

"This is what Rebecca wanted," Emerson said firmly. "There are various documents that need to be signed, by all of you, in order for me to release her accounts to you, and transfer her stocks and property to your names. I've prepared copies for you to look over."

"It's got to be a mistake," Maddie said, although it was clear from Becky's recorded message that she knew exactly what she was doing and why.

The lawyer stood, and moved around the table,

placing a thick brown folder on the table in front of each member of the family. "A copy of the video, and a transcript, is enclosed in each of these packets. When you've had a chance to digest this information, contact me, and we'll finish the paperwork."

Maddie looked shell-shocked. They all filed, silently, out of the conference room. Becky's children left the lawyer's office without once glancing in the direction of the Delaneys.

In the outer office, Janet, Joseph, Ted, and Jordana gathered around the lawyer, asking him what they should do next, but Maddie hung back. Warner was glad to see that even Janet seemed to realize this wasn't the time for histrionics. He saw tears glistening on Maddie's eyelashes and went to her, taking her small, cold hand in his.

"I've got to get out of here. I can't talk to them yet. Not until I've had time to think about all this," Maddie said desperately, with a wave of her hand that encompassed the room, the people in it, and the surprising events that had just transpired.

"That sounds like a good idea," he said, quietly.

Warner sent a silent nod toward the elderly lawyer as they left. He carried the strangely heavy brown accordion file under his arm.

"Where to?" he asked, as they emerged from the two-story house that served as the law offices.

"I don't know," Maddie said, dazed, "Patsy's?"

"Sounds good," he agreed as he opened the car door for her. He knew she was truly in shock, when she didn't comment on the polite gesture. Maddie always made fun of him when he observed the old-world courtesies his parents had taught him. He would explain that it was automatic for him to open the door for a lady, and she'd say it was preposterous, and last time she even ran around the car to open his door for him in return and then asked him if it made him feel stupid, or perhaps just impatient at the wait.

Today, however, she just slid into the car seat and waited for him to come around to the driver's side. "I could really use some of Patsy's cooking," Maddie said as he got into the Toyota.

"That's perfectly understandable," Warner said, and he meant it. "Just sit back and relax. We'll be in Allentown in twenty minutes."

"Thanks for getting me out of there. I definitely cannot deal with my family right now," she said. Then she lapsed into silence, though not for very long.

She tried to take his advice. At least he thought she did. But she couldn't seem to sit still. "I can't believe that just happened. It feels like a dream, or a strange kind of nightmare," she said. "What was Aunt Becky thinking?"

"She couldn't have known how your family would react," he said soothingly.

"I guess so," she agreed. "I must admit that even I thought Becky's death would make Mom mellow out a little. But it didn't. She's as obsessed as ever."

"I suspect your aunt thought it would be some time before her will would be read. She probably thought she had time to tell you all about her plans."

"You may be right," Maddie said, nodding. "But did you see Damon and Rachel? They looked so hurt. I felt bad for them."

"Hmm," Warner murmured, but he kept his thoughts about her cousins to himself. Family was family, and he had no right to say what he was thinking, which was that her loyalty was misplaced. Maddie didn't need to hear him talk about how childish her cousins were. Their reaction annoyed him more than anything else that had happened at that bizarre meeting.

Luckily, she dropped the subject before he was tempted to tell her what he really thought. But it came up again when she told Patsy about the day's events.

"You should have seen my cousin Damon's face," Maddie said, after she told her friend about the bequest. "It was clear he thought that somehow I influenced Aunt Becky's decision, but I didn't. I swear, I never asked her to do this. It wouldn't have occurred to me."

"We know that, honey," Patsy reassured her.

But she continued, as if her friend hadn't spoken, "What am I going to do with a house?"

Warner couldn't keep it inside anymore. "Damon Tanner is forty-three years old. He moved out of his mother's house over twenty years ago," Warner said, growing irritated all over again as he remembered her cousin's nasty reaction to the news of Maddie's bequest.

"Still . . ." Maddie said. "Maybe she should have left the house to her kids. They grew up there."

"They don't need it. Both of them own their own very comfortable homes. What would they do with that big old place?" Patsy asked. "Other than sell it."

"What am I going to do with it?" Maddie asked, baffled.

"I'm sure she meant well," her friend answered.

"She said it could be your home base," Warner explained, for Patsy's benefit. "I think she intended to make sure Maddie always had some place to come home to."

"That's nice. I always liked that woman," Patsy said, nodding once, in approval.

Warner agreed. "Me too."

"She's a sweetheart," Maddie added. "But I wish she hadn't done this. My mother is never going to accept it. And I don't have the slightest idea how to take care of a house. I've never even owned an apartment. I've always rented . . . when I wasn't living in a dormitory, or some other temporary lodging."

"Maybe it's time you learned then," Patsy said, encouragingly.

"Why? What good will it do? If I ever settle down, it won't be *here*."

"Have you got someplace else in mind?" she asked.

"I don't plan to live anywhere specific. My work takes me somewhere new every year or so, and I like it that way. Great-Aunt Becky knew that. I thought she understood." She looked so forlorn, Warner's heart went out to her. But she was wrong.

"Maybe she understood more than you think," Warner commented. "She was as sharp as a tack. I wouldn't ignore her advice, if I were you."

"What advice?" Maddie asked, confused. "Live here?"

In response to her questioning look, he could only shrug his shoulders. He didn't know what he meant. Warner just wanted to chase away that worried look in her eyes.

"I can't," she said, adamantly. "Even if I wanted to at some time in the future, I certainly don't have that option right now. I have to go back to work as soon as I figure out how to straighten out this mess. I have a *life*."

"I'm not saying that you shouldn't go back to work," Warner said. "I'm just saying you shouldn't discount what your aunt said. She was no fool."

"I know that, Warner. I'm well aware of that fact, but this . . . this is just a big honking mess. My mother is going to have a stroke, or have a nervous breakdown, or both. I can't live in Becky's house. And even if Mom wasn't against it, I'd still have a big problem with this. I don't want to live here. I need a house like I need a hole in the head. It's so . . ." she floundered, casting about for the words to describe her predicament, and came up with "big!"

"I understand," Patsy said soothingly. "You've spent the last ten years living out of carry-on luggage, with almost everything you own packed inside it. A house that size won't fit in there."

"Exactly," Maddie said, missing out on, or choosing to ignore, the sarcastic undertone in her friend's comment.

"You know, you could try to think about this another way," Patsy suggested. "There are a lot of people out there who would kill to have your problem."

"I know," Maddie wailed. "On top of everything else, I feel like the most ungrateful person who ever lived. But I can't pretend to be happy about this. That would be completely dishonest."

"Okay, so happy isn't an option," Warner said. "But how about not going off the deep end until you've given it a little time to sink in? You can handle this, Maddie. It's not the disaster you're making it out to be. You'll figure out what to do, and do it. Okay?"

"How exactly am I supposed to figure that out? Tell me," she ordered.

"I don't know. You just will," he assured her. "If you stop freaking out."

"That's your advice?" she asked. "Don't panic?"

"It won't help," Patsy chimed in.

"I can't think straight," Maddie said. "I'm all mixed up. All I can think about is what my mother is going to say to me when I get home tonight."

"You can't worry about her," Warner said. "You have enough problems of your own without adding your mom's feud with a dead woman to the list."

"He's right," Patsy said.

"Okay, so what do I do first?" she asked.

"Drink up?" he suggested. "You've got a lot to think about."

"Then can I panic?" she said facetiously.

"No," Warner said implacably. "Why would you?"

Patsy jumped into the debate. "I don't know how, but you've got to carry out your aunt's wishes."

"I want to," Maddie said, obviously frustrated. "I mean, I loved her and I also know Becky did this because she loved me. She was trying to help. I wouldn't want to disrespect her or her memory."

"You'll figure out a way," Warner assured her.

"I hope so," Maddie answered fervently. "I really don't want to disappoint her, if she's watching. But my mom is going to go absolutely insane. I know it."

Patsy and Warner couldn't argue with that. Maddie was probably right, and there was nothing that any of them could do about it except wait for the storm to pass.

CHAPTER SEVEN

No matter what Maddie said, her mother remained adamant. She thought Maddie should sign the house over to her cousins immediately. Maddie was tempted just to give in and do what Janet wanted, but her conscience wouldn't allow her to betray her aunt's trust like that. She kept hearing Becky's words about having a place to come home to. She didn't agree that it was something she needed, and if her aunt had asked her before she did this thing, Maddie would have told her she didn't want it, but she couldn't turn a deaf ear to the old woman's last request. As Patsy had said, she had to try and fulfill Great-Aunt Becky's wish. Somehow.

A couple of days after the reading of the will, Maddie and her mother sat drinking tea in the living room in a rare peaceful moment. She probably shouldn't have done it, but she was carried away by the normalcy of it—sitting in the white wooden chair at the table she'd eaten breakfast at every morning before school while Janet braided her hair. Maddie just couldn't resist taking advantage of the unexpected opportunity to make an appeal to her mother's sense of right and wrong. "It was an old woman's dying wish that I take her house. How can I refuse that? It would be like spitting on her grave."

Janet winced. "Rebecca was my mother's sister, and I wouldn't expect you to show her disrespect, but I can't help feeling that there's more to this than what we see. I know you loved her, and she loved you, but I believe it would be dangerous for you to accept that house. Who knows what kind of hex the place might be under?"

"Whatever you *think* she did, you should forgive her now. It's just common decency."

"She forfeited her right to common decency when she turned her back on God—and her family."

Maddie didn't think Rebecca Tanner had turned her back on her family. It was Janet who had ostracized her. But this wasn't the time to debate the issue. "You're asking me to do the same thing. I can't believe you seriously expect me to walk away from this. It would be like turning my back on her."

"Keeping that house can't bring you anything but bad luck," her mother persisted.

"Mom, I know you feel very strongly about your beliefs, but I think you're letting your pain and your hurt over an old argument affect your judgment in this case."

"You're wrong," Janet said stubbornly.

"Please, can you just *try* to look at the situation from my point of view? Just . . . just, I don't know . . . imagine that you are me for one minute. It shouldn't be that hard. You know me."

"Honey, I'm sorry—"

"Wait!" Maddie cut her off. "Just try it. I'm begging you."

"I can't," Janet said sadly.

Maddie threw her hands up in the air in exasperation. "Would it kill you to look at this realistically for once? This just can't go on forever. The woman's dead. You've got to put this ridiculous feud to bed, once and for all."

"I can't change the way I feel. You have never taken me seriously about this, but I know what I know. Your great-aunt Becky was not right. There was something 'off' about her, and I wasn't the only one who saw it, either. Plenty of people noticed."

"Dad didn't seem to have any real problem with her."

"Your father was always willing to give her the benefit of the doubt because it was clear that she loved you, loved all of us, but that didn't make her any less dangerous, in my opinion."

"Mom, do you know how irrational you sound when you talk like this? You've become obsessed."

"Will you stop with all the psychobabble, Maddie? I'm not obsessed, nor am I irrational. I knew this woman for a lot longer than you did and I saw what life did to her. When she was young, she was full of life and love and spirit, but over the years she became bitter and cynical."

"We toasted life together, less than a year ago, on New Year's Eve, Mom. She was still full of spirit . . . and she wasn't bitter, that was just the way you saw her. She could be a little sarcastic, sure, especially when you were around, glaring at her, or talking about her as if she wasn't there, but there was nothing evil about it. That was a perfectly natural reaction to the situation *you* put her in. When we were alone, she told me stories about herself when she was young—and you and Dad, too. She helped me to see you as a person when you—" Maddie stopped herself, just in time, from telling Janet how much her mother's behavior had embarrassed her for all those years. She didn't want to hurt her mother, so she hurriedly finished the sentence. ". . . before I ever thought of you that way." It had been her great-aunt that had helped her to accept her mom as an individual in her own right. If it hadn't been for Rebecca Tanner, Maddie might have ended up despising her mother throughout her adolescent years and perhaps even beyond that.

Apparently, her mother was able to guess at what she hadn't said. "Do you really think that telling me you sat around talking about me is somehow going to make me feel better?" she asked, rhetorically. "She defended me?" Janet added, indignant. "That's the whole problem with that woman right there, and if you can't see that, then you are the one who isn't being rational."

"Great-Aunt Becky was not the problem, Mom. I promise," Maddie said wearily. "You could see that, if you tried."

"You're saying I'm the one with the problem, I know that, and I'm trying to tell you, you're wrong."

"Fine." Maddie gave up. "I get it, Mom. If I do take the house, you're going to spend the rest of your life trying to make me regret it. Great."

"That isn't what I meant," Janet said defensively.

"What did you mean then?" Maddie demanded.

"I can't let you make a mistake like this. I couldn't just sit back and let you do that. Don't you understand?"

"No. I don't," Maddie said baldly. "I'm going for a drive." And she left.

She hadn't been behind the wheel of a car in a

long time and she couldn't believe how free it made her feel. One moment she felt trapped and desperate, and the next, thanks to Enterprise Car Rental, she felt as though she could go anywhere, and do anything, she wanted.

Sun-warmed wind whipped across her cheeks through the open window. Perfect, puffy white clouds floated across the blue sky, all the way back to the horizon. The vibrant green cornfields of eastern Pennsylvania rushed past her window, the last of the corn ripening on the stalk in neat rows that extended from the side of the road back toward the darker green of the tree line. At the side of the road, the fluffy white heads of the Queen Anne's lace bobbed on strong green stalks and multicolored wildflowers dotted the long grasses and the yellowing scrub brush.

She had forgotten how much she loved to drive. Maddie felt comfortable in her own skin as she hadn't in days.

Except when she was with Warner Davis. Something about being with him soothed and reassured her as nothing else did.

He'd been a rock at the reading of the will. He might not really belong to her, but sometimes, as in the lawyer's office, she felt as though he really was family. Not the family she'd been born into— the one she had no choice but to live with—but the family she chose. Their marriage might not be authentic, but their relationship was one of the few truly solid things in her life. It seemed perfectly natural, after she'd driven for an hour and a half, to turn the car toward Warner's house.

Calmly, she decided it was time to leave her parents' house. She couldn't stay there.

The obvious answer to her problem was to move into Warner's place. He would put her up while she figured out what to do, she was sure. On her visits stateside, she often stayed with him rather than her parents. She had a drawer full of clothes in the bureau in his guest room, and he always said she was welcome anytime. She believed he even meant it.

His house was lovely, homey, and comfortable. Maddie had always appreciated having an open invitation, and even more than that, someone who was always pleased to see her. Best of all, it provided the perfect excuse not to go home to Mom. She loved her parents, of course, but her visits home were never without incident. She didn't suppose Warner would be all that surprised at her sudden appearance on his doorstep. He had to know that she was not going to be able to last long at her mom's place under the circumstances. He was probably just wondering when she would reach the end of her tether.

Legally, it was her house, too, he insisted. Maddie knew she had no real right to the house, but it was fun to think of it as hers. Maybe Great-Aunt Becky was right, at least partially, and she would enjoy owning her own home. But if Maddie ever did consider getting a place of her own in the States, the only space she could imagine occupying was an apartment in a big city like Manhattan, perhaps something similar to her friend Jennifer's home. She would have to settle for something a lot less luxurious, of course, given their respective pay scales, but she could envision herself, someday, choosing to come back to someplace like that to live.

She could not conceive of anything that could induce her to come back to the town of Richland in the heart of Haycock Township. She was out, and she intended to stay out. Of that, she was absolutely certain.

She did have to admit that she felt her heart warm as she turned onto Warner's street. His house was an adorable eighty-year-old charmer on two acres of land that included a small orchard composed of a couple of cherry trees, three pear, and a variety of apple trees, one of which she had planted the first time she ever visited him here. The cedar shingles had been painted cornflower blue for as long as she could remember, although he did repaint the window shutters a different color every three or four years. At the moment they were white to match the traditional white picket fence that fronted the property.

She hadn't bothered to call Warner to tell him she was coming. She knew where he hid the spare key in the fake rock, so Maddie figured if he wasn't home she'd just let herself in and wait for him. She'd stopped to buy a couple of bottles of wine at the liquor store on the way. She would go ahead and start drinking without him, if she had to. Luckily, his car was in the driveway, when she arrived. She couldn't wait to see him.

As she parked on the street in front of his house, she remembered how excited he had been when he first bought it. He'd been so happy and proud as he gave her the tour. And she was happy for him, though she thought it was strange that, by some twist of fate, he ended up living ten minutes from the house she grew up in. Warner felt right at home in Richland from the very beginning, and he never could understand why she didn't love her hometown.

Warner was raised in Easton, fifteen miles away, which was the big city compared to this tiny, rural township. The things he liked best about his new home were the very things Maddie found so stifling about it. She quickly realized that he didn't mind that his new neighbors were so intrusive. He chose Richland largely because everyone was so curious about everyone else's business. He said it felt like a solid, old-fashioned community.

It wasn't that Maddie didn't have some good memories of growing up here. She actually felt, even if she was not exactly comfortable in the town she was born in, at least her house was the one place on earth that she never questioned she belonged. As insane as it was that the whole family allowed Mom's eccentricities to wreak havoc on their lives, Maddie was one of them. No matter how far away she went, or how long she was gone, when she walked into her childhood home she fell right back into the routine—if one could call the madness that surrounded the Delaney family routine. But right at the moment, she could not handle the added stress of living with her mother on top of the bombshell that had just been dropped on her. She had to get out of that house—and into this one.

Maddie hurried up to the front door, mentally rehearsing her entrance line, *Save me, Obi-Wan Kenobi, you're my only hope*. But when she reached the front door of Warner's house, she saw, through the stained-glass panels that composed the top half of the door, that the light wasn't on in the foyer. She stood just listening for a moment. Nothing. No music, no sound at all. She knocked on the door, and waited. When he didn't answer, she felt conflicting emotions—disappointment that he wasn't there to greet her, but also satisfaction at the thought that maybe he was out having a little fun for a change. Warner needed a night out more than any two people she knew. What's more—he truly deserved it.

She moved away from the door and looked up

at the second floor. She couldn't see any lights anywhere, but all of the curtains were closed, so if he was upstairs in his bedroom, she wouldn't be able to see. But she was sure that if he was up there, he would have heard her knocking and answered the door. It was more likely that Warner had gone out. Perhaps in someone else's car. Yes, that was probably it. Someone came and picked him up and took him out somewhere. But where? He never went anywhere except his food co-op, and places like that.

"Maybe he's out getting lucky," she murmured aloud, as she let herself in the front door. There was a light shining from the kitchen, at the back of the house, and she headed in that direction, flicking the light switch on in the hall as she went by. There was some evidence that Warner had cooked for himself, and perhaps the "friend" whom Maddie had imagined he'd gone out with to "wherever." Some pots were soaking in the sink, filled with soapy water, and dishes were drying in the rack. The most telltale sign, however, was the faint scent that still pervaded the room, of garlic, onions, tomato, and . . . chocolate. Warner had not only prepared a meal here recently, he'd been baking! Maddie went on the hunt for leftovers.

She felt a sudden strong craving for his fantastic homemade chocolate chip cookies. They were delectable, a guaranteed cure for what ailed her. . . . In fact, they were her favorite food in the world. She conducted a thorough search of his neatly organized kitchen cabinets and then the canisters on the counter, but couldn't find any sweets. She rifled through the drawers and poked about in the stainless steel refrigerator in a last-ditch effort. As she explored, she became more and more convinced that that faint, tantalizing hint of chocolate in the air was definitely the unforgettable aroma of Warner's famous cookies.

Where could they be? He had to have made a pretty large batch. There were too many standing orders from his friends, family, nieces, nephews, and neighbors for him to bake less than thirty or forty at a time. When Maddie was home at Christmastime, Warner whipped up sheet after sheet every day.

She had asked him then, "Does your house always smell like this? I don't remember."

He had laughed. "No. Only about once a month or so, when I get the urge to bake."

"You're wasted in the art department," Maddie told him. "You really should be a chef."

It wasn't the first time she had suggested he make that particular career move. He had always, even in college, enjoyed cooking, but, he said, he didn't want to do it for a living—that would take all the fun out of it.

"It would be fun for the rest of us," she retorted, speaking around a mouthful of some fantastic confection that he had made.

"I would love to spend my life providing you with finger food," he said. "But somehow I don't see that as the respectable profession my parents always hoped I would pursue." She had giggled and he had laughed and, remembering that conversation, Maddie smiled again.

Now, she took a cursory look around the small but elegant dining room with its gleaming hardwood table and comfortable antique chairs. Warner had found the furniture in this room—table, chairs, and the low, matching breakfront—in a thrift shop, and refinished them himself. A large wooden carving board and antique pewter candlestick holders placed atop the long, low, gleaming wooden break-front offset the cut crystal bowls he had inherited from his grandmother. Along with the tasteful modern art on the walls, it was just enough to give the room a masculine feel—nothing overwhelming, just a sense that this was a place where a man lived and ate. Since Maddie didn't think he'd hide the cookies in the breakfront, she moved on toward the living room.

When she opened the door, the lights were dimmed, the television aglow, and Warner and a woman were sitting on the couch together—very close together. He bolted upright, and the woman gasped fearfully. "Oh!" Maddie nearly jumped a foot.

Maddie could imagine how the other woman felt, since her own heart was still racing from the shock of finding them in there, and she apologized profusely. "I didn't realize there was anyone here," she said shakily. Realizing that that explanation might not be quite adequate, she went on. "I didn't mean to intrude. I'm Maddie . . ." She caught herself just before she said her married name. ". . . Delaney," she announced instead, just in case Warner hadn't mentioned her existence to his date. "I just dropped by to—" she started to elaborate, then thought better of it. "Well, *that's* not important now." She backed toward the door, talking all the way. "I'm sorry," she said again. "I'm just so embarrassed, because I saw the car out front, but I didn't see any lights on inside the house, so I just assumed that Warner was out, and . . ." She just couldn't seem to stop talking. "I *did* knock. I guess I should have rung the doorbell. Sorry."

She had already backed halfway through the doorway when Warner stood and said, "Maddie, stop! It's okay. Come back here. I'd like you to meet my friend, Samantha Wheeler." She stood in the doorway, half in and half out, not sure whether to go forward or back, as Warner drew Samantha up off the couch. He and Maddie stood facing each other awkwardly. Then Warner cleared his throat and came forward to draw her back into the room, toward the woman he'd been necking with on the couch.

"Maddie, this is Samantha, a good friend of mine." He turned to the tall, beautiful woman who was waiting expectantly for him to complete these awkward introductions. "This is Maddie. I think I may have mentioned her to you?"

"No, I don't think so," Samantha said, without rancor, and she smiled and offered Maddie her hand.

"Oh," Warner said. He looked taken aback by her answer. "Well, we're very old friends—" he started to explain.

"We went to college together," Maddie chimed in. "And grad school."

"That's nice," Samantha said. "And you stayed in touch?"

Warner couldn't take it anymore. Maddie watched him as he teetered, and then made his decision.

"We're married," he blurted out. "Maddie's work takes her all over the world so we don't see too much of each other, but her parents live here in Richland, so when she comes home we see each other, about once or twice a year, usually."

"Oh?" Samantha didn't look too shocked to Maddie. Her smile had been replaced by a look of inquiry, but at least she didn't seem to be angry. Warner was an extremely lucky man.

He went on in a rush, "It's sort of complicated."

"Not really," Maddie said. "It's simple, really. We got married in grad school, but it was never a *real* marriage. It was just for scholarship money, and taxes, and stuff like that. Not to cheat on our taxes, or anything sordid. Warner can explain it better than I can, but you know how they say two can live as cheaply as one. Well, it's even cheaper than that, so we got married and we haven't gotten around to getting unhitched. That's all there is to it."

Samantha still looked somewhat confused, but she only said, "I see."

Maddie didn't think she did. See. But the woman wasn't rushing to judgment, and that had to be more than Warner could have hoped for, given the unhappy look on his face.

"It's an unusual situation, I know," Warner said, apologetically.

"No, no, I'm sure it's perfectly sensible," Samantha Wheeler said.

"Yes, exactly!" Maddie grabbed on to the word like a drowning man grabbing for a lifeline. "It is sensible. Warner is nothing if not sensible. He has always been like that. Neither of us was ready for marriage and we had years more of school ahead of us, so we decided to do it. Get married. Just until we fall in love, or something. Not with each other," she hastened to add. "With someone else," she finished falteringly, looking helplessly at Warner. He mouthed the words *Shut up!* at her, and she clamped her lips together obediently.

Samantha looked from her, back up at Warner, as if she knew he'd sent the silent message, but she just went on smiling graciously at him and at Maddie. She was obviously taking this whole awkward situation in stride. "Yes, well, I should be getting home," she said. "I'm sure you two have a lot to talk about."

"No, no, I don't think so," Warner replied. "Right, Maddie?"

"It's just my mother," she mumbled. "That's all."

"See, I told you, Sam," he said to Samantha.

"Right," Maddie said. "I'll go."

"No," Samantha said firmly. "Maddie, is it?" Maddie nodded. "You stay. Talk to Warner. Obviously you wouldn't come looking for him if you didn't need him." Maddie shrugged. "I told the sitter I'd be home early, anyway." Samantha cut off Warner's protests before he could voice them. "Really, it's all right."

Warner wasn't going to give up that easily. "Just give us a minute. One minute. I'll be right back." He didn't wait for an answer, just strode to the door, grabbing Maddie by the elbow on his way and towing him along with her. "Let me just see what this is about. I'm *sure* it's nothing."

She was propelled out into the hallway while Samantha watched, without batting an eye. "Nice to meet you," Maddie called back to the other woman over her shoulder.

"I'll be right back," Warner said. Out in the hall, he let her go, abruptly, as he turned to face her. "What?" he demanded, his voice lowered, but still forceful. "What are you doing here?"

"Mom is driving me crazy about the house and we had another argument this afternoon. I almost said something terrible to her, so I decided to take a drive before things got out of hand," she explained in a rush. "And then I drove over here."

"Uh-huh. And just what did you think I could do about it?" he asked.

"Nothing, really," she mumbled, looking down at the ground, back toward the living room door, and anywhere but at him. "I just needed to vent."

But he had already realized what she was there for. "Maddie! You can't come barging in here every time you and Janet have a fight. This is ridiculous."

"I'm sorry," Maddie said, with sincere regret. "I

didn't know. I thought I could camp out here for a day or two, just until things cooled down, you know. I'm really sorry."

"You don't have to keep apologizing. It won't help anything," he said harshly. "The damage is done."

"I know. I totally screwed up. But I can't take it when you're angry at me," Maddie answered him. "Please say you'll get over it in a day or two and I'll get out of here."

"And go where?" he asked. "Home?" She didn't answer. "You'd better stay here tonight."

"Won't she think it's a little strange?" Maddie asked in a whisper.

"She doesn't seem to," Warner answered, looking back at the door to the living room. "I'm sure she won't," he added, definitely.

"But—" Maddie started to argue.

"Don't!" he said. "I'm going to go follow Sam home in my car and talk to her. Hopefully I can explain this to her satisfaction. It's partly my fault. I should have told her about you before. As soon as you go home, in fact. But I put it off because things were going so well between us."

"If I'd known—"

He cut her off. "No, I don't want to hear it. There isn't time now. Just . . . come on with me." He went back into the living room and Maddie obediently followed him.

"Sam, I'm going to explain everything to you," he said as soon as he reached the woman who stood waiting by the couch.

"You don't owe me any explanations," she said.

"I think having my *wife* show up out of the blue entitles you to a conversation," he retorted. "And I would rather tell you what's going on here than have you come up with your own interpretation.

This is not what it looks like. Maddie's just an old friend who happens to need a place to stay tonight, so she's going to stay here while you and I go to your place and have a little chat."

Samantha mulled it over for a minute and then agreed. "That's fine." She was remarkably calm, under the circumstances, Maddie thought. If their situations had been reversed, Maddie didn't think that she would have been able to stay so cool. No wonder Warner liked this woman. If what Maddie had seen here tonight was any indication, Samantha Wheeler was almost too good to be true.

CHAPTER EIGHT

Warner had always assumed that Radu must have mentioned his marriage to Samantha. His best friend had certainly known about the arrangement—but it was such ancient history, and so completely unconnected to his life after graduate school, that they never really discussed it. Since Warner never knew what Radu thought of his pseudo-marriage, he had no clue how he might have characterized the relationship to his wife, and since Samantha had never mentioned it, Warner left it alone. But, after Maddie's sudden arrival, Warner wished he'd explained to Samantha about his wedded status before. He'd been waiting to get onto firmer footing with her before opening up that can of worms, but perhaps that hadn't been necessary. Whatever her reaction might have been then, anything would have been better than this. He hated having to explain.

He was a big chicken, that was it, Warner realized. Nevertheless, it took the entire drive to Samantha's place for him to work up the nerve to tell her the story. He followed her in his car and, when they reached her house, she invited him in for coffee, which he brewed while she paid the baby-sitter and checked on the children. The short reprieve was welcome, as it gave him the time he needed to gather his thoughts.

"I know it looks a little odd," he started when they were seated across the kitchen table, steaming mugs of fresh brewed coffee on the table in front of them. "So I want to explain about Maddie."

"You don't have to," Samantha said. "She's charming."

"Yes, okay, but that's beside the point. You deserve an explanation for what happened this evening. Our date, and her showing up, and everything. The thing is, it's a complicated situation. When Maddie and I were in college, I realized there were certain benefits to being married and she . . . and we . . . I mean . . ." he stammered to a halt.

"Warner, you don't have to explain anything to me," Samantha said gently. "I think I understand."

"Yes, I do. I should have told you before this because . . ." He took a swallow of the hot coffee. It scalded his tongue, but he welcomed the little jolt of pain. It seemed to steady him. "Tonight shouldn't have happened."

"It wasn't that bad," she said softly.

"Radu told you about me being married?" he asked.

"If he did, I don't remember." She shook her head. "No, but, I think I knew. It seems to me I heard somewhere that you were married. Maybe I even knew her name. I guess I just assumed you were divorced."

"No," he said, shaking his head. "I thought about it a lot over the years, but when she came home to visit, she was always on her way to Greece or England or India, and it never seemed like a good time to bring it up. She generally comes home on the holidays, and all the paperwork has to be done on weekdays so . . ." He knew it sounded like he was making excuses, and Warner needed Sam to believe him. She had to truly understand the situation. After what Radu had done to her, Warner didn't want her to have any doubts about him. More importantly, he didn't want her to think he was anything like her missing husband. "We're just friends. We've always been friends," he said emphatically. "Nothing more," he hastened to add. "Platonic friends."

"I get the picture," Samantha said laughingly. "You're friends."

"Uh-huh," Warner muttered, embarrassed, but relieved that the whole thing was out in the open.

"And you're married," she reiterated.

"Yes, but—"

"I get it," she interrupted, before he could start babbling again. She didn't look hurt, or disappointed. In fact, he would have sworn she was laughing at him, except that Sam didn't do that. She didn't have a mean bone in her body. Sam was one of those rare people who just didn't seem to need to put anybody down.

"Maddie's here because a relative of hers died recently. Her great-aunt. And she had to be here for the reading of the will."

"That's too bad." She didn't sound very sympathetic. She was listening attentively, but he could have been talking about the gross national product or the price of wheat in the Ukraine, something that didn't concern her at all.

"They were very close."

"Mm-hmm," she murmured. She appeared serene. Warner was relieved that she was taking the news so well, but he wondered if she was just covering up her true emotions. She'd gotten pretty good at hiding her feelings after Radu left.

"Maddie's a linguist. She was supposed to be in Cairo for the next six months, or a year, translating some ancient scrolls."

"That's . . . different" was Samantha's only comment.

He examined her face closely, but she just listened, patiently. She appeared to be reserving judgment.

"I know it must seem sort of strange that she's staying at my place, but she does that sometimes. She and her mother have a rocky relationship," he said.

"Warner, you are the nicest guy." There was no mistaking the warmth and approval in her voice now.

He breathed a sigh of relief. "Thanks, Sam. I'm so sorry about all of this."

"Don't be," she said and he believed she really meant it.

"So you're okay with all this?"

"Sure. Why not?" She truly didn't appear to be fazed by the sudden appearance of his wife on his doorstep.

"So," Warner said, with another sigh. "Good."

"So," Samantha echoed. "What other surprises do you have in store for me?"

"That's pretty much it. I'm an open book."

"I think it's a little odd that this woman whom you've barely seen in the last ten years showed up tonight—of all times," Samantha said.

"Maddie always has had terrible timing," he conceded.

"Right," Sam said sarcastically. "How did you end up as friends?" she asked. "That's got to be an interesting story."

"Why?" Warner asked.

"I just don't see you two hanging out with the same crowd," she commented.

"We did. Pretty much," he replied.

"Really?" She sounded a little surprised.

"Why is that so hard to believe?" he asked.

"I just can't picture the two of you together, that's all. She doesn't seem like your type."

"Do I have a type?" Warner asked. It was his turn to sound surprised.

"Well, I've known you a long time, and I've met a couple of the women you've been interested in. Dates of yours. None of them were anything like the woman I just met at your house."

"How do you mean?"

"For one thing, they were all brilliant," she said. "Real intellectuals."

"Maddie's specialty is dead languages," he reminded her. "That's about as academic as you can get. Actually, she's a genius." Warner could have kicked himself as her smile faded.

"I believe you," she said. "I didn't mean to imply that she wasn't . . . smart. I meant that the women you dated were all sort of . . . well . . . excuse the expression, but they were a lot more . . . formal. I've never seen you with anyone whom I could imagine just dropping by your place without an invitation. I can't even imagine doing that, and I think I'm a pretty good friend of yours."

"Is that all you see yourself as?" he asked, disappointed. "A friend?"

"Friends are good to have," she replied.

Before Maddie showed up, Samantha had been melting into his side on the couch, slowly moving closer and closer. "That's true, but . . . tonight, I thought, I mean I hoped, that we might be getting past that point."

"I didn't think you would ever be able to forget Radu was my husband," Samantha said.

"I've been working on that," he admitted. "In the end it wasn't as hard as I thought it would be." He smiled down at her, ruefully, and something in her eyes caught his attention, a spark of something more than affection.

"It wasn't?" she asked, breathlessly. He felt his face grow warm at the expression he thought he could see in her eyes. There was definitely something there, he thought. Something he'd been waiting to see.

"I really did have a good time tonight," she said, confirming his suspicions. The warmth spread down, through his body. "The movie was just getting good when we were . . . interrupted. I'll have to rent it and watch the ending sometime."

"You should," Warner said. It was a romantic period piece, the perfect date movie, a friend had told him. "Maybe we could try to get together again when you do, rent the video, I mean? Then we can take up where we left off."

"I thought that was what we were doing," Samantha said ruefully.

Surprised, Warner looked up, scanning her face. "We are?"

"I thought so," she said, lowering her eyes.

"Definitely. Yes," Warner agreed, jumping up and out of his chair. He was around the table in seconds, standing by her side. She looked up at him, smiling.

She liked him. Maddie was forgiven. Her arrival hadn't ruined anything after all, it had just caused a slight delay.

He held out his hand and Samantha took it in hers and stood up. It could have been a very awkward moment, but for once he didn't stop to question his good fortune—or to think. He lifted her chin and looked deeply into her eyes, and found all the encouragement he needed. There could be no mistaking that look. It contained a definite invitation.

He slipped his arms around her and bent his head to kiss her. She greeted him with pleasure, her eyes closing, her lips molding themselves to his, her body leaning into him. Now that they had made this sudden, momentous change to their relationship, it felt perfectly natural, almost inevitable. All his worrying had been for nothing. She was as hungry for him as he was for her, pliant in his arms, and as eager to kiss as to be kissed.

Warner didn't press his luck. After only a minute, he drew away slowly, detaching himself an inch at a time from her embrace, reluctant to release her so soon.

His hands still at her waist, hers on his chest, they each drew a deep shuddering breath. "Wow," he said softly. "That was . . ." He cleared his throat. ". . . worth waiting for."

"I know," Samantha replied. She looked as shocked as he felt. "I never . . . Radu never mentioned what a great kisser you were."

"Really? And I thought he couldn't keep a secret," Warner quipped.

"Ha, ha," she retorted, slapping him lightly on the arm. "You know what I meant. He gave me the impression that you were a little uptight. You know." Warner looked at her curiously. "He said you were a prude," she clarified.

"Me?" he exclaimed, astonished. "You thought I—" He shook his head. "Whatever gave you that idea?"

"Well, you were never very demonstrative with your girlfriends, and you never got very serious with any of them."

Warner could have explained about his rules; how, over the years, he held back because he'd never felt ready to make a commitment before. He nearly did tell her that each time he met a woman or got involved with her, he found himself drawing away if she seemed to expect more from him than a casual relationship. He was tempted to explain that he had never wanted to give anyone the impression that he was free when, technically, he wasn't. If he were honest, he'd have to admit that none of the women he had dated had made him wish he were free, before this. He almost said it . . . that he could never bring himself to let go before.

He wasn't ready then. Or maybe he'd been waiting for this woman.

Warner didn't want to bring up the subject of his wife again, though, so he contented himself with saying, "Maybe Radu should have gotten the facts before he speculated about my love life. I can tell you right now, I've never had any complaints."

"Who's complaining?" Samantha asked, slipping her arms around him again and reaching up to kiss his cheek. "Not me."

"Good." He kissed her again.

He kept his emotions under control this time, determined to go home before things got too passionate between them. They could continue this discussion another time, when he didn't have a crazy lady—whom he happened to be married to—waiting for him at his place. He let his hands drop from their perch on her shoulders and took a couple of small steps back, away from temptation. They had barely touched each other in all the months since Radu had been gone. A few more days, to straighten out *both* of their marital situations, wouldn't hurt. He was pretty sure.

CHAPTER NINE

Maddie waited uneasily for Warner's return. She paced across the kitchen floor, into the hall and the living room, and then wandered upstairs, but she just couldn't seem to settle anywhere. Every time she started to sit down, she got right back up again. She was too tense to stop moving. Warner had not looked happy with her when he left. She giggled nervously as she remembered his face when she'd walked in on him and Samantha, his eyes clouded over, the edges of his mouth turned down, his nostrils actually flaring in frustration. He looked very different from the Warner she was accustomed to seeing.

She had to admit, his girlfriend seemed all right. She was pretty cool about having her evening interrupted, anyway. Maddie couldn't wait to find out more about the woman. She was very attractive. When she first saw *that* Samantha, she felt a twinge of something that could only be described as . . . envy. She didn't generally mind being so petite, but tall, elegant, beautiful women made her feel somewhat childlike. Then there was that pro-

prietary air that Ms. Wheeler displayed when she
put her hand on Warner's arm. That had trig-
gered something akin to jealousy in Maddie. She
knew it was petty, but she couldn't help feeling
that the woman had invaded her territory.

Maddie had never thought much about Warner's
love life. She knew he dated. They'd even talked
about it a little over the years. She told him about
her best, and worst, encounters. They didn't really
keep secrets from each other. He knew about her
most embarrassing romances and she thought she
knew a good bit about his various relationships.
This was different, though. She'd never seen, or
even imagined, him actually seducing someone.
Suddenly she saw her husband in a whole new
light. Solid, predictable Warner Davis making a
booty call? Even though she'd seen the cozy setting he'd created in the living room, the lights
turned low, a romantic movie flickering on the
television screen, still, her mind refused to accept
the truth. Not only because she had never really
pictured him with another woman, but also because she'd never seen a woman look at him the
way this woman did.

Maddie could accept that Warner had urges. He
was a normal, healthy male. But it was inconceiv-
able that he would indulge in a casual relationship
with the incredible woman she had met tonight.
Then it hit her. Warner had to be in love. It was
the only feasible explanation for the scene she'd
stumbled upon here tonight, and for her feelings
of resentment. She sensed a change in him. That
was why she felt so strange. He wasn't her Warner
anymore.

She called Patsy, hoping to get some more information about the woman. "Why didn't you tell
me Warner had a girlfriend?" she wanted to know.

"I didn't know. I swear. Who is she?"

"Her name's Samantha Wheeler. Do you know her?"

"Yeah, I think so. Tall, right? And really pretty? Two kids?"

"She has kids? She doesn't look like the type. She was too perfect."

"We don't all walk around in sweat suits and hair nets all day long, you know. That's just me," Patsy said flippantly. "And the hair net's for work. I'm required to wear it. By law."

"Well, I can't imagine Samantha in a hair net," Maddie said.

"I remember now. That's where I know her from. Mrs. Hutchin's salon. You'll be happy to hear that she dyes her hair."

"I don't care about that. What's the deal with her ex?" Maddie asked. "Why'd she dump him?"

"She didn't. He left."

"You're kidding!" Maddie exclaimed. "Who would walk away from her?"

"A friend of Warner's apparently. I remember the story now. Jamie told me all about it. Seems Samantha was married to this Indian guy, or I think he was half Indian, half black. Anyway, he grew up with Warner, in Easton, and a couple of years ago, they decided to buy a house, so Warner found it for them. A nice little place, over toward Hellertown."

"Yeah, yeah," Maddie said impatiently.

"Anyway," Patsy continued, "they're settling in, seemingly the perfect little family, and suddenly he just took off. The husband. I never really talked to him, but he looked like a perfectly normal guy. I can't figure out how anyone could do that. Wait until you see the kids. They're gorgeous. A boy and a girl who is just a little doll. She comes with her mother when she gets her hair done, and she is so sweet—"

"I'm sure she's adorable," Maddie interrupted. "But let's stay on track here, Pats. Samantha Wheeler's husband walked out on her and then what happened?"

"Nothing, as far as I know. No one's seen him since."

"My God, that's horrible. How long ago was this?"

"I think it was at the beginning of the year some time."

"She seems to be holding up pretty well," Maddie commented.

"She is. She still gets her hair done. I guess she's trying to keep it together for the kids. She's lucky to have Warner as a friend."

"From what I saw tonight, he's more than just a friend," Maddie reported.

That was a mistake. Patsy got excited. "Really? What did you see?"

"Get a life, Pats. I'll talk to you, later. Bye."

"I want details," she warned. "Next time. Bye."

When Warner arrived home, Maddie had reconciled her conflicting emotions. "Hey, stranger," she said, as he let himself in the front door. "Did everything work out okay?"

"Yeah," he said grudgingly. "No thanks to you."

Maddie reproached him. "You should have warned me."

"Warned you about what?"

"That you were seeing someone. I didn't mean to intrude."

"So it's my fault that you barged into my house tonight with no warning?" he said dryly.

"Well, if I'd had any idea that there might be

some action in your crib, I would definitely not have just burst in on you," she replied.

"Are you saying you would have called before you dropped in?" he asked.

"Definitely," she lied. He raised one eyebrow, turning his usually boyish expression sardonic. Maddie had always found that particular expression adorable on him. She modified her answer. "Well, probably."

"Face it, you never even thought about asking before you moved in," he said, without rancor

"You were the one who insisted I stay," Maddie pointed out.

"Of course you can stay," Warner said. "That's not the problem."

"It might be. Samantha seemed pretty cool tonight, but eventually she's going to start wondering what's going on between us."

"You don't know Sam. She is very easygoing. She would never get upset about anything like this."

"I don't care how mellow she is, no woman likes it when some other woman moves into her man's house."

"Maybe not," he conceded. "How long *were* you planning to stay?"

"Why? What happened to 'stay as long as you like, this is your house, too'?" Maddie asked teasingly.

"Well, I just assumed . . . I mean . . . whenever you've visited before it's only been for a few days. Don't you have to get back to work?"

She loved making him all flustered. Warner was so staid most of the time, it was fun to push his buttons whenever she could find them.

"Eventually. Yes. But I can't go now." She turned

and walked away from him, into the living room, and threw herself into her favorite chair—his leather recliner. "I spoke to the admin offices at the university yesterday, after I found out about Great-Aunt Becky's house, and asked how much time I had. They said they were still working on my paperwork and they didn't know when it would be straightened out. I told you I was having problems with the Egyptian authorities about my work visa, didn't I?"

"You might have mentioned it," Warner said wryly.

"It seems that the university is taking over the battle. They suggested that I work from here, as well as I can. I've got a copy of the cartonnage with me and they'll send me the support materials over the net. I can use the reference library at Penn. This way, they're able to save part of my salary—I'll be freelance, and so technically not on staff at all. Since I can't go back right away without a valid visa, it seemed like the most sensible solution."

"How long?" he asked, impatiently.

"A month or so, maybe." He looked shocked. "Which is good for me, because it's going to take me at least . . ." She paused, looking up at him. "I'd guess about a month or so to straighten out this situation with my new house. Unless, of course, you'd like to take care of that for me—"

But Warner was shaking his head. "No way, Mad. I don't mind being your mailman, or your hotelier, or even, on occasion, your banker, but I cannot be responsible for your house."

"I was afraid you might say that," she said ruefully.

"So." He looked pensive. "A month," he mused, aloud.

"I could rent a room," Maddie suggested. "Or something."

"Oh, stop with the poor pitiful little homeless waif routine," Warner replied. "You have plenty of places where you can borrow a bed, not to mention that you can always go back to your own bedroom in your parents' house. They didn't kick you out. You left."

"I can't stay there, Warner. Don't make me."

"I never made you do anything you didn't want to do in your life," he snapped irritably. "I would like to see someone try it, though."

"Someone's a little bit grumpy, tonight," Maddie teased, as if his snappishness had nothing to do with her. She smiled tolerantly. "It's no wonder, it's past your bedtime."

"I'm not grumpy," Warner said, but she sensed that her teasing had done the trick. He was softening. He could never stay angry with her for long, thank goodness. It wouldn't take much for him to get over his annoyance with her. He was halfway there already.

"So is it really okay for me to stay?"

"For now," he said. "But you'd better behave yourself," he added, sternly.

"I will. I promise." Maddie crossed her heart. "I'll fix things up with that Samantha woman, too."

"Don't help me," he said quickly. "And don't call her that," he added, as an afterthought.

"Okay, okay. Don't get grumpy again. Come on. Let's get you into bed," she urged. "You'll feel better in the morning."

"I doubt it," he muttered, under his breath.

Maddie pretended not to hear him. "Upstairs, hubby, dear. I'll tuck you in."

"You will not," he growled, but he followed her obediently up the stairs.

He left her at the door to the guest bedroom, which doubled as his studio, and she watched as he walked the few feet down the hall to his bed-room.

"Good night," she called softly.

"Night, Maddie. See you in the morning," he said as he closed the door.

She started to get ready for bed, shaking her head over the events of the evening. What a disaster!

When she decided to take refuge at Warner's place a few hours ago, Maddie hadn't even considered the possibility that Warner might not welcome her with open arms. He was always there for her. That wasn't supposed to change. Ever. He was her rock.

She always figured he would get married and settle down eventually, and she expected to be part of it—especially since she'd have to give him a divorce in order for him to marry someone else. Maddie had even joked with him about giving him away at his wedding. She wanted him to get married in the two-hundred-year-old white clapboard church at the corner of her street, to a bride dressed in an old-fashioned confection of satin and lace . . . not this gorgeous, icy female with legs that came up to Maddie's chin.

Somehow, she always thought she'd be there when he met the woman who would be the second Mrs. Warner Davis. She had been equally sure she would like the person he chose, without reservation. He had such a great heart, he deserved someone who was as warm, and sweet, and giving as he was. More importantly, he needed someone who was as different from Maddie as he was. She had always felt he ought to be with a girl who loved to cook with him, and who was lively, and cute as a button. An elementary school teacher, or a librarian, would be the perfect match.

Maddie knew she was much too wild for Warner. Her visits, he told her, turned his life upside down. So she pictured him with a woman who would fit right in with his circle of friends, and his work, and his house, and his oh-so-normal family. His mother had always treated her as if she were some kind of freak. The woman did not like her at all. Maddie could understand that. She knew she wasn't a good influence on him. In their relationship, she was the wicked and wanton woman who had swooped in and snatched him out of the arms of that nice girl-next-door that he was destined for. His next wife had to be someone who would share in his simple life in a way Maddie never could.

She was too restless, too unconventional, and much too flighty to move into Warner's lovely little house, or to reflect well on him at dinner with the dean of the art department, or to become a soccer mom. That was what he needed. She knew that. Still, this woman he was dating was not, at least at first glance, the kind of sweet soul that he should be with.

She might have felt sorry for her, given what she'd just learned of the woman's history, but Samantha Wheeler was too self-possessed, too together, and much too tall. She was an amazon. Warner would never be able to handle her. She would redecorate his house, Maddie was sure. She would take over and he would let her. Worst of all, she would not allow his friendship with Maddie to continue. It was obvious, from the assessing look in her eye this evening, that she found Maddie lacking in some way.

Maddie knew she wasn't the right *wife* for Warner, but she considered herself his very good friend. Maybe he was the one who got the worst of the deal in this phony marriage of theirs, but it wasn't as if he didn't get anything at all in return. She loved him.

She also added a touch of excitement to his well-ordered, monotonous life. If it weren't for her, he would be a totally conventional guy; living in this tiny little town, and working in the insular world of the local college. He hardly ever met anyone new, and never did anything more daring or adventurous than adding butterscotch chips to his famous chocolate chip cookies. He needed her. Just like she needed him.

Samantha, she was pretty sure, was not going to see it that way, though. Women like Ms. Wheeler, admirable as they were, did not approve of women like Maddie. She was the type of woman who always balanced her checkbooks and did her laundry every week (before she even ran out of socks and underwear). Maddie doubted that she'd be interested in exploits such as camel-trekking in the Thar Desert or going into areas that the U.S. State Department had designated unsafe for American tourists. She would definitely not be thrilled to receive a phone call in the middle of the night from foreign officials who needed verification of Maddie's identity.

Maddie had to admit that she was assuming a lot based on one ten-minute encounter with the woman, but she was relatively certain that she read the situation correctly. She would have to get to know Samantha, of course, to be sure. She *might* be mistaken, and if she was, she could give Warner her blessing, and a quick divorce. But if she was right, Warner had to be warned. She couldn't hand him over to someone who wouldn't let her keep watching over him, and bringing a little excitement into his life. She wanted to share the job with his next wife, not give it up completely.

The next morning, at breakfast, Maddie apologized again for interrupting his session with Samantha.

"Session?" he echoed.

"Date? Whatever," she amended. "I hope I will get to meet her again soon under happier circumstances."

"Don't count on it," he retorted. "Samantha and I don't know each other that well yet, and I already had to explain you once. Tonight was our first date without her kids. I will not be making excuses to her for your behavior again, at least not until the wedding, if I have my way."

Maddie froze, her pancake-laden fork halfway up to her lips. "Wedding?" she queried.

"Just a figure of speech," he said blandly.

She put the fork down. The lump in her throat would not allow the passage of even Warner's light, fluffy hotcakes into her esophagus. "Very funny," she said. "So you don't want me to get to know her, huh? Why? What are you trying to hide?"

"Oh, for Pete's sake, Maddie, this isn't a plot," he said, aggravated. "It's just common sense. I don't want my wife hanging out with my girlfriend, okay?"

"Are you sure that's all there is to it?" she asked.

"Yes," he said firmly. "So let it go."

"Mm-hm," she murmured, picking up her fork again and inserting a sweet, delicious bite into her mouth now that her heart had left her throat and she could swallow again. For a couple of minutes, the only sound in the room was the gentle clinking of silverware against dishware, and the chirping of the birds outside his window.

"Oh, all right," Warner finally said in disgust. "We'll have lunch next weekend. Okay?"

"I can't wait," she said, biting into a croissant with relish.

"You had better behave yourself, Maddie."

"Who, me?" she asked, trying to look hurt and slightly offended and probably failing miserably since she was neither of those things.

"Yes, you," he said, with that *how do I let you talk me into these things* tone of voice that Maddie was so familiar with. "And you had better not make me regret this," he said threateningly. "Because if I do, so will you."

She batted her eyelashes at him and finished off her breakfast. "You don't have to worry about me," she promised.

CHAPTER TEN

Maddie held on to her rental car for three days, clinging to it as if it were her security blanket. When she finally called Enterprise to tell them to pick it up, Warner decided to take it as a sign that she was ready to open up a dialogue with her mother and perhaps work toward a resolution of some of their issues. He prayed it wasn't just because she had grown so comfortable staying with him that she didn't feel the need for wheels anymore.

Warner had tried to mediate between Maddie and her parents years ago, but it had not been a success. In fact, it was a total failure each time he even attempted to get them talking, and eventually he learned not to interfere. The Delaney family had their own unique way of interacting. Outsiders, no matter how well intentioned, could not break the code. At this juncture, with Maddie in his guest room, freaking out about her job, her new house, and her life in general, there was nothing he could do to facilitate communication between her and family. He would just have to wait.

She drove him to work most days, and then used his car until it was time to pick him up. At night, they shared the Toyota. She didn't go out often and Warner tried not to think about it too much. There was nothing he could do, and no point in worrying about what was coming next. He'd learned, in the last ten years, that she would work things out in her own way, and in her own time. He couldn't begin to predict what she might do in her current situation.

Maddie's rare visits home, while exciting and entertaining, were always a bit stressful. He'd come to expect that. It was no big shock that she had affected his relationship with Samantha—and he had to admit that that seemed to be working it-self out anyway. As uncomfortable as he was at the prospect of having Maddie as a semipermanent houseguest, it wasn't completely without an up-side. In the last week, since Maddie had moved into his place, he had started to spend more time at Samantha's house. He felt right at home there. Sabrina and Eddy were always so happy to see him, it was easy to imagine becoming a part of their life.

So far, he was still going home every night. He couldn't imagine Samantha sleeping with a mar-ried man, even if it was him. And, with Maddie staying at his place, he was reluctant to begin a sex-ual relationship without first officially ending things with her. He had not gone without sex for the past ten years, but when he did get involved with a woman, it was understood that the relationship was casual. Before this, he had always ended it if it looked as if it were getting serious. He never wanted a woman to fall in love with him. And he had never fallen in love with any of them. He never felt as though he had been involved in an illicit affair before, either. Maybe he would not have felt that way if Maddie had been in another country, or on another continent, as she usually was, but now she was right there, in his house, every night when he came home and every morning when he woke up. It wasn't a real marriage, and he didn't owe her anything, but he couldn't bring himself to break his vows while Maddie was actually sleeping under his roof.

He tried to tell himself that whatever he did with Sam was not forbidden. Maddie knew about Samantha, who knew about her, and both of them appeared to accept the situation for what it was. Still, Warner felt like he was being unfaithful. To both of them. He had to put an end to it. He had to ask for that divorce. He also had to decide whether to ask Samantha to marry him. It was past time to act. The big question was, what should he do first?

He had planned to discuss divorce with Maddie when she arrived back in the States, but he had put it off. Now, Warner decided that getting that paperwork started was his first priority. Maddie had to be expecting it by now. She knew that he was serious about Samantha. She'd even begun to act a bit jealous. If he hadn't known how possessive she was, he'd have been flattered. However, he'd seen Maddie wage war over the last chocolate chip cookie on the plate. He suspected her behavior had more to do with sour grapes than with her feelings for him. She did not like to share her things.

At breakfast on Friday, a week after she moved in, the perfect opportunity finally presented itself. He'd been listening to her side of the conversation with Cairo University every morning that week, and he noticed that, this time, she hung up the phone with an air of finality.

"What's up?" he asked as she came to sit at the kitchen table.

"It looks like I don't have to go back to Egypt any time soon," she announced as they sat down to eat.

"Oh?" he asked, trying not to sound perturbed.

"The university is happy to have me do the work from here. It's easier than being on staff, especially with the Egyptian government putting up all these roadblocks," she explained.

"Can you do that?" he queried.

"I don't see why not. I've been doing it. And they're happy with the progress I've made so far, so . . . I guess I've just joined the electronic age."

"You don't sound too unhappy about it," he commented.

"I'm not, I guess. It's not what I expected, and I had been looking forward to living there, but after all the bureaucratic nonsense I went through, I think I'll be happier just visiting. Every few months, I'll probably have to go over and show them what I'm doing."

"Are they paying enough for you to do that?" he asked.

"They'll pay for it," she said. "They'll use some more of the grant money. Probably the money they're saving by not having me on staff."

"Sounds good," Warner said.

"Yeah. The only thing I regret is that my assistant will think I was run out of the country, which I was, basically."

"But you've still got your dream job," he pointed out.

"That's the most important thing," she agreed. "I don't want to be petty about this." She smiled at him over the rim of her coffee cup. "I can't help it, though," she said playfully.

"Uh-huh," he murmured.

"It did work out pretty nicely," she mused. "I can deal with the house now."

"You lucked out," Warner said. He was happy for her, of course, but he was also a little nervous about what all this meant for him. He didn't mind having her as a houseguest, exactly, but he didn't see himself putting her up for weeks and weeks. Her very existence was putting a distinct strain on his relationship with Samantha. Maddie's presence would almost certainly cause the other woman to cut him loose, eventually. And that was a risk he was not willing to take.

"I guess I can move into Rebecca's house once I clear out a bedroom," she said, as if she had read his mind.

"Oh?" This time Warner was sure he was not successful in keeping the eager, hopeful note out of the syllable.

Maddie flashed a knowing look at him. "I don't know exactly how long it will take. I've been over there twice, looking it over, and there's a lot of work to be done. Aunt Becky was a pack rat, and she didn't throw out anything for the last few years, from the look of things."

"I see," Warner said, nodding encouragingly.

"I've been there before, of course, plenty of times, but I never noticed it when she was alive. I guess that was because it was her place then, and now it's mine." She swallowed hard. "I have to figure out what to do with that big old house."

"It's a nice house," he said consolingly.

"Yeah, but I can't help wondering why in the world she kept all that stuff. The newspapers alone will fill a Dumpster and there must be a hundred empty shoe boxes. What could she possibly have intended to do with them? You can hardly walk in any of the rooms. She seems to have been literally living in the living room."

"I take it your cousins have no interest in helping you clear the place out?"

"Nah. They gave me a list of things they'd like to keep, though. When I find them."

"You know you're welcome to stay here as long as you need to," Warner said. Surprisingly, he meant it.

"Thanks," she said wryly. "I know you don't want your girlfriend getting the wrong impression about us."

"I told you before, Sam understands," he replied. "But I have been meaning to talk to you about that."

"About what? Samantha?" she asked. "I don't think she'd like it if she found out you were talking to me about her."

"Not her. This has nothing to do with her. I'm talking about us."

Maddie looked up at him, surprised. "What about us?" she asked.

"Well, I've been meaning to talk to you about a divorce." It was much easier than he'd expected to say the words.

"Wow." She sat, looking down at her hands, apparently digesting the news.

The silence between them grew until, after a minute or two, he finally spoke. "I'm assuming you expected this. It's been on my mind for a while."

"Knew what? That you wanted a divorce? I guess I knew that you would want one someday, probably before I did, but not . . . right now."

"Now is as good a time as any," he replied.

"Does this mean you're planning to get married?" she asked.

"Not right at the moment, no. But eventually, I will. I hope."

"So there's no urgency," Maddie said.

Now that he'd finally brought it up, Warner felt it was important to deal with this, to get it over with. "It's not like I need to be divorced right this minute, no, but I do want to get the paperwork started right away."

"Did that Samantha put you up to this?" she asked.

"Of course not. She doesn't know anything about it," he answered. "And don't call her *that* Samantha."

"Sorry," she said. "I told you she wouldn't like me living here."

"She really doesn't have anything to do with this," Warner insisted. "This is something I've been meaning to talk to you about, but the opportunity never seemed to present itself. You're always coming and going so quickly, and it seemed easier to wait until you were going to stick around for a few weeks. Now that you're here for a while—the timing seemed perfect."

"How long?" Maddie asked him. "You said you wanted to ask before this. How long have you wanted a divorce?"

"A couple of years, I guess. What does that have to do with anything?" he inquired.

"Just curious. I didn't realize that our marriage was a problem for you," she said, pouting. Warner realized he'd hurt her feelings, which surprised him.

"It wasn't a problem, exactly. It was just . . . I guess it made me feel like I didn't have as many choices. It still does."

"I thought we were going to stay married until one of us found someone else."

"We were, but I don't think it makes sense any-more," he replied.

"Can I take that to mean that you and that . . . you and her are getting pretty serious?" she asked.

"It's not beyond the realm of possibility," he hedged.

"So you're changing the rules, just like that?" she said, in a huff.

"It's not *just like that.* I told you this is something I've been thinking about for quite a while," he tried to explain.

"Do you really think you have to do this? For her? If she's really interested in you, then our fake marriage shouldn't matter to her."

"It's not her. It's me," he retorted. "We are friends. Good friends. And that will never change, no mat-ter what. But we don't need to be married anymore," he said.

"God, I hate this. Why can't things just stay the way they are?" Maddie protested.

"Nothing has to change between us." He tried again to reassure her. "It's not like we were ever re-ally husband and wife."

"It's already started changing," she said unhap-pily.

"We'll go on, as friends, just as we have for the past ten years. It's just a legal technicality," he re-torted.

"If it's just a technicality, why can't we wait?" Maddie asked. "I thought we weren't going to bother with a divorce until one or both of us actually wanted to get married."

"That was the plan. Ten years ago. But things change. Back then, marriage seemed like a distant possibility. Now, it's not."

"It is for me," Maddie said, under her breath.

He ignored that. "Why wait?" he said simply. "We

should just get it out of the way. While you're here in the States."

Maddie nodded. But he didn't think she meant it. Sure enough, a minute later, she said, in a small voice, "I didn't know it was such a problem for you."

"It wasn't a problem," he told her. "Not really. It's just something I've had to deal with more and more over the years. It's not exactly the norm, Mad."

"It never was *the norm*," she replied. "It worked, though."

"Yeah," he conceded. "Not always, though. People ask questions. Sometimes it's awkward."

"People?" she echoed.

"Friends. Family."

"Women?"

"Occasionally. This is such a perfect opportunity for straightening things out. I don't want to miss the chance."

"Are you sure?" she asked. "I mean, it must come in handy sometimes. It does for me. I can't tell you how many times I've flashed my wedding ring at some guy and gotten rid of him without a fight."

"That doesn't always work," Warner reminded her.

"I know, but sometimes it does. You must have women hitting on you now and then that you just don't want to deal with."

"You don't have to be married to be unavailable. You can just tell them you're not interested."

"And that's all it takes?" Maddie asked.

Warner thought back to the last time a woman asked him out. "Pretty much," he said, nodding.

"I think it's different for girls," she said. "And anyway, I'm not a very good liar. If I wasn't really married, I don't think I'd be that convincing."

"You're not *really* married," he pointed out. "We're just pretending."

"Maybe it's not exactly real, but I do feel married to you," Maddie answered. "We've been together forever."

"I know what you mean," Warner said. "I do," he insisted when she looked at him skeptically. "But I don't want to use you—or this relationship—as an excuse anymore."

"An excuse for what?" she asked.

"For not getting too close to anyone. I'm ready to make a commitment. I want a family."

"I didn't think men had a biological clock," she taunted.

"Well, I do," he said, smiling.

"That's because you're not a man, you're a girl."

"One of these days, you might be glad you're free, too," Warner told her.

"I don't think that's very likely," Maddie said doubtfully.

The brunch was the following Sunday morning, and Warner was not looking forward to it, especially not after that conversation. Both Sam and Maddie were much more eager to have this little get-together than he was.

From the barbed comments that they made to him about each other, he surmised that neither woman liked the other very much. In fact, they obviously disapproved of each other.

But there was no escaping it. Both insisted they would like nothing better than to get to know each other. *Be careful what you wish for*, he wanted to say—to both of them. Warner knew better, however, and he kept his mouth shut, and made reservations for the three of them at his favorite café in

Philadelphia, about a forty-five-minute drive from Richland. He liked the idea that this showdown, or whatever it was, would occur on neutral territory.

They didn't even consider driving there together. Maddie drove with him to the Pelican, so she could take the car afterward, and visit the University of Pennsylvania. It was agreed that Samantha would drive him home. The first hurdle crossed, and relatively painlessly at that, Warner was pleased to note—they arrived within minutes of each other at eleven o'clock that Sunday morning. They walked together into the restaurant, Warner sandwiched between them, and he groaned, mentally, at the symbolism of it.

"From what Warner has told me about your work, it sounds fascinating," Samantha said, after they were seated at a corner table in the trendy, but comfortable, café.

"I like it," Maddie said. "I've been meaning to ask Warner . . . what do you do?"

"I'm working at the elementary school," Samantha answered.

"You're a teacher?" Maddie asked, impressed.

"No," Sam admitted ruefully. "I'm the secretary to the principal."

"How long have you been doing that?" Maddie asked.

"Since the end of August, right before the current school year began," Sam said, not exactly warming to either the conversation, or the woman across the table.

"So what did you do before?" Maddie tried again, gamely.

"I worked at home," Sam replied stiffly.

Warner prayed that Maddie would be tactful, Sam was quite defensive about being a homemaker. But he didn't need to worry.

"Great!" Maddie said. Samantha looked as surprised as he was by Maddie's enthusiastic response. "Maybe you can give me some pointers," she continued excitedly. "I'm going to be working on my new assignment from home, and I've been thinking a lot about how to arrange it. Did you work regular hours, nine to five, Monday to Friday or something like that, or did you prefer to keep it open? I tend to get absorbed in my work, and I'm afraid that if I don't set certain hours for myself, I'll end up working all the time."

"I was raising my children," Sam said dampeningly. "It's a twenty-four-hour-a-day job."

"Oh." Maddie obviously didn't know how to respond. "That's different then. Mothers don't keep office hours," she tried to joke.

"No, they can't," Samantha replied, harshly. "But it is important to be organized. Actually, that's the only way to get everything done."

"I can imagine," Maddie said, though she clearly didn't have a clue what Sam was talking about. Warner could have enlightened her, but he didn't dare risk it. If he tried to explain Samantha's career as a homemaker to Maddie, he was afraid he might sound patronizing to either one or the other. They wanted to meet and get to know each other better, they said, so he arranged it. Beyond that, it was up to them to get together.

"As far as your work is concerned . . ." Samantha said, "I don't know anything about the specifics, but I can imagine that it is crucial that you are organized in your approach, too."

"Yes, I guess it is," Maddie said, but without conviction. "When I was working in an office, there were other people there to get the documents I needed, or find phone numbers, or answer the phones. I never had to buy my own paper clips before. I went to Staples, over in the Quakertown Mall, but there were too many choices and I didn't end up buying anything."

"You should sit down at your desk, or wherever, and think it all out first," Sam told her. "Make a list of what you need, before you go shopping."

"That sounds like a good idea," Maddie replied. "I'll try it. Thanks."

"I never thought of it, but I guess I was self-employed," Sam said, smiling for the first time that morning. "It's mostly common sense."

"Warner can tell you, I don't have a lot of that," Maddie confessed. "I tend to fly by the seat of my pants."

"I wish I could feel comfortable doing that," Samantha said. "I have lists for everything. I have to plan *everything* or I can't get anything done. Partly it's because of the kids, you know. I can't just run out to the store or whatever because I'd have to take them with me, which is a production in it-self."

"How old are your little boy and girl?" Maddie asked.

"Eddy is eight, and Sabrina is six."

"They're adorable," Maddie commented. She had met the kids at Warner's place and, of course, she hit it off with them right away.

"Thank you," Samantha said, nodding. Warner was there when the children told their mother about Aunt Maddie's stories and the candy she gave them and he could tell that Samantha wasn't thrilled by their instant liking for the woman he was married to. But he had to give her credit, she hadn't said anything to discourage their feelings for Maddie. She only said, "Isn't that nice?"

Children were drawn to Maddie. Warner was sure it was because she was so carefree and genuine—two qualities he had always found appealing in her, even when they made his life difficult. He was sure Samantha didn't appreciate those particular character traits, however. She even had different names for them. She told him she thought Maddie's behavior was irresponsible and childish. She couldn't understand what he found charming about it. "You've known her longer than I have, of course," she said more than once. Only the night before, when they were talking about this brunch, she had said it again, adding, "I hope there's more to her than I think there is."

As the waiter took their orders, he watched the two women. Each was trying her best, he thought, but so far they hadn't found any subject they could talk about for more than a minute or two. They were just too different. Warner had been afraid something like this would happen. He really didn't want them to end up liking each other even less after this encounter. The silence at the table stretched out to a minute and a half.

"Bri, Samantha's daughter, plays the violin," he said, to prod them into conversation. Sam usually liked to talk about her children.

"Really?" Maddie said. "That's wonderful. She's only six?"

"She's the best in her class. Way ahead of the other kids her age," he bragged.

"She's learning the Suzuki method. Have you heard of it?" Samantha asked.

"I think so, is that where they teach children to play by ear?"

"Yes, they try to teach music in the same way that children learn language. You're a linguist, right? So you must know something about that."

"I don't know much about how children learn language. My concentration is on ancient languages, most of them dead. No one has spoken them in hundreds of years."

"The inventor of this teaching method, Suzuki, got the idea for it while watching a child learn how to walk. His parents were constantly encouraging him to try again, and even when he fell down, they praised him for trying again and again. He learned in small increments, but very quickly. And Suzuki noticed that learning language was a similar process, so he thought that if learning to play an instrument was handled in the same way, it would occur naturally. The parent learns to play with the child, and you listen to tapes of the pieces you are learning regularly, so that it becomes a part of the child's daily life, like walking and talking."

"You play, too, then?" Maddie asked.

"A little."

"She's learning, right along with Sabrina. She keeps a little ahead," Warner interrupted. Sam shot a warning look at him and he subsided, taking a swallow of his Bloody Mary.

"How old was she when she started?" Maddie queried.

"Four years old," Sam said, with maternal pride.

"That's incredible. Does Eddy play, too?"

"No, he's the artist in the family. I started him on the piano, but he didn't enjoy it at all. His dad is completely tone deaf, so that may have something to do with it."

"They're both so bright," Maddie said, and there could be no doubt that she was completely sincere. "I was telling them about my work in Egypt, and they told me about Hippocrates."

"Eddy did a report on him last year. He wants to be a doctor."

"That's great," Maddie said enthusiastically. Talking about her kids had finally loosened Sam up a bit, and that was all Maddie had been waiting for. They had found their common ground.

"His uncle is a paramedic, and between that and the television, he's pretty interested in emergency medicine. I like the doctor idea, but he can't decide between being a paramedic and flying a helicopter, or being a zoologist."

"I was the same way," Maddie said. "I think I alternated between wanting to be a fireman and an astronaut until I was eighteen or so."

Samantha surprised Warner by laughing. "I had a friend like that, Marina Alonzo. She must have changed her major six or seven times."

"Me too," Maddie said. "I didn't know what I wanted to be when I grew up. I still don't, exactly. I love my work, but I don't think that choosing a profession is all you need to do to be a grown-up."

"True," Samantha said, and Warner could see that Maddie had finally gone up in her estimation.

On the way home, she confirmed it. "I can see why you like her, now," she said. "She's obviously very intelligent, and at least she knows her limits."

He was relieved, primarily because the ordeal was over, but also because it wasn't a disaster after all. The two women were almost friendly by the time the check came, and that was more than he had dared to hope for.

"You were very quiet," Sam commented.

"This was your thing, yours and Maddie's. I didn't really think I had much to add," he replied.

"Well, thank you. It was very pleasant."

"You're welcome." He was sure that Maddie was going to mention the divorce, but since she didn't, he didn't say anything. He'd tell Samantha at some point. But this didn't seem like the right time to mention it. She was happy. Maddie seemed equally satisfied. He decided to let well enough alone.

CHAPTER ELEVEN

Maddie was starting to think her mother might just be right. Perhaps Becky's house—her house, now—really was cursed. Her aunt's bequest was causing her nothing but grief. Since she'd gotten the sad news of her great-aunt's death and been forced to make this unexpected trip home, her luck had taken an abrupt turn for the worse. Warner wanted a divorce, neither she nor Cairo University could seem to make the Egyptian government see reason and let her back into the country, and the house itself, when she visited it, seemed just a tangible reminder of what she had lost. It was so big and empty without Becky in it.

For the first time, about a week after the reading of the will—when the papers had all been signed, in triplicate and quadruplicate in most cases—she went over to the big old house that her great-aunt had lived in. She wandered through the rooms, used the bathroom, and made herself a cup of tea on the old-fashioned stove. Alton Emerson had assured her that all that was left to do was to wait for the tax notice that the government would send her, but the house didn't feel like it belonged to her.

She rented a safe-deposit box in which to keep her copy of the deed, and all the other official-looking pieces of paper that were part and parcel of property ownership. She made another visit to figure out exactly what kind of cleaning and repair work was necessary to make the place habitable. She brought an electrician with her to check the wiring and he said it was old but sound. He suggested she might want to update it in a few years, or if she did some remodeling.

"It's fine, though," he told her. "You might want to get someone in here to find out where that breeze is coming from." It did sometimes seem as though a chill wind blew through the rooms. But she hadn't found the source. She made a mental note to check it out, soon, but she had more pressing matters to attend to. It was not going to be easy to sort through the possessions that Becky had accumulated over her lifetime, or to clear out the items such as her clothes, and even furniture, that had meant something to her.

On her third trip back, a couple of weeks later, Maddie didn't feel any differently as she surveyed her inheritance. If anything, she felt as though this piece of property owned her. It was older than most of the houses on the street and was built of stone, rather than brick. She didn't know much about architecture, but she thought it more elegant than most of her neighbors' homes. It was two stories tall, with a high peaked roof, lots of windows to let the sun in, and a huge old-fashioned oak door wide enough for two people to walk through side by side.

Becky had told her it was built in the 1800s, which was why the doorways, other than the front door, and staircase were narrower than usual, and the rooms were so large and square. The front door opened into a spacious foyer, and an arched entryway led from there to the hall, which ran through the length of the house. The living room opened off the hall to the right through another archway and the dining room to the left. Beyond the dining room lay the kitchen and beyond the living room was the library, both of which could be reached through the front rooms, or through doors at the back of the hall. The stairs to the bedrooms were surprisingly small and narrow, but Maddie loved the carved posts and rounded handrail of the banister.

Upstairs, there were four bedrooms, also built on a larger scale than she thought they usually were in more modern houses. Becky hadn't been using the second floor much, it seemed, in the last few years. They were not as well kept as the rooms downstairs, and the paint and wallpaper were fading or peeling. But Maddie could see how attractive these rooms would be with a little sprucing up. Each had a distinct feel to it. The master bedroom had a window seat built under the large bay window that faced south. Damon's old room had built-in hardwood bookshelves lining the inside wall. Rachel's former bedroom had a small marble fireplace on one side, and shared a huge walk-in closet with the guest room behind it.

Maddie didn't think they built houses like this anymore, although perhaps the rich could afford to construct homes on this scale. It was too bad she couldn't appreciate her good fortune more than she did. As Patsy had said, there were people who would truly have loved owning a lovely house like this one. She wished she was one of them.

Maddie told herself to be practical, and set to

work cleaning it out. She probably should have started with one of the bedrooms, so she could keep her promise to Warner to move out of his house soon, but instead she started with the rooms downstairs, going helter-skelter through the mess piling up old newspapers and magazines.

When she got to the living room, she came to an abrupt halt. It felt echoingly empty without Great-Aunt Becky's presence to bring it to life, though almost all of her things were still in place. Maddie's cousins had removed a few items, but had asked her, through her lawyer, if she would be interested in disposing of the rest of the house's contents, including those in this room. She had sent back a positive answer in the hope that it might begin to repair the chasm that had opened up between them ever since the reading of her great-aunt's last will and testament. Maddie figured she didn't need anyone else out in the world sending bad vibes in her direction.

Lately, Maddie felt at times as if she were channeling Janet Delaney. She was becoming superstitious, and found herself, at odd moments, thinking about chanting some mantra to ward off the bad luck that dogged her these days. Not only did she have to take care of a house now, she had to empty it out first. What's more, there was no one to help her do it. She had never felt so alone.

Her parents, of course, wouldn't come near the place, and her brother and his family weren't much better. She didn't blame Teddy or Jordana of course. They were both so busy with work and the kids that even if they hadn't been afraid of offending her mother—they probably would not have been able to offer much more than moral support. And *that* was the one thing she had more than enough of.

Which was why she stood in the doorway on a Wednesday afternoon staring at her aunt's sofa, remembering the last time she had seen the spritely old woman, last New Year's Eve. That time she'd been here by choice. She could have spent the holiday with Warner, or in New York City with Jennifer, or with Patsy and her husband, or plenty of others. She wanted to have the intimate get-together with her great-aunt on the most festive night of the year because it felt right to start her thirty-second year on earth that way. It had been one of her favorite nights ever.

As she started to sort through the stuff that covered the tables, chairs, and even the floors, she remembered how they danced, and drank, and talked until dawn. Becky told her the old stories—the ones she'd heard before—about the three great loves of her life; the man who died in World War II; the white man in the sixties who went with her to Washington, D.C., to hear Martin Luther King, Jr., speak about his dreams; and her husband, whom she married when she turned forty, and never regretted marrying, but who had been very much her third choice.

They talked about the amazing things the older woman had lived through throughout the century, and the way the world was still changing so quickly. Maddie talked, too. Becky wanted to know everything about her work and her life. New Year's Eve had seemed like the perfect time to review the choices she had made, both good and bad, and to relive her adventures.

It had been a fantastic night, and the memory made her smile even while tears ran down her cheeks. "Snap out of it!" Maddie told herself, and started cleaning again, more slowly here, where her great-aunt had spent so much of her time over the past few years. She almost felt as though Becky were there, could almost hear her whispering in her ear, "Live your life the way you want to, child. Follow your heart."

Maddie found herself kneeling on the floor in front of a pile of gardening magazines, listening hard, not sure whether she'd imagined, or remembered, the words. She shook herself, figuratively, and stood, looking hopelessly at the various piles she'd made all over the room of all of Becky's old mail and magazines, newspapers and catalogues, and thought she'd never be able to handle this on her own.

For the next week, Maddie tried to find help. Patsy was supportive, but she was extremely busy, too. So were all of Maddie's other old friends—Warner among them. Those who hadn't moved away to settle elsewhere, as Jen had, were working, or looking for work, or raising young children, or caring for elderly parents. She knew she shouldn't complain, but Maddie couldn't help feeling as though she'd been abandoned.

She finally lined up some teenagers to help her after school, but they didn't last past the first night. They said they heard strange noises, and demanded to be paid for their few hours of work. She tried to convince them to come back again, but they refused. She was tempted to call her cousins and insist that they help, but she knew it would be pointless. She had no alternatives left. She couldn't afford a professional cleaning crew, even assuming that she could get one to do the job. She didn't really need anyone else to confirm her fears about the house, anyway.

Ghosts, or not, Great-Aunt Becky's house was a little scary. Maddie found that she didn't like to be there alone. She heard noises, sometimes. Old houses did settle, and ancient wooden floorboards were supposed to squeak, but she also thought she heard distant laughter and faint voices, which made her more than a little uncomfortable.

She especially disliked working in the place after the sun began to set. At dusk, or worse, after dark, the air in the house took on a different feel. It moved around her, as though a window had been left open. The slight breeze the electrician had noticed blew constantly through the creaky old place, but from where, and to where, she couldn't tell. She checked every room in the house and couldn't find any opening that might explain the strange air currents.

During the daylight hours, she was able to attribute these odd occurrences to her own overactive imagination, but as the shadows lengthened throughout the afternoon, Maddie found herself rushing to finish her work—whether it was washing down the walls or packing up half a century's worth of Becky's memorabilia.

Her aunt had amassed quite a collection of items that Maddie didn't think she could bear to part with, including photos, albums, books, dolls, and other knickknacks and jewelry boxes, which Becky seemed to have collected for years, certainly since she was a young girl. Maddie loved the old sequined and beaded dresses and purses in the cedar closets, some of which were probably valuable. She also planned to keep the ancient record player, and the even more ancient gramophone, as well as various other antiquated appliances. There were some beautiful old pieces of furniture, too.

She stored her favorite stuff in two of the rooms, one upstairs and one down, while packing up and throwing away as much of the rest of the clutter as quickly as she could. There were years' and years' worth of accumulated magazines, receipts, and other assorted paraphernalia. It cost too much to have it all hauled away at once, so she discarded four or five large plastic trash bags at a time, by the curb, for the regular garbage men to remove. It was the most economical alternative Maddie could find, but it was also a slow process that required that she dropped by at least once a day.

Inside Becky's house, she felt closer to her great-aunt, but she felt far removed from any other human contact. It was unsettling. She listened to her great-aunt's records, and moved about her kitchen and bedrooms and attic, and felt as if, at any moment, the woman she had loved almost more than her own mother would walk around a corner and say, "Hi."

She carefully omitted any mention of the house when she spoke to her family, even though she and her mother had started talking on the telephone nearly every day. She ignored Janet's many references to her inheritance, which was not easy as she seemed as determined to bring up the subject as Maddie was to avoid it. She had work, as well as the house, to take care of, which gave Maddie a great excuse to linger on at Warner's, but she realized that she was just prolonging the inevitable by staying.

There was so much going on in her life that she wasn't ready to deal with, and his comforting presence—and fantastic cooking—might give the illusion that the many changes she was having so much trouble accepting could be warded off, but she couldn't hide forever. He wouldn't let her, and honestly, she didn't want to.

It took her two weeks to work up to it, but Maddie finally moved into her house in mid-October. It was still not really livable, but it had been almost three weeks since Warner asked for the divorce, and she figured it was time for her to get out of his hair, so both of them could get on with their lives. Foolishly, she decided to try to explain that to her mother.

"It was time," she said. "He needs his space."

"Maddie, Maddie, Maddie," Janet said sorrowfully. Maddie could picture her shaking her head reproachfully on the other end of the telephone line. *"Now* you decide to be sensitive and supportive? When he's got a girlfriend? What did I do wrong?"

"Of course I'm supportive of his relationship with Samantha. I love Warner. I want him to be happy," Maddie said.

"I want him to be happy, too," Mom echoed. "But with you. I knew that house was cursed."

"Oh, leave it alone, Mom, will you?" Maddie pleaded. She wanted to get along better with her mother, but at moments like this she felt that it was never going to happen.

She found a surprisingly sympathetic listener in Samantha, who was one person who definitely approved of her move into the new house. Maddie tried to spend as much time with the woman as she possibly could. They were both doing their best to get to know each other. If Warner was going to be with Samantha, then Maddie wanted to be friendly with her. And Sam was always supportive and even empathetic when Maddie spoke to her about Janet.

"The real problem is, it never ends. There are candles to burn and blessings to say, and incense to ward off spirits and sickness, not to mention protective charms and all kinds of rituals for every possible occasion," Maddie told Samantha over lunch about a week before Halloween. She had been surprised when Samantha actually called her and invited her to have lunch, just the two of them, without Warner. She said it would give Maddie an opportunity to vent. "I have a mother, too," she confided. "She's not quite as off-the-wall as your mother, but she's got her own problems."

"I can relate to Mom's desire to believe there's more to life than what we see, but she's driving me nuts with this stuff," Maddie whined.

"My mother doesn't believe in anything she can't see and touch. She has no faith in anything. Least of all, me. I've been thinking about your situation, and I thought it might help for you to know that what you're going through isn't unusual. Mothers and daughters have problems all the time," Samantha said. "At least your mother's . . . hobby is harmless. She's just highly suggestible."

"I'm suggestible. Mom's a raving maniac," Maddie responded. "But I think I know what you mean," she conceded. "It's not as if she's hurting anyone."

"I've met her," Samantha said, sympathetically. "At church. She's sweet."

"She really is. Church is actually the perfect setting for her. She is very spiritual and her faith is terrific. If she had just become ultrareligious, I could handle that, I think. There are a lot of women her age who have turned to religion. But Janet isn't like other women. She recognizes the notion that most of the stories in the Bible are probably fiction. Great fiction, but fiction. She doesn't make that distinction with this other stuff she believes in. She is way too into astrology, for example."

"It does seem a bit extreme," Sam agreed.

"The mere existence of a holiday like Halloween suggests that there was a time when people were more in touch with . . . should I call it the spirits? But I don't want to think about that stuff. Not at this time of the year. You can't turn on the television without seeing some gruesome horror movie. I don't need to hear about it from my mother. It's everywhere."

"I know. My kids love it, but I am just looking forward to getting through it and on to the more cheerful holidays."

"I like Halloween, and trick-or-treating, but this year I feel the same way you do. My great-aunt's house has got these really spooky vibes, and I don't need my mother telling me every day that the place is haunted on top of that. She's going to drive me around the bend."

"It's easy to imagine strange things like that at this time of year," Samantha said pleasantly.

"My imagination is active enough, thank you. I don't need any help in that area."

"And if you did, I doubt that it would be your mother you would go to," Samantha said.

"You speak the truth, sistah," Maddie proclaimed. In a rare moment of solidarity, they smiled at each other in complete accord. It didn't last, however.

"You have to stop letting your mother push your buttons," Samantha advised.

"I tell myself to ignore it, but then she starts talking about Venus in Saturn or something, and I lose it. I know that millions of people believe in astrology. I've worked with some, and studied cultures where astrology was considered a bona fide science, so it's not like I don't believe there could be something to it, but she's over the top."

"I never have understood why people like it," Samantha said flatly.

"Well, a lot of people do. Knowledgeable people. Scholars, not just kooks. I've read a lot about the subject in the course of my work, and I'm aware there are convincing arguments on both sides. But my mother actually believes her horoscope is accurate. She lives her life by it. That's what I don't get."

"I don't get any of it. How can a woman like your mother, an educated woman, fall for that stuff?"

"Obviously there are all kinds of real psychic phenomena. At this time of year, it's not all that difficult to believe in lots of paranormal phenomena, ghosts, and demons, and angels and all. But I've never personally experienced anything like that. Although . . . every evening at my new house, I do hear these strange noises—" Maddie began.

"As you said, an overactive imagination can be a problem at this time of year," Samantha interjected.

"It's not my imagination. At least, I'm pretty sure it's not."

"It must be," Sam insisted. "There is no other rational explanation."

Maddie disagreed. "There is the possibility that Great-Aunt Becky is trying to contact me from the other side."

"Sure," Samantha said, clearly under the impression that Maddie was joking. "In that case, I guess you don't have anything to worry about, though. She wanted you to have the house."

"You're laughing," Maddie tried to explain, "but it is another rational explanation."

"You're not serious?" Sam questioned.

"I don't know. Maybe," Maddie responded. "Becky's death was unexpected. Maybe she had something important that she meant to tell me before she died. Or maybe she just wasn't ready to move on from this plane of existence."

"You can't believe that." Samantha clearly didn't. "Don't you think that it's more likely that you're not quite ready to accept your aunt's death? It is only natural that you might feel as though you didn't get to say good-bye."

"That does sound reasonable," Maddie said. But she doubted it. It wasn't just the strange noises she heard in Rebecca's house, it was also the way she felt when she was there. It was not a feeling that she could imagine her subconscious mind would create. It was a frightening sensation, and she wasn't one of those people who enjoyed being frightened.

"I'm not like your kids," she tried to explain to Samantha. "I don't *want* to believe in ghosts and mummies and bogeymen. It's like we were saying before, I can understand the popularity of horror stories, and I suspect those books and the movies serve a purpose. I read somewhere that novels like *Dracula* are actually explorations of the psyche, and I can understand that themes like death and immortality should be explored, but I'm not the kind of person who considers being scared out of my wits an enjoyable form of entertainment. I know you know what I'm talking about."

"Definitely," Samantha averred. "That's why I'm trying to get you to pull yourself together. You must know that this is your mother's influence over you. Your whole life she's been telling you that these things exist, but you know they don't. When you're thinking clearly, anyway."

Maddie wasn't willing to go that far. "I try to keep an open mind. There have been documented clairvoyants, and prophets, in every culture and in every epoch of history. I just don't think my mother happens to be one."

"And what about you?" Samantha asked, reasonably.

"Me? I don't have any psychic abilities. No. But I could be the recipient of a message, maybe. Everyone can, probably."

"I don't think I can," Samantha retorted.

"In primitive cultures, even today in the Native American tradition, it isn't uncommon," Maddie pointed out.

"This is the twenty-first century," Sam said. "And you and I are definitely products of our times."

Maddie thought her new friend was being somewhat narrow-minded, but she also knew that further debate on this subject would be pointless. She wasn't going to change Samantha's mind. Not today. And she couldn't afford to antagonize the other woman. Their tentative friendship was in a very delicate phase. She decided to change the subject altogether.

"I was wondering if you'd lend me your kids on Halloween. I'd love to go trick-or-treating, and people look at you funny if a grown woman shows up on their doorstep without children in tow," she joked. Samantha didn't laugh, though. "Warner told me you have a costume party to go to, or something," Maddie added.

"Yes. Muriel Landsdowne's having a party," Sam confirmed.

"So, how about it?" Maddie asked. "We can all have dinner together, and then I can baby-sit while you and Warner go there. I've been wanting to do something for you two to make up for that date I interrupted."

"Well," Samantha said, slowly, "okay."

"Great, you won't regret it!" Maddie vowed. "Gotta go." She left before Sam could change her mind. She found that she was uncomfortable talking to Warner's girlfriend for more than an hour or so. Perhaps she was in denial, but she could not see what Warner found so enticing about the woman. Samantha could not have enthralled Warner so thoroughly with that body of hers alone. True, it was a fantastic body, but he just wasn't the type of guy to fall for a great pair of legs.

It wasn't that Maddie couldn't see the attraction. Samantha was not only beautiful, she was smart, and decent, and much nicer than Maddie herself. Only a really sweet person would make the effort to befriend her boyfriend's wife just because he obviously cared about her. What confounded Maddie was that the woman didn't seem to have much of a personality. She wasn't unique in any way. In a word, she was boring.

If she had to guess, Maddie thought it was Samantha's kids that had pushed Warner over the edge. It was obvious that Warner was completely in love with them. As in, head over heels. They were adorable. Seeing him with that little girl was like watching one of those really sappy diaper ads with the gorgeous dad trying to fill in for the gorgeous wife while she was at some awards dinner. Even Maddie could see that her husband was a man who ought to have children, and—unlike most of her female friends—she didn't usually go soft at the sight of a handsome man dangling a baby on his knee. Instead, she immediately wrote men like that off as weekend dads with too much baggage to suit her, or as the property of women who could make better use of them than she could, and therefore—by her rules—untouchable.

But Maddie couldn't believe Warner would marry a woman just to get an instant family—no matter how fabulous that family might be. It wasn't in his nature to do anything that selfish. He had to be in love with the mother, too. Maddie just needed to figure out what it was that he saw in Samantha that she could not. Then she could give him his freedom, as well as her blessing, without reservation. Warner deserved a woman who would challenge him, take him out of himself. He was such a sweet guy. The woman who ended up with him had to make sure that he occasionally had a good time, because he couldn't do it for himself. He just wasn't built that way. Maddie admired his capacity for taking care of others, but with it came a tendency toward self-sacrifice, and he couldn't be allowed to subjugate his own needs to fulfill the needs of those he loved. Someone had to make sure that he had some fun in his life.

His first marriage hadn't been much of a bargain. He got her, always taking, never really giving much back. He helped her out of jams, and listened to her complain about her mother, and put her up when she came into town, and fed her, and coddled her. And he did it all without complaining, much. He deserved better the second time around. If she had anything to do with it, Warner was going to live happily ever after this time.

A SPECIAL "THANK YOU"
FROM ARABESQUE JUST FOR YOU!

Send this card back and you'll receive 4 FREE Arabesque Novels—a $25.96 value—absolutely FREE!

The introductory 4 Arabesque Romance books are yours FREE (plus $1.99 shipping & handling). If you wish to continue to receive 4 books every month, do nothing. Each month, we will send you 4 New Arabesque Romance Novels for your free examination. If you wish to keep them, pay just $16* (plus, $1.99 shipping & handling). If you decide not to continue, you owe nothing!

- Send no money now.
- Never an obligation.
- Books delivered to your door!

We hope that after receiving your FREE books you'll want to remain an Arabesque subscriber, but the choice is yours! So why not take advantage of this Arabesque offer, with no risk of any kind. You'll be glad you did!

In fact, we're so sure you will love your Arabesque novels, that we will send you an Arabesque Tote Bag FREE with your first paid shipment.

**Call Us TOLL-FREE At
1-888-345-BOOK**

* Prices subject to change

THE "THANK YOU" GIFT INCLUDES:

- 4 books absolutely FREE (plus $1.99 for shipping and handling).
- A FREE newsletter, *Arabesque Romance News*, filled with author interviews, book previews, special offers, and more!
- No risks or obligations.

INTRODUCTORY OFFER CERTIFICATE

Yes! Please send me 4 FREE Arabesque novels (plus $1.99 for shipping & handling). I understand I am under no obligation to purchase any books, as explained on the back of this card. Send my **FREE Tote Bag** after my first regular paid shipment.

NAME

ADDRESS _____ APT. _____

CITY _____ STATE _____ ZIP _____

TELEPHONE ( ) _____

E-MAIL _____

SIGNATURE _____

Offer limited to one per household and not valid to current subscribers. All orders subject to approval. Terms, offer, & price subject to change. Tote bags available while supplies last.

Thank You!

AN103A

ARABESQUE

Accepting the four introductory books for FREE (plus $1.99 to offset the cost of shipping & handling) places you under no obligation to buy anything. You may keep the books and return the shipping statement marked "cancelled". If you do not cancel, about a month later we will send 4 additional Arabesque novels, and you will be billed the preferred subscriber's price of just $4.00 per title. That's $16.00* for all 4 books for a savings of almost 40% off the cover price (Plus $1.99 for shipping and handling). You may cancel at any time, but if you choose to continue, every month we'll send you 4 more books, which you may either purchase at the preferred discount price. . . or return to us and cancel your subscription.

* PRICES SUBJECT TO CHANGE

THE ARABESQUE ROMANCE CLUB: HERE'S HOW IT WORKS

THE ARABESQUE ROMANCE BOOK CLUB
P.O. BOX 5214
CLIFTON NJ 07015-5214

PLACE
STAMP
HERE

HALLOWEEN

CHAPTER TWELVE

Warner Davis was a happy man. Around his kitchen table were gathered all the people he loved best, busily carving out jack-o'-lanterns. They looked somewhat bizarre at the moment, but that was to be expected on All Hallows' Eve. Eddy was dressed as Spider-Man, and Sabrina had chosen to be a princess. He and Samantha had decided to do the couple thing, and dressed as the Frankenstein monster and his wife. She had on a long white semitransparent dress, and a wig of black hair, streaked with white, that had to be a foot tall. While Sam got the kids and herself into their costumes, Maddie had painted Warner green and stuck bolts to his neck with Krazy Glue. She swore they'd come off with a little nail polish remover. He wasn't sure he believed her, but she had gotten totally caught up in the spirit of Halloween and he hated to discourage that. She had been a bit subdued lately.

She had always loved holidays. All holidays. They were her religion. Maddie believed in celebrating life more than anyone he had ever met. She was a truly joyous person. It was one of the things that had, over the years, made her visits home so special. She had chosen, tonight, to wear a mermaid costume. It was made of green cellophane as far as he could tell. It covered her from her chest to her feet, and the tail trailed behind, branching out into a tail fin that, when she walked, waved behind her somehow suspended a few inches above the ground. Sequins glued to the material, or plastic, or whatever it was, made her look both shiny and scaly, though he'd talked her out of covering her nut-brown shoulders and her face with the same green makeup she had used on him. Unlike Warner and Samantha, she wasn't dressed for a costume party. She just did it for the fun of it.

He had missed her a little since she had moved into her aunt's place a couple of weeks ago. When she offered to take Samantha's children trick-or-treating so that he and Sam could get to their party early, Warner was touched. It was just like her. He couldn't help noticing that Samantha was a little bit suspicious of Maddie's motives, though. The two women didn't have anything in common, except for him. When they were together, they were always on their guard. Both of them. Samantha's nervousness around Warner's soon-to-be-ex-wife was very apparent in the polite, even formal, manners she displayed toward the other woman. Maddie, of course, responded by behaving even more unconventionally than usual, so the already extreme differences between the two of them were exaggerated to a ridiculous degree.

"Oil and water," Patsy said, when she first saw them together. "You'll never get them to mix."

But here they all were, laughing and joking about their costumes, and dinner and candy and Halloween pranks they remembered from when they were young. Everyone was looking forward to the evening ahead. Even Samantha seemed to have loosened up a little. She might not trust Maddie's motives completely, but Warner knew she appreciated the gesture she made in offering to baby-sit.

"Let's light the candles," Samantha said.

"And turn out the lights," Maddie suggested. "For the story." She had promised to tell the children a tale about jack-o'-lanterns when they finished making theirs. "The man responsible for our tradition of carving a face in a pumpkin and placing a candle inside was just an ordinary guy, an Irishman named Sam Hain, who lived a long, long time ago. He did something dastardly—that's how they talked in those days, but in Gaelic, of course," she told Bri and Eddy, who were listening intently.

"What's Gaelic?" Bri asked.

"One of the few dead languages that Maddie doesn't speak," Warner said in an undertone to Samantha.

"Ancient Irish. It used to be spoken in Ireland, but not that many people speak it anymore. It sounds like this: *Pogue ma hone.*" That last was aimed directly at Warner, and he had a pretty good idea of its meaning before Maddie translated. "Kiss my you-know-what."

"Not in front of the children," Samantha warned. "They pick up on every little thing you say, especially the stuff you really don't want them to repeat."

Maddie looked at the cherubic faces watching the exchange and grimaced. "It went right over their heads," she answered.

"Don't bet on it," Samantha said knowingly.

"What did he do?" Eddy asked, impatient at the interruption.

"No one knows. But as Sam grew old, he began to fear that he was going to be punished for whatever it was that he did. He was pretty clever, so he wasn't worried about getting caught by anyone in this world, but he was afraid that God wouldn't let him into heaven when he died. Sure enough, one night, the devil came to get him."

She paused, looking into the young faces that were hanging on her words, and smiling. *"Bang!"* she yelled, pounding on the table at the same time and making the children jump, and Sammy and Warner as well. "He distracted the devil, and jumped out of the window and ran away. The devil was after him, right away, but he had just enough of a head start to get to a great big tree nearby, and he jumped up into the branches."

" 'Do you think that climbing up there will stop me?' the devil asked, and climbed up quickly after him, using his long clawlike fingernails and toes to walk straight up the side of the trunk.

"Sam Hain jumped down, grabbed two sticks that lay at the bottom, and put them on the ground in the shape of a cross, because he'd learned that that was the one way to stop the devil from coming near you. Sure enough, the evil one couldn't climb back down after that. He was stuck up in the tree.

"Sam was, as I told you, a very clever fellow, and he decided to try and strike a bargain with the devil. 'Sure and I'll let you down, if you promise never to take me to hell,' he said. After a minute, the devil agreed to the deal, and Sam uncrossed the sticks and let him down out of the tree. He was frightened, of course, because everyone knows that making a deal with the devil can be a very tricky business, but the evil one kept his side of the bargain, and left Sam alone.

"After that, Sam didn't worry about being good at all anymore, because he knew he was going to heaven. Sometimes he was good, and sometimes he wasn't, depending on what he felt like doing at the moment. When he died, he went straight up to the pearly gates expecting a warm welcome, but he was told that heaven was closed to him, because of his bad behavior.

" 'Where am I supposed to go then?' he asked. But they had never had this particular situation occur before, and they didn't know what to tell him. Finally he left. He was very unhappy, as you can imagine, but he thought at least that he was better off where he was than in the everlasting fire down below. So he wandered about for a few decades, or perhaps centuries, growing lonelier and lonelier with nothing whatsoever to do.

"Eventually, he decided to go to hell after all, because he was so bored and lonely, but the devil refused to let him in. 'A deal is a deal,' he said. 'I promised never to take you to hell, and I never will.' He was pleased, of course, to see Sam Hain suffering so, and he laughed as he turned him away.

"Not knowing what else to do, and feeling he just couldn't stand wandering aimlessly about the earth forever, Sam went back up to heaven and begged for God's mercy. 'We can't let you in,' said the angels at the gates. 'But your prayer for mercy has been granted. Because you weren't an evil fellow, we can give you this little bit o' light to keep you company.' They gave him a little light, which some people say was God's grace, and others say was that little piece of his soul which was pure and good.

"He put the light in a hollowed-out gourd, and went back down to earth. There, he found, as he walked about, that sometimes people could see his little light, especially on All Hallows' Eve, when the curtain between the world of the living and the world of the dead is lifted, for a little while. That gave him something to do at last, and he's wandered ever since, scaring and thrilling people when he can, and especially on Halloween.

"And that's why we carve pumpkins and put candles in them," she finished the story.

"Cool," said Eddy.

"I don't get how a holiday about death became a kids' celebration. How did *that* become this?" Samantha said, waving a hand toward the kids, the punch bowl full of candy, the bright orange pumpkin, and the cookie sheet covered with white pumpkin seeds that Warner had just roasted in the oven and was sprinkling with salt.

"It's not really that odd when you think about it," Maddie said.

"I have thought about it, that's why I brought it up," Sam snapped.

Maddie ignored her surly tone and answered her question with a question of her own. "Have you ever been to an Irish wake? It's a heck of a party."

"Yes," and "No," Warner and Sammy said simultaneously.

"The Irish always send off their dead in an upbeat way. So it isn't that surprising that they would invent a ritual like this," Maddie explained. "Besides, a lot of cultures have similar traditions. Think of Cinco de Mayo, from Mexico, and that Shinto spirit holiday from Japan. They are all family related, a sort of communion between the newest, youngest generation and the ancestors. I think it makes perfect sense that it evolved here in America the way it did."

"Thank you, Professor," Warner intoned solemnly.

"Sorry, sorry. I get carried away when it comes to stuff like this," Maddie excused herself.

"Admit it," Warner teased. "You just like Halloween because you can dress up in some slutty outfit and get free candy."

"Oh, I confess," Maddie said happily. "It's heaven, isn't it?"

Samantha shifted in her chair and Warner was careful not to look in her direction. He had not had an easy time persuading her to dress up, or to go out. Most importantly, it had taken a day and a half to convince her that she should let Maddie take the children. She was afraid they might see costumes she thought inappropriate, or behavior—such as the pranks they'd all just been talking about—that might give the children ideas. Not to mention her concern at the idea that Maddie would let the kids eat all the candy they collected at one time.

"She's not an idiot," Warner told her.

"I know, but . . . she's not a very careful person," Sam argued. "And she knows nothing about children."

"She'll be careful with your kids," he promised.

Sam gave in to the subtle pressure, but she still had some serious reservations about the plan. "Well," she said now, "I agree that it can be fun, but only if we remember the rules. Safety comes first."

"I know," Maddie reassured her. The children nodded.

"I don't think there's any real danger," Samantha said, as much to herself as to them. "But you kids will behave yourselves, and listen to Maddie, right?"

"Yeah," the children chorused. Maddie nodded again.

Warner recognized his cue to act. "We should be going," he said, coming around the table to offer Samantha his arm.

"Okay," Sam said reluctantly, rising slowly. She got as far as the kitchen door.

"If you need us, just call. The number's by the phone."

"Okay," Maddie said blithely.

Warner gave Sam a quick kiss on the cheek that was part encouragement, part reassurance that she was doing the right thing, and gently tugged her out the door.

"Bye, guys," Maddie said. "Have a good time."

Warner ushered Samantha out of the house and into the car, saying, "I'm sure they'll be fine," as she looked back at the house, a concerned expression on her face. "Maddie would never let anything bad happen to the kids," he assured her.

"I know," she said unconvincingly. "I just hope she doesn't tell them too many horror stories or she'll never get them to bed tonight."

"We can call from Muriel's and tell her that, if you're really worried about it," he offered.

"No, I'm sure it will be all right," Sam answered. "Let's just enjoy ourselves."

"We will," he promised.

The party was in full swing when they arrived. A lot of their friends and mutual acquaintances were there and they circulated, greeting people and admiring some of their costumes. Warner had been worried that no one would know who they were supposed to be but everyone seemed to recognize them. They received a lot of compliments on their outfits. The food was good, and the company excellent, and Sam relaxed and seemed to forget about Maddie and her earlier anxiety as they mingled and chatted, and got caught up with people they hadn't seen in a long time. Warner was just happy to be there with her.

Samantha was so beautiful, so poised and charming. Even dressed as the monster's bride, she looked amazing. Or maybe she looked even prettier than usual tonight because of the getup she was wearing, Warner thought. Her almost almond-shaped eyes were thickly outlined with kohl, her lips were painted white, and still her face glowed as she laughed and flirted and danced with him. This was a side of her he hadn't seen in a long time—possibly since before Radu left.

They danced closer and closer as the night wore on. After midnight, the crowd on the dance floor thinned out as people went home, until only a few couples were left, dancing to soft jazz and other mood music. The lights dimmed and Warner enjoyed the silky feel of her body against his. His lips settled on the spot at the base of her neck where there was a slight hollow. It was just the width of his index finger, and his fingertips replaced his lips to stroke the soft coffee-colored skin gently, measuring the length and depth of the tiny dip between her chin and her shoulder. His mouth found hers and their tongues dueled, playfully.

He imagined he could taste her excitement, just as he tasted her skin. His own ardor rose slowly, first just a slight thrill at the pleasure of being able to caress her gently with his hands and mouth, growing to a stronger desire to take all of her this way, and finally a wave of possessive delight at the thought that nothing remained between them. She belonged with him in a way no one else ever had. *Thank you, Maddie,* he thought.

Why he thought of Maddie at that moment, he didn't know, but once he did, he couldn't seem to get her out of his head. A quick glance at Samantha's face assured him she hadn't noticed that his attention had wandered from her. A satisfied smile played over her mouth and her head was tipped to the side to expose her throat to his questing lips. But he was still distracted even as he continued to nibble at her skin.

Why did Maddie have to come home now, all of a sudden? The other times that Warner thought he might have found someone, she had been far away: exploring an ancient tribal burial ground in Africa, or writing a treatise for an archaeological society at some venerable old institution in Europe. Those relationships had had a fair chance, unlike this one. Even though he sometimes blamed Maddie, or rather his marriage to her, for their failure, those impediments were theoretical. Now, when he had finally found someone that made him forget his pseudo-marriage, she had to come back and stay for longer than ever. Her presence was intrusive and unsettling.

He wished she would go away again and stop making him think about her. Compared to her, *of course* Samantha seemed a little dull. It certainly wasn't her fault that she was an ordinary hard-working mother of two small children. She didn't have the time to jet all over the world, even if she had the inclination. Luckily, she didn't feel deprived or unfulfilled. She was content with her life. That didn't make her less exciting than Maddie. It made her more appealing to him. Much more appealing. She was sweet and gentle and intelligent and dignified. She was a woman who inspired confidence in a man rather than constantly challenging him to be something he wasn't. She didn't play games.

Maddie wasn't a player either, but she made him feel off balance with her whirlwind visits. Just thinking about her rootless lifestyle made him dizzy. She often made him feel as if he were some rigid, conventional bore, just by being herself. She wore her every emotion on her expressive face. While he liked her openness, Samantha's reticence was more restful. It was all Maddie's fault that Sam seemed uptight when she was around. He didn't know why he was comparing the two of them anyway. Maddie and he were going to be divorced, officially, as soon as possible. And she would disappear again. Then he was probably going to ask the beautiful, pliant woman in his arms to be his wife.

"That was fun," Sam said in the car on the way home. "Maybe I should throw a party. I can't believe how long it's been since I last saw some of my friends. Not since . . ." Her voice trailed off.

"Since Radu left," he finished for her. She nodded. It was the first time either of them had mentioned her missing husband in months—other than when the children brought him up.

"I think I'm ready," she said. "A few people asked me if I'd heard from him tonight, and it didn't make me want to run screaming from the room like it used to."

"That's good," Warner said tentatively.

"I think I'm over the stage where I want to climb into bed and pull the blankets over my head whenever I think about him."

"It had to happen sometime," he said encouragingly.

"It's hard enough to split up when you have some kind of warning," Samantha said. "This way, there's no time to get used to the idea. All of a sudden, he's gone."

"It's not an easy adjustment to make. For anyone," Warner agreed.

"One of the worst things about it is that no one knows what to say," she went on.

"It's difficult. No one wants to say the wrong thing and maybe make it worse," he said.

"I know. But it doesn't make it any easier. For a while, I honestly felt like all of our friends were really his friends, not mine, except for you. You stuck by me."

"Maddie and I are getting our divorce," he blurted out suddenly. When Sam didn't react, Warner didn't know what to think.

"Maddie mentioned it," Sam answered.

"Oh? Good," he said. "I didn't want to say anything because . . . well, because—"

This time she finished his sentence. "Because you didn't want to bring up divorce before I did. I understand that. And I appreciate it," she told him.

"Really?" he asked, pleased to find they were so attuned to each other. "That's great!"

Warner drove through the black night, happy and satisfied. He looked forward to a future full of nights like this one. He glanced over at Sam, thinking she might have fallen asleep, and was surprised to see she was staring out of the window, lost in thought. She didn't look very happy.

"You look about a million miles away right now," he said.

"I'm here," she replied. But she still didn't sound happy.

"Is everything all right?" he asked.

"Sure, fine. I was . . . just wondering if Maddie ever got the kids to sleep?"

"Oh," he said, vaguely dissatisfied by her response. He decided that they were both suffering the aftereffects of coming down from the party. Warner didn't realize until much later that night that Samantha still hadn't said anything about getting a divorce from Radu.

Before that thought could occur to him, they arrived at Sam's house, where they found Maddie sound asleep, in Samantha's bed, the children, in their pajamas, on either side of her. He woke her up and he and Sam put the sleeping children in their own beds, while Maddie went to the bathroom to splash her face with cold water.

"Maybe we could throw a party of our own," he whispered to Samantha, as they stood in Bri's doorway, watching her sleep.

"Maybe," she said softly. She didn't sound overly excited about the idea.

Maddie came down the hallway, looking a little less sleepy. She stopped when she reached them, as they stood in the doorway to Bri's room. "Did she wake up?" she asked.

"No," Warner said. "She's dead to the world."

Maddie stuck her head into the little girl's pink and red bedroom, and looked all around. "Is anything wrong?"

"No. We're just looking," Warner answered.

"At Sabrina?"

"Yes," Sam said.

"She is very cute when she's asleep. They both are," Maddie commented. "Nice and quiet, too." She stood with them for a moment. "Interesting hobby," she said.

"We like it," Warner said, smiling.

"Did they give you any trouble?" Sam asked, beckoning to them to follow her and leading them back downstairs.

"No, of course not. They're really good kids," Maddie replied. "They sure have a lot of energy, though. They tired me out." Warner noticed that she still looked sleepy.

Sam must have seen it, too. "Do you want a cup of coffee?" she asked. "Before you hit the road?"

"Can you put a splash of whiskey in it?" Maddie suggested. "This was a G-rated evening."

"Sure, why not? I think I'll have one, too," Sam said.

"Me too." Warner wanted to join this party. Or rather, he wanted to keep it going. He didn't want the evening to end.

While Samantha made their Irish whiskeys, he told Maddie that he had told Sam about the divorce.

"Oops," she said guiltily. "I thought you told her already," Maddie said. "So I mentioned it."

"I know. Sam told me."

"Sorry."

"No, it was okay, she understood that I didn't want to pressure her to get a divorce. But tonight she said she thought she was definitely getting over him."

"That creep," she said. "I'm sure Sam was waiting to see if you were going to be available before she went ahead with her divorce."

"I'm available," Warner said. "I've always made that very clear to her."

"How clear could it be when you were married?" Maddie queried.

"She knew it wasn't a real marriage," Warner answered. "And I think she knows me well enough to know I'm not the type to play around."

"But you were her husband's best friend," Maddie commented. "She might have thought that that made you two friends, too."

Warner paused, struck by the observation. "I guess so. Originally. But not since . . ."

"Since when?" she asked, looking up at him curiously.

"Since the night you came back," he replied.

"Oh," Maddie said.

"Do you think that she thinks that I'm not that serious about her?" he had to ask.

"I don't know," Maddie answered. "I don't know Samantha all that well. I guess my impression is that she's just as interested in you as you are in her. Maybe more. She isn't exactly the type to be looking for casual sex, either. Not like me."

She winked. He smiled and shook his head. She was teasing him. Maddie was terrified of commitment, afraid of being tied down, and even more afraid of being loved, so she sabotaged most of her relationships the moment the guy gave any hint that he felt anything beyond friendly affection for her; but she didn't sleep around. She required both knowledge of, and respect from, her sexual partners. It was just too dangerous, in this day and age, not to be a little bit discriminating. Even for a throwback to the sixties like Maddie Davis, sex was not something to be taken lightly. For her, love was even less so.

"I'm sure she's thrilled you're finally going to be free," Maddie teased, checking the door to make sure Sam wasn't coming.

Warner didn't want her overhearing this conversation, either, so he decided to change the subject. "Did you and the kids get a lot of candy?"

Maddie refused to be diverted. "Did she ask you to marry her?" she taunted. Which reminded him that Sam hadn't been as happy to hear the news of his divorce as he expected. "Not yet," he said, sticking his tongue out at her.

"She will, I'm sure," Maddie said, making a face at him.

"I hope so," he replied, lightly.

She stuck her tongue out at him. "That's what

you get for being such a great guy. Women just won't leave you alone."

"I think I can live with that," he said, laughing.

"It's gotta be tough," Maddie said, shaking her head. "I feel for you, guy."

"Thanks, babe. I appreciate your support," he said in the same flippant tone.

"Support for what?" Sam asked, as she came back into the room.

"Nothing," they both said at the same time.

"Really, it was nothing. We were just joking around," Warner said, not wanting her to feel left out. He couldn't tell her what the joke was. It was too embarrassing. "Maddie likes to give me a hard time."

"Seems like you enjoy it, too," Sammy said.

"Men are like that. They want to be the butt of our jokes. That's why they do all of those annoying things they do," Maddie explained.

"You've uncovered our secret!" Warner exclaimed. "You can never let on that you know, however, or they will come and get you."

"They? Who?"

"The guys," he said.

She smiled, and yawned. "It's been fun, but I'd better be going. It's late."

"Thanks again for watching the kids," Sam said. "I really appreciate it, Maddie."

After she left, the house seemed too quiet. Warner was sorry this evening had to come to an end. It had been a great night.

"It's late," Sam said.

"I know, time to go," he replied. "But it was fun, wasn't it?"

"Yes, it was."

"We'll have to do it again, soon," he said, and

gave her a kiss on the cheek. "I know where we can get a cheap baby-sitter."

"I don't mind paying," Sam answered. "I don't want to impose on Maddie too much."

"Don't worry about that," he told her. "She doesn't mind."

"I do," Sam said. "I don't want to take advantage of her."

"Believe me," Warner assured her, "she owes me."

"She doesn't owe me anything," Sam insisted. "And they're my kids," she added, forestalling any argument he might make.

"Okay," he said, though he wasn't sure what he was agreeing to. "It's up to you."

He left Sammy's house feeling that something had gone wrong at the end of the evening, somewhere, but he didn't know what. Or why.

CHAPTER THIRTEEN

Warner stopped by Maddie's house on his way home from work one day about a week after Halloween. He was her first official guest since she'd taken residence in her new house, and Maddie couldn't help thinking that that was just the way it should be. "I'm glad you dropped by," she greeted him happily when she found him standing in her doorway.

"How are you?" she asked as she ushered him into the living room, thrilled at the prospect of having company as the sun went down.

"I'm good," Warner responded. "I've been trying to imagine you settling in here, and I couldn't quite picture you as Susie Homemaker, so I thought I'd stop by and see this with my own eyes."

"In that case," she said, "are you hungry? Do you want something to drink?"

"Sure, I could use a little something. If things get hairy around here, I may need the fortification," he said.

"I hate it when you're pompous," Maddie complained. "What would you like? I've got wine, iced tea, and a bottle of vodka."

"I'll have a glass of wine," Warner answered.

"Would you like some cheese and crackers with that?" Maddie asked, in her best hostess manner.

"Okay," he accepted. As she turned to go to the kitchen, he added, "It's not that spray-on cheese, is it?"

"Ha, ha, ha," Maddie said sourly. "Laugh it up, funny boy." But she smiled as she went into the kitchen. Maddie couldn't help it. She loved him, even when he was being obnoxious. She poured him, and herself, a glass of wine and took it and the cheese platter out to the living room.

She felt all grown-up, placing the shining stainless steel cheese slicer next to the smoked Edam cheese with its thick brown wax covering, and the wedge of glistening Brie on the coffee table.

He wandered about the room, looking at the various pieces of furniture and knickknacks she'd decided to keep. Seeing the house through his eyes, Maddie didn't think it looked too dilapidated. "You've done a lot here," Warner complimented her.

Maddie glowed at him. "I think it's starting to look pretty good. I'm kicking around the idea of keeping the place, maybe turning it into a bed-and-breakfast." She didn't hold out a lot of hope that that plan could work, though, since she had no idea how to do it, or what was involved. "I can't see myself living here, but I don't want to disappoint Great-Aunt Becky."

"What, do you think she's watching?" he teased.

Maddie shook her head, disappointed by Warner's lack of imagination. "It's the principle of the thing," she explained. "You should understand that.

You used to be a man of principle yourself." As soon as the words came out of her mouth, she knew she had made a mistake. She hadn't meant to say that.

He raised an eyebrow at her. "Used to be?" he queried.

"Forget it," Maddie said dismissively. "I didn't mean that. It was just a bad joke." She hadn't meant to impugn his character. It was just that, lately, she'd felt as if she'd seen a side of him that she hadn't known about. It was all that Samantha's fault. Maddie had never doubted Warner for a minute before.

"You must have meant something," Warner persisted.

"No, I didn't, so let's just . . . sit here and enjoy our drinks. Eat some Brie," she ordered.

"Okay, okay," he said, mildly. "But I still want to know what you meant by that remark." He caught her gaze and wouldn't let her look away.

"You seem like you've changed," Maddie answered, reluctantly. "But it could just be me."

"Changed how? In what way?" he pressed.

"Can't we just drop this?" Maddie pleaded. She didn't want to tell him what she'd been thinking about him and his desire for an instant family.

"Why? If you've got something to say, I want to hear it. God knows, you've never held back before."

"Okay, you asked for it." She took a deep breath. "I'm probably all wrong about this," Maddie hedged. "But I get the impression—and I'm probably way off track here, so you can just tell me to shut up if I'm wrong, but . . . I get the feeling you're sort of rushing into this thing with Samantha."

"Me? Rushing?" he said incredulously. "Boy, are you barking up the wrong tree. We're taking it really slowly. Her husband left her less than a year ago, and she's understandably nervous about jumping right into another relationship."

"Not her," Maddie said out loud, though her inner voices were urging her to just shut up and agree with him. "You." He looked at her curiously and she couldn't stop herself from continuing. "You've convinced yourself that you're in love with her. That you've finally found your soul mate, your other half. That's why you suddenly decided to divorce me."

"First of all, there was nothing sudden about that decision. I've been thinking about it for a couple of years now at least."

"You never mentioned it to me before," she said sardonically.

"It's harder than you might think," he said. "I didn't want to hurt you."

Maddie was far from convinced, but she didn't argue the point. "Okay. Even assuming that that's true, I don't understand, why the big rush? Samantha hasn't even got her divorce started yet."

"She will," Warner said confidently.

"Have you proposed?" Maddie asked.

"Not yet. As you said yourself, it's a little early for that," he answered.

"But you're definitely planning to marry this woman," Maddie stated.

"I'm leaning that way," he said, grinning. "There's nothing wrong with it, right?"

"This fast?" she queried.

"It's not that fast. Samantha and I have known each other for years."

"Yes, but she was married to your best friend at the time. Doesn't that seem a little strange to you?"

"Not at all," Warner said, shrugging. "And I can't

believe that *you* are judging me like this. You've never even had a relationship that lasted for more than a month."

"You have, though. And they never work out. I don't know why, exactly, because I'd marry you for your chocolate chip cookies alone, if we weren't already married. But somehow, you have managed to avoid the trap for all these years."

"Trap?" He raised an eyebrow at her. "Nice," he said sarcastically.

She ignored that. "You've never rushed it like this before, either. Don't you think you're being a little hasty?"

"No, I don't," he answered. "And I can't believe you're saying this to me. Out of the two of us, I'm not the one who leaps first and looks after. That's your department, Maddie."

"Maybe I'm saying this badly," she said. "Aren't you even a little bit nervous about marrying a woman who isn't even divorced from her first husband yet? Let alone playing Daddy to her kids! That doesn't strike you as wrong, somehow?"

"I'm not playing at anything," he argued. "I'm trying to help them. I love them. There's no law against that, is there?"

"Don't ask me to give you my blessing, that's all," Maddie said.

"I wouldn't," he assured her. "You are not going to make me feel guilty about this, Maddie. I know how your mind works."

"What do you mean by that? My mind works just like everyone else's," Maddie said indignantly.

"Right," he said sarcastically. "Lots of grown-up women leave the country in order to get away from their mothers. You spend your life traveling the globe and sleeping on other people's couches and you're going to give *me* advice. I don't think so."

"All right, all right," she said, holding her hands up in surrender. "Sorry."

But he wasn't done. "You are the only person I know who would act like her best friend is committing a crime when all I want to do is have a family, like a lot of people my age," he concluded his diatribe.

"I didn't say it was a crime . . ." she said, smiling.

"Fine," Warner said, subsiding. "Just don't . . . Just cool it."

"Fine," she agreed.

They sat side by side on the couch, neither one of them looking at the other. Maddie had not intended to say anything to him about all this, and she didn't know how, or if, she could fix it now. Warner was the person she cared about more than anyone else in the world; whether he believed it or not, she only wanted him to be happy. That was why she even bothered to try and tell him that Samantha wasn't the woman for him.

Who is? the little voice in her head taunted her. *Certainly not you. Marrying you, as it turns out, didn't work out so well for him. Did it?*

But it was the perfect setup, she argued with herself. She wanted so badly to tell him what she was thinking—how perfect it was that they had each other as friends and as partners. They loved each other, and yet each of them was still free. They supported each other's dreams, but were not codependent. They hardly ever even fought. Why in the world would he want to screw all that up?

But Maddie knew she was going to have to let it go. Their arrangement just didn't suit him anymore. Apparently, it hadn't been right for him in a while. Even though it hurt a little to think that Warner had not been as happy with their relationship as she had been, if that was the way he felt, she certainly wasn't going to get in his way. Whether she agreed with him or not. Maddie opened her mouth to tell him so when suddenly she heard it. A distant laughter, like a group of children in a school yard.

"Did you hear that?" she asked him.

"What?" Warner said, but his eyes held an expression she was familiar with. She'd seen that look in her own face, in the mirror, in this house.

"That," she said, as the sound came again, this time carried on that mysterious breeze that always confounded her.

"It's probably just coming from outside," he said, not trying to deny that he knew what she was talking about. "From a neighbor's yard," he theorized.

"Come on upstairs," she said, jumping up off the couch and grabbing his hand to pull him up after her. "To the upstairs window," she explained when he looked at her, puzzled. "I've looked and I can't see where it's coming from. Maybe you'll spot something. I just want to know what I'm dealing with."

"Are things still going bump in the night?" he asked.

"No bumping," Maddie said coolly. "But I do hear . . . other things."

"Like what?" he asked indulgently.

"Like what you just heard."

He followed her, reluctantly. She was just happy that the voices, or whatever they were, hadn't faded away yet. Sometimes she only heard a faint burst, or two, and then nothing. But today, she made it to the back bedroom before the sound stopped.

"Look!" she commanded, leading him to the window. "I can't figure out where it could be coming from. Can you?"

He stepped up to the uncurtained window with confidence and looked outside. Maddie knew what he saw. A lake, in the pasture of the farm behind the house, and, to either side of the house, cornfields.

"Maybe it came from out front," he said.

"They designed the house so that you could not possibly hear anything from out front," Maddie reminded him. "The main road is out there, remember? And you can't even hear the cars going by."

"Right," he said pensively. "So, what is it?"

"That's what I want to know," Maddie said. "It's weirding me out."

"Maybe you should get your mother over here. That's her area," Warner said thoughtfully.

Maddie nixed that idea. "I would never ask her, and even if I did, she would never come."

"You won't know until you try," he admonished her.

"I know," Maddie said firmly. "It is not a possibility. Even if I were inclined to encourage this nonsense of hers, which I'm not, Janet Delaney wouldn't come into the house if it were the only one left on the planet."

"You are as pigheaded as she is," he said, shaking his head.

"Hey!" Maddie exclaimed in protest. "You're supposed to be on my side."

"I am," he assured her. "I'm just saying—"

Maddie covered his mouth with her palm. "Stop right now. While you're ahead."

He removed her hand. "Okay, okay. So what are you going to do?"

"Do?" she asked, looking at him blankly.

"About the . . . noises, or whatever? About the house?"

"You think I need to do something about it?" she asked. "Like what?"

"Well, I don't know. You're the one who said it was freaking you out."

"It is," Maddie assented. But at the moment she was feeling more relieved than anything else. It wasn't her imagination. He heard it, too.

At that moment, the air around them stirred. She'd grown somewhat accustomed to the sensation, but she still recognized the strangeness of it. "Feel that?" she asked. "That . . . breeze."

"Uh, maybe," he said, standing very still.

The air caressed her cheek again. "There. That," she said. "I've checked, there aren't any windows open, or holes anywhere that I can find. I've been from the attic to the cellar looking."

"That's strange. But it doesn't seem very scary, or anything."

"No, I guess not. Still, I wish it would stop," Maddie said. If she was going to be stuck with a house in Haycock Township, she wanted one without any connection to the paranormal. She'd had enough of the occult and the otherworldly growing up in her mother's house.

"It probably will," he said.

Over the next half hour, the house slowly subsided, or perhaps Maddie just became less sensitive to its eerie little quirks as she and Warner drank a couple more glasses of wine each. There was something about having him there that made her feel safe and comfortable, despite the fact that he had confirmed her worst fears. Only Warner could make the house's strange vibrations seem less creepy with one offhand observation. She loved him.

Maddie, being Maddie, didn't think. She said it aloud. "I love you, honey." It was only after the words came out of her mouth that she realized what she had said. Warner didn't seem to think anything of it, which was good. But she still felt bad about what she had said to him earlier. It might be true that he was rushing into this, and then again, it might just be that he knew what he wanted. The last thing she wanted was to get in the way of his happiness. She just wished she could be as sure as he seemed to be that Samantha Wheeler was the key to that happiness.

"About the divorce . . ." Maddie started, her voice trailing off as she realized she had no idea how she planned to finish that sentence. She had been Mrs. Maddie Davis for most of her adult life. She didn't want it to end. But she was going to have to give up the right to the name. She'd never really had it anyway. She had just been borrowing it.

"Yes?" Warner prompted.

"I don't know. I just wanted to say that . . . I guess it won't be any problem to get one, right?"

"It should be easy. The process seems pretty straightforward," he told her.

"And so, then what?" Maddie couldn't resist asking. "Are you planning to propose right away?"

"Maybe." When she looked at him disapprovingly, he added, "Probably. I'm thirty-three years old, Maddie. It's time I settled down."

"I'm thirty-two. So what? It's just a number."

"I want a family," Warner said in explication. "We've talked about this before. I know you don't think much of the institution, but I've always planned to have kids someday."

When they had first talked about getting married, all those years ago, Warner told Maddie that he did want a real family someday. At twenty-two, kids seemed a future, very distant, possibility for both of them. She assumed it was some kind of warning about getting too attached, and she promptly forgot all about it.

"Fine," Maddie said soothingly. "I'm all for it. I just don't think you should rush into . . . anything."

"This, from the woman who is out the door the second a guy even says he likes you. You are not exactly the first person I'd go to for advice about relationships," Warner said.

"I'm not—" Maddie stammered. "I'm just saying that I think you should think about this."

"I've thought," he stated.

"I like Samantha and all, but are you sure she's the one for you?"

"Why wouldn't she be?" he asked, offended.

"No reason. I'm not saying she isn't. I just can't help thinking that you seem . . . I don't know, a little desperate. That's all."

"Uh-huh," he murmured, though he clearly didn't agree with her assessment. "And *that's* why you don't want me to marry Sam?"

"No. I mean yes. I mean I don't know," Maddie answered. "I think Samantha's nice. I just think you two should get to know each other better before you take a step like marriage."

"I don't need to think about it," Warner said. "No, I don't mean that. I don't need to think about it more than I have, more than I am. I've thought about it a lot," he stated definitely. "This is what I want."

"Just because you're thirty-three?" she asked again. "I didn't know you had a deadline."

"Not really. I did think I'd be married before this," he said. "Not to you. To someone who wanted kids and a backyard and everything."

"Men have kids at seventy, or later," she commented, trying not to sound hurt by his dismissal. The thing was, it shouldn't hurt because she never thought they had a real marriage either. She certainly hadn't thought about having kids, with him or anyone else. She wasn't ready to make a commitment to a cat, let alone a man.

"Maybe they do, but it still isn't in my plans," Warner replied.

"You're not doing this because you're lonely, or anything like that? Right? Because you *can* be in a relationship without getting married to the woman."

"I'm aware of that," Warner said dryly. "And to answer your question, indelicate as it was, no, I am not doing this because I'm lonely, or horny, or anything like that. I'm *thinking* about marrying Samantha because she's incredible and she makes me feel really good."

"Ooh, so it's a sex thing," Maddie said, understanding at last. "Now, *that* I can comprehend."

"No, it's not a sex thing," Warner protested. "And by the way, did I ever tell you that you've got the emotional maturity of a twelve-year-old boy?"

Maddie smiled. "Touchy, touchy, touchy," she accused.

"God, woman, you're incorrigible," he said, shaking his head. "I don't know why I even try to talk to you."

"You don't want to talk? We don't have to talk. We can just sit here," she offered. "You're probably right, anyway. I'm never going to understand why you would want to marry anyone else."

"Ha!" he exclaimed triumphantly. "I knew it. This is just like what happened with Tommy Lamont. Admit it."

"What?" Maddie said, confounded. She didn't remember anyone named Tommy Lamont.

"You weren't even interested in the guy until he dumped you for Cheryl Tompkins," he explained. "You are a great big dog in the manger."

"I am not," Maddie retorted, stunned.

"You're kidding, right?" Warner asked.

"I am not kidding. I'm not a dog in the manger. I want you to be happy, that's all. I don't want you to marry this woman for all the wrong reasons and then regret it later. Like you did with me."

"What?" It was his turn to look shocked. "Whoa . . . back up. I don't regret our marriage."

"You don't? Then what have we been talking about?" Maddie asked.

"Not regret." He answered so quickly that she didn't doubt that he was telling the truth.

"Oh," she said, somewhat deflated. "So . . ."

"So, let's not make this a bigger deal than it really is," he answered. "It's time. That's all."

"Yeah, okay," she agreed.

When she walked him to the door and said good-bye, Maddie felt as if she were bidding farewell to an era. She gave him a peck on each cheek, then a quick kiss on the lips. He tasted like wine.

"Bye," she said, stepping back from him.

"Old man," she added.

"I'll see you," he said back. "Kid."

She smiled weakly, and watched him walk to his car, then waved good-bye as he started the car. As she stepped back through the door into Becky's house, it occurred to her that he was the one who needed a place like this. She could picture him there with Samantha's kids much more easily than she would ever see herself being comfortable in the big old house.

But tonight, for a change, she actually felt less like an intruder than ever before. Maybe it was because Warner had been with her this time to experience the eerie sensations that made her feel that the house had a life of its own. The spirit that inhabited the hundred-year-old structure seemed more welcoming of her somehow and she went into the living room feeling almost as if she wasn't alone.

CHAPTER FOURTEEN

Warner wasn't sure what had changed between himself and Samantha, but something had definitely happened. There was only one thing he could think of that could create this kind of distance between them, and that was her husband. But she didn't mention that he had contacted her. He finally asked her about it at dinner one Friday night in the middle of November. "Have you heard something from Radu?" he asked.

"No," she said surprised. "Why? Have you?"

"No, of course not. I would have told you if I had."

"Me too," she said instantly. "Of course," she added.

"So if it's not that, then what has been bothering you?" Warner probed gently.

"Nothing," Sam insisted. "I've just had a lot on my mind, lately."

"Like what?" he asked.

"Oh, you know, work, the kids, Thanksgiving, et cetera."

"Work?" he said skeptically.

"Being a secretary is harder than it sounds," she said.

"It just seems like you've been . . . sort of unhappy, lately," he pressed.

"Well, I'm not," she answered.

"So there's nothing wrong?" he asked again.

"Nope. Nothing," she continued, giving him a perfunctory smile as she went back to eating her meal.

The kids were already tucked into their beds upstairs. They had had pizza, and Warner played with them and gave them their bath. Then he read them stories until they fell asleep, while Sam straightened up and cooked a slightly more sophisticated dinner for the two of them. It had become their Friday night ritual and he thoroughly enjoyed the whole evening.

Warner couldn't have said which was his favorite part: eating pizza with the kids and tucking them in, his second dinner—the adult dinner featuring wine and grown-up conversation with Sam—or afterward, when he and Sam made out like teenagers on the living room couch for hours. It was foreplay unlike anything he'd ever experienced. They never discussed sex, but they seemed to be in perfect accord about waiting. For what, he didn't know. But they hadn't actually consummated their relationship. Not fully.

They touched, kissed, caressed, and tasted each other, from forehead to fingertips. He wanted badly to make love to her. He even fantasized about it. But there was something holding him back. And it appeared that, whatever it was, it was holding Samantha back, too, though she was just as eager as he was to mess around.

As unfathomable as the situation was, the arrangement had its advantages. He hadn't felt this kind of excitement and energy with a woman since high school. And it didn't feel manufactured, or phony—

it just was what it was. He loved to run the backs of his fingers across the swell of her breast, and he loved it even more when she skimmed her fingernails over his shoulder blades and down his back, but he didn't feel the need to push things. The limits to their lovemaking had evolved naturally just as the rest of their relationship had.

This strange form of abstinence was yet another of the many firsts he had experienced with Samantha. She was not only the first woman he could imagine himself walking down the aisle with, she was also the first he could conceive of growing old with. Perhaps it was because she was the first woman he ever dated that he felt completely relaxed with. Usually, a few months into a relationship, he'd start to grow bored. No matter how much he liked the woman, once the thrill of getting to know her had worn off, he found her predictable, unexciting. But with Samantha, the romance continued. It showed no sign of waning. Ever.

These Friday nights confirmed his belief that she was the one he'd been waiting for. And it wasn't just this one night a week. Every time he saw Sam, he felt the same way. When he was away from her, he was almost as certain. Even Maddie's barbed comments couldn't shake his confidence that this was right. This was the relationship that he'd been dreaming of for years. It was perfect.

Tonight, as they had almost every Friday night for the past six weeks, they cleared up together after dinner, and went into the living room. This was, by far, his favorite room in the house. As much as he liked Sam's deep red kitchen that, with its oak cabinets and tiled floor, looked both modern and yet warm at the same time; and Eddy's room, with its sports posters and slanted architect's desk; and as much as he admired the frilly pink and white room she'd created for Bri; and the elegant master bedroom done in shades of lavender and gold against cherry-wood furniture, he liked it in here best.

Sam called it the family room, which seemed very apt to Warner. It was clear that more than one generation had inhabited this space. Eddy's remote control cars and robots and dinosaurs were lined up on one wall, while Bri's dollhouse occupied another. The children's videos and DVDS, such as *The Power Puff Girls Movie* and *Explorers*, were mixed in with Sam's collection of chick flicks and serious films. The Nintendo and X-Box and Playstation games were shelved next to her CD collection.

"*Sense and Sensibility* is on HBO tonight," she said, handing him the remote.

"Sounds good," Warner said, taking it and turning the television on. She left to go check on the children, as he searched for the channel she wanted. He didn't care what they watched. He just liked sitting in here with her, necking on the couch. This was the heart of the house. Every Friday night, he tried to picture what he would add to the eclectic mix if and when he became a part of this little family. Radu's presence had been virtually wiped out, except for some photos. Warner couldn't even remember what his best friend had contributed to the decor. An old recliner, perhaps. He thought he had seen one in here at some point. And maybe a pile of *Sports Illustrated* magazines in a box. Try as he might, he couldn't actually remember the room looking any different. Perhaps that was why Radu had left. Maybe he didn't quite fit into the Norman Rockwell portrait of a family.

Warner knew he wouldn't have that problem. He couldn't wait to make the picture complete again.

"They're fast asleep," Samantha said, when she returned a minute later. She sat down on the couch beside him, kicking off her shoes as she slid into his open arms.

They kissed, long and deeply, his hands rediscovering the familiar terrain of her back, her waist, and her hips, while she slid her hands down across his chest, and inside his shirt. He slipped her T-shirt up, out of the way, and undid the front clasp of her bra to free her breasts into his waiting palms. He nuzzled them, and encircled one hard-peaked tip with his lips, before she pulled his mouth back up to hers. Tonight, however, she cut their make-out session short. After just a few minutes, she pulled away.

"The movie's starting," she said, in explication.

"Tired?" he asked.

"A little," she answered. As if there were some invisible barrier between them, they let each other go, sliding apart slowly and gently, until they were seated side by side on the couch, their bodies touching only at the hip. They sat so close together that he could feel her heart beating. He was sure she could hear his heart, too, still pounding away, but they focused their attention on the television.

If her husband, or his wife, or anyone else, had walked in on them then, they'd never have guessed at the passion they'd displayed a few minutes ago, he thought as his heartbeat slowed to its normal rate. Sam was already enrapt in the movie, cool and untouchable, her legs curled up under her, and her eyes glowing in the flickering light from the television screen. She was a very single-minded woman.

She didn't look at him as she asked, "How is Maddie doing?" The question came out of nowhere.

Or maybe it didn't. Maybe it was because of Maddie that Sam had been acting oddly lately.

Warner managed to keep his composure and answered calmly enough, "She seems fine. But she says her house is haunted."

"Sounds like Maddie," Sam said, smiling. "Or her mother."

"Don't let her hear you say that," he cautioned. "I made that mistake when I dropped by her place the other night, and she nearly bit my head off."

"You dropped by her place?" Sam asked. Her tone was matter-of-fact, but he suspected the question was a loaded one. Was she jealous?

"On my way home from work on Wednesday," he answered. "I thought I told you."

"No, you hadn't mentioned it," she replied.

"It was sort of funny, actually. She may be right. That house has a very weird vibe."

"Oh, please," Sam said disparagingly. "You can't be serious, Warner."

"I felt it. And I heard . . . something. We both did."

"I hope you didn't encourage that notion," Sam chided him. "Her mother is bad enough, always talking about the moon, and the stars. The only sensible thing Maddie ever did in her life was to get as far away from that mother of hers as she could."

"You think so?" Warner asked, surprised. "I always thought it was sort of sad. Her mother is eccentric, sure, but there's not a mean bone in the woman's body."

"She's nutty as a fruitcake," Samantha persisted. "And Maddie's not much better."

I thought you were starting to like her better, Warner wanted to say, but he kept his mouth shut. It was the only thing he could do.

"I'm not surprised that she thinks that old house is haunted, but you? Aren't you a little old to believe in ghosts?"

Warner had just said something very similar to Maddie. He hadn't realized how harsh the words sounded until he heard Sam say them. He was surprised at the urge he felt to argue with her, but he knew he couldn't. The timing was wrong. They couldn't have that particular debate at the moment. The woman next to him was waiting for an answer to her question.

"I've got to tell you, she is definitely not imagining things. There is something strange going on in that house." When she looked at him skeptically, he nodded. "I did hear . . . and feel . . . something."

"Well, that must have made her day," Samantha said, starting to rise.

Warner stood, too. "Where are you going?"

"I thought I'd make a cup of tea," Sam said stiffly. "You want one?"

"I'll get it. You sit and watch your movie."

She hesitated, then nodded. "Okay, thanks," she said, relenting. The standoff was over.

"It's my pleasure," he asserted. Warner leaned down and kissed her wetly on the neck; then he headed into the kitchen, whistling.

That nagging sensation that something was wrong between them had retreated to the back of his mind. On a night like this, the future seemed to spread itself out before him. He would make this family his own, and they would all live happily ever after. He was sure of it.

When he brought Sammy her tea, she seemed more relaxed, and Warner stopped worrying, finally, about the tension between them. It was probably nothing, except perhaps a guilty leftover from that moment at the party when he'd been distracted, in the midst of kissing Sam, by thoughts of Maddie.

He could justify the slipup. He loved both women. He just loved them both in different ways. Maddie was his friend, and she'd been closer to him, until now, than any other woman he knew. But Sam was going to be much more than a friend. He wanted to make a life with her and her children. He wanted to make them into the family he'd always imagined he would have.

Warner went home that night convinced that he had figured out what had been nagging at him was his own conscience. It wasn't Sammy who was acting differently. It was him. *He* was the one who had pulled away. He wouldn't do it again, he told himself. He had made his decision. He knew what he wanted—to make this relationship with Sammy work for them both.

That night he dreamed of Maddie. He woke up in the wee hours of the morning in a panic. He couldn't remember everything about the dream, but he remembered she'd slipped away from him, growing smaller and smaller, until he couldn't even see her anymore. It left him with a sense of loss.

It was probably perfectly natural, he told himself. They were getting a divorce, after all. Everyone said that that was a traumatic experience. Even if it was common, these days, psychologically speaking, it caused people to feel depressed. And even though he and Maddie hadn't really been married, they had been together for a very long time. It made perfect sense that he'd feel this way. He was changing. They were changing. He was moving on.

He could tell Maddie that nothing would be different between them a hundred times, or a thousand, but that didn't make it true. She would no longer be his wife. She might not even be his best friend anymore, if Sam took over that role. *Of course* his subconscious was sending him subliminal messages. He'd been in denial, and it was time to stop and admit that he was experiencing something completely new and different. He was transforming his life.

Over the next week, Warner noticed that, although they tried hard to be friendly to each other, Sammy and Maddie didn't like each other much. He didn't know whether theirs was the natural antipathy of two women with very different personalities, or if they, unconsciously, felt like rivals, or both. Whatever the reason, they would probably never be good friends, no matter how hard they tried. There were just too many obstacles preventing them from achieving a rapport.

For one thing, Maddie was a free spirit, a child at heart, while Sammy was very much an adult. For another, they were proud of who they were, which gave each woman a distrust of the other. And then there was the fact that he'd been so close to Maddie for so long. That definitely did not help the situation. They would tolerate each other, and probably even continue to pretend that they liked each other, but they would never be close.

He would always love them both for trying, though.

It was just as well they were determined to get along, because he didn't plan to give up either one. No matter what Maddie, or even Sam, had to say about it, he had no intention of losing either his best friend, or the woman he loved. Warner wanted both of them to be a part of his life, and he was determined to arrange it, somehow. He couldn't imagine saying good-bye to either of them. So he wouldn't. It was as simple as that.

CHAPTER FIFTEEN

The week before Thanksgiving, it snowed. Maddie loved the snow, but the storm could not have come at a less convenient time. She had hired a roofer to repair a portion of the roof that had suffered water damage and they had agreed to get right on the job, since it was the beginning of their slow season. However, the snow made working on the slanted slate roof impossible, and the job hadn't been going particularly smoothly even before the snow impeded their progress. A series of bizarre mishaps had plagued the first stages of the repair work. A bucket fell on the boss's foot, and broke his toe, eliminating him as a worker, and requiring that he relayed his orders up to the roof through his less experienced supervisor. Then, one of the men slipped right through a damaged slate, which would not have been so unexpected, except it was in the section of the roof that had not suffered any water damage.

Needless to say, the repair work had gone slowly after that. Everyone was extremely cautious about where they stepped or what they did. She had worried that the work was going to be delayed already, without the unseasonable weather to throw the men off schedule. Maddie wanted to have the renovation completed by the new year. She planned to do a lot of the work herself, painting and papering the walls and sanding the floors, but she needed professional help with some of the remodeling. The electrical wiring was a little hinky and the plumbing—while built to last—contained some quirks. She had consulted a broker who said she could probably rent the house to a family, but to do that she had to make it really comfortable. Having the work done now would also lessen the chance that it would require a lot of maintenance later on, when she wouldn't be around to handle it.

Unfortunately, the house didn't seem to want to be fixed. It was probably a figment of her imagination, but she couldn't help wondering if someone wasn't trying to tell her something.

"Like what?" her friend Patsy asked.

"If you hit me with that hammer one more time, I'm going to fall down on your head?" Maddie suggested.

"Oh, yeah," Patsy said sarcastically. "You could hit that old place with a bomb and it wouldn't make a dent. That house is just like the old lady who lived in it. Steel, through and through."

"Aunt Becky was a doll!" Maddie exclaimed, insulted by the characterization of her favorite relative as some kind of battle-ax. Sure, Becky was acerbic and demanding, but she was also a sweetheart who only did what she thought was best for those around her.

"Absolutely," Patsy agreed without hesitation. "But she was a tough lady. Don't be offended, I meant that as a compliment. She never let anyone, including your mother, ever get her down or push her around. She was indomitable."

"Yes, she was," Maddie said, mollified. "She was my role model."

"Ha!" Patsy snorted. "You may have admired her, I know I did, but a role model? For you?"

"Sure she was," Maddie said, puzzled by her friend's tone. "I wanted to be just like her."

"In what way?" Patsy asked, still with that undercurrent of laughter in her voice.

"Strong, independent, different," Maddie listed. "I do what I want to do, when I want to do it, and I don't answer to anybody. Just like her."

"Oh?" Patsy said, still teasing. "So where does running away from home fit in? What about dealing with your mother? Can you see Becky ever backing down from a confrontation with anyone? Let alone flying to another continent to avoid dealing with it."

"I didn't run away, I left Richland, by choice, because I needed something this dinky little town didn't have to offer. The work I love."

"All right," Patsy said soothingly. "No offense intended." When she saw that Maddie didn't look placated, she added, "I didn't mean to upset you. Maybe I'm just jealous because you travel all over the world, alone, having adventures I can't even imagine and not needing anyone to come home to, not even needing a *home* to come home to."

"First of all," Maddie began, "you've got more guts than any two people I know. I can't even begin to picture you turning your back on the business you dreamed of owning, and poured so much of yourself into building. I *really* can't see you dragging your family from place to place, lugging your kids from one city to another, instead of living in that comfortable home you made for them. You are much too good a mother, and wife, to ask them to do that. I think that is not only brave, it's . . . beautiful."

"Thanks, Mad."

She wasn't done. "Secondly, why does everybody have to choose just one thing or the other? I want it all, some day. What about all the times you've been to visit me? What about our week in London last year? We had a good time, didn't we? You get to have adventures, and have your home and family. And I get to share your home and family when I'm here. We can both have the lives we want. They are *not* mutually exclusive. I can be me, and you can be you, without it being any kind of competition, right?"

"Okay," Patsy agreed, but she wasn't very convincing.

"What's wrong with that?" Maddie pushed.

"Nothing, but . . ."

"But what?" she asked. "What is it?"

"I *sort of* agree with you, but if we're truly going to be honest here . . ." Patsy hesitated, before continuing. "I've got to admit that I don't think you can have it both ways. I don't want to hurt your feelings, Maddie, but . . ."

"Go ahead, I'm tough, I can take it," Maddie joked, inwardly apprehensive at what her friend might say.

"Maybe it's not Becky's house that is trying to tell you something, maybe you're trying to tell yourself something."

"I don't know, Pats," Maddie said, shaking her head. "That sounds a little crazy to me. I may be a little screwy, but I don't think I'm schizophrenic."

"Of course not. Forget it. It's not important. You're fine. I'm fine. We all got to do what we gots to do, right?" Patsy replied. "Like I said before, I'm just jealous because when I leave here, I've got to go be a soccer mom, and when you leave you get to commune with the ancients or, at least, talk to grown-ups."

"Maybe it used to be that way, Pats, but things are changing. And I don't like it."

"That's life, babe," her friend said. "That's just the way it is. There's nothing any of us can do about it."

But Maddie wasn't ready to give up. She hated the feeling that she had lost control of her own life. Supernatural powers might possibly be at work in Great-Aunt Becky's house, but the forces affecting Warner were all too human. And she didn't have to just sit back and take it. She could do something about his situation.

The more she thought about it, the more Maddie was convinced that it was her duty to bring him to his senses. Now, before it was too late. All she needed was a plan.

On Sunday, after church, she invited him over to her place. "If you don't have plans with Samantha?" she said.

"No, we usually get together on Friday," he told her.

My God, she's got him on a schedule for sex, now, Maddie thought. She was quite surprised to learn, after a couple of glasses of wine, and some gentle probing, that there was no sex, scheduled or un-scheduled.

"We're in a holding pattern," Warner explained. "What with the divorce and all."

"She's not a virgin, is she?" Maddie asked, tongue in cheek. She regretted her snide tone when he looked at her reproachfully.

"We decided it would be less complicated if we

waited," he replied. "What's with all the interest in my sex life anyway?"

"I just assumed . . ." she said, at something of a loss for words. "I mean, it's not like you never had lovers before."

"This is different," he said, shaking his head. "You wouldn't understand."

"I think I do. You can't fool around with your best friend's wife?" It was a bad joke, and it fell completely flat.

"It's not that, exactly. Sam isn't like the other women I've dated. She's special."

"I get it," Maddie lied. "This is a test, right? Of your commitment."

"Maybe," he agreed reluctantly. "I guess you could call it that."

"Are you sure about this, Warner?" she asked. "It sounds sort of backward to me." When he looked at her curiously, she asked, "If she loves you, don't you think you should be . . . um . . . intimate by now?"

"We are intimate," he retorted.

"But not having actual sex? Don't you think *doing it* might strengthen your relationship?" she pressed.

"I don't think so," he said. "This works for us."

"I can't argue with you about *us*." She made little quotation marks around the word with her fingers. "I don't know Sam well enough to judge her motives," Maddie conceded.

"That's right," he averred.

"But I do know you," she went on. "And I don't think this arrangement is good for you."

"Me? I'm fine," he insisted.

"I think you've got things a little mixed up," Maddie countered. "I know Samantha is your ideal woman and all that, but I think the real reason you're divorcing me and marrying her is that she's unattainable. She's got that ice goddess thing down cold, have you noticed?"

"No, she doesn't," he said, annoyed.

"It happens to all of us, at one time or another," Maddie persisted. "We can't resist what we can't have."

"Maddie, what the hell are you talking about?" he asked.

"You. And Samantha. I never understood why you were so into her. Actually, that's why I invited you over here tonight. To talk about it calmly and rationally. Not like last time," she hastened to add. "This isn't just my gut talking. It's my brain, too. I know I can make you see reason. You're the most sensible guy I know."

"I don't know whether you're trying to be insulting or if it's just coming out that way," he retorted, annoyed.

"Just let me explain. I've been thinking about this ever since we talked, and I don't believe that you are really in love with her. I'm not being a dog in the manger here. I promise. I'm really concerned about you."

"Don't be," he said.

"I can't help it. You have always been really serious about relationships, and all, and I admire that about you. You know what you want. It's just who you are. But I can't help thinking something is out of whack here, especially when I see the two of you together. She isn't right for you."

"That's for me to decide. Not you."

"I can't just stand by and watch while you make the biggest mistake of your life," Maddie said. She took a deep breath. "So kiss me," she ordered.

One minute, Warner looked like he was about

to get up and leave, and the next, his chin dropped down to his chest. "What!"

"Kiss me. I want to show you something," Maddie answered calmly.

"Woman, have you lost your mind?" he asked, astounded.

"I'm serious," Maddie told him. "If you're so sure of your feelings for Samantha, then kissing me shouldn't be any big deal."

"I'm not going to kiss you," he spluttered.

"Why not? What are you afraid of?" Maddie taunted.

"I'm not afraid of anything. I'm just not going to go along with this wacky scheme of yours. What do you think it will prove anyway?"

"Just that you're not really in love with Sam," she declared.

"How?" he asked. "Forget it, I don't want to know," he continued, before she could answer. "This is ridiculous."

"If I'm wrong, I'll be happy to apologize," she said. "But I don't believe you can do it." She moved slowly toward him.

"What do you think you're doing?" he asked.

"If you don't kiss me, I'll just have to kiss you," she warned.

"No, you don't," he said firmly.

"Yes, I do," she countered.

"Fine," he said suddenly. He reached out and pulled her to him. Now that he was actually doing it, Maddie wasn't sure this was such a good idea. But she couldn't back out now. "If it will shut you up," he said, just before he lowered his mouth to hers. She had kissed Warner before: at their fake wedding, when they said hello, when they said good-bye, on birthdays, and New Year's Eve, lots of times. But this kiss was something else. Maddie thought that her head might explode.

Maddie hadn't expected to feel such hunger at the touch of his lips on hers. His mouth was hot, his arms hard around her. She felt herself surrendering immediately to the force of his assault. And it wasn't a gentle kiss. He was very annoyed with her. His frustration was evident in the breath that escaped his nostrils, rushing past her cheeks. He was an angry male animal, and the fact that she was pliant in his arms did not seem to appease him at all. He kept on. His mouth slanted over hers for a long, long time.

She hadn't expected *not* to feel anything; after all, she loved Warner. So she wasn't surprised that his kiss had an impact on her. What with him asking her for the divorce, and everything else that had been going on between them lately, her feelings for him were right on the surface. She was concerned for him, confused about letting him go, adrift at the thought that their relationship was about to change. She knew that kissing him would be an emotional experience. She just hadn't counted on her body's physical response. She hadn't anticipated the force of her feelings.

When he finally let her go, Maddie felt limp. "Satisfied?" he asked, his voice hoarse.

"I guess so," she whispered. This wasn't what she had wanted. She had thought if she could seduce him, he would admit that it wasn't really Samantha he wanted, but just the comfort she offered. Everyone needed to feel that bond with another human being sometimes. Maddie's plan had been to demonstrate to Warner that any woman would do, that Warner was only imagining that there was something more between himself and that woman. But her plan seemed to have backfired on her. Warner looked fine, while she felt as if she'd been punched in the gut. She couldn't seem to catch her breath.

Maddie had been so sure this would work. That was why she was willing to offer herself to prove that Sam wasn't for him. She was certain their friendship was strong enough to withstand this test. And afterward, he could give up on this pipe dream of his, this fantasy that he had finally found the woman he'd been searching for. He would agree with her that it was the desire to be a part of the family he'd been hoping to find his whole life that had blinded him to the fact that Samantha was not the girl for him.

Unfortunately, he seemed unmoved, while she felt as if her world had turned on its axis. "I'm sorry," she said, finally. "I guess I was wrong," she added in a small voice.

"That's it?" he asked. "That's all you have to say?"

"Don't be mad," she pleaded. "I was only trying to help."

"How?" he asked.

"I thought if I seduced you . . . you would realize you couldn't marry her."

He shook his head. "Maddie, I don't know where you get these crazy ideas."

She licked her lips. "I don't either. Sorry. But I honestly thought you couldn't kiss me without feeling anything. I guess you really are in love with her."

"I could have told you that. In fact, I believe I did."

"I know, I know. You don't have to rub it in," she mumbled.

"I think I do," he said. "You can't go around doing stuff like this. Do you even realize how nuts it sounds? Are you really that scared?"

"Scared? Me? I just didn't want you to make a mistake, that's all."

"Come off it, Maddie. You are so afraid of change that you were thinking about sleeping with me just so I wouldn't get married!"

"That's not it. I was doing it for you," she insisted.

"You were doing it because you don't want to lose your escape hatch."

"Give me a little more credit than that. My intentions were good," she said.

"I know your heart was in the right place, honey, but you've got to stop acting like . . . like . . . an idiot!"

"Okay, okay. I get it," she said.

Maddie couldn't help wondering if he might be right. She'd been a bit surprised when Patsy called her a coward the week before, although both she—and Warner!—had alluded to it before. This was, apparently, how she was perceived, even by her closest friends. Hadn't they been saying, for years, that she acted like a child: afraid of commitment, running from responsibility, and her mommy? Maddie had always just shrugged off their comments, taking them as jokes, as jealousy, even as concern for her rootless state, but now she finally understood. It all came together in her mind.

They really did think there was something wrong with her. And maybe they were right.

The revelation didn't change anything. Nothing at all. Except her vision of everything and everyone. Suddenly Maddie saw herself, and the people around her, in a whole new light. For a couple of days she tried to go on acting as if nothing had happened, but she had become very aware of the effects of her behavior—and especially the childish way that she sounded when she spoke to her mother.

Janet was more concerned than ever about Maddie's inheritance since Maddie had moved into Becky's house. Mom's dire warnings of impending disaster annoyed Maddie, but as she listened to herself belittling her mother's beliefs, not to mention her very real fears, Maddie felt embarrassed and ashamed. She was responding to this woman, who deserved both her love and respect, with all the maturity of an adolescent. However ridiculous Maddie might think her mother's theories, Janet did not deserve to be demeaned by her only daughter.

Then there was Warner and his new girlfriend. Maddie thought back over the last couple of months, and realized that she had been constantly testing *him*, and trying to annoy *her*. She was mortified. She had no right—none at all—to judge Warner or to try and cast doubt on his choice of a lover, or a wife. It was up to him.

She went to see Patsy a couple of days later, and told her all about her stupid plan, and how it had backfired. "Poor Warner. I can't believe I made him kiss me."

Patsy laughed. "If that's the worst thing you ever do to him, he'll be lucky," she said.

"Don't say that. I'm not going to do anything bad to him ever again," Maddie vowed. "But I don't know what to say, or how to act anymore. I am a terrible person."

"So you found out that you're not perfect. We all have to accept that, eventually. Well, most of us," Patsy quipped. "You too."

"I've been behaving abysmally for years," Maddie wailed.

"You're not *that* bad," her friend said. "Don't go off the deep end about this."

"But you're the one who told me I was being childish and irresponsible," Maddie said.

"Me? I did not," Patsy protested. "I would never say anything like that."

"I'm paraphrasing," Maddie clarified.

"Oh, well, okay. I might have said something a little bit like that. But I didn't mean it in a negative way. You're taking it all wrong."

"How could you not mean it in a negative way? How can you call someone irresponsible in a positive way?" Maddie demanded.

"I might have said something like . . . Wow, that was stupendously irresponsible."

"And how would that make it positive?"

"If I said stupendously, that makes it sort of a compliment, doesn't it?"

Maddie had to laugh. "You are twisted, Pats."

"Just trying to help."

Maddie sobered up a moment later. "I really do have to make some major changes in my life," she announced.

"You are, babe. You've got the house, and you're fixing it up nice. That's all good."

"But I didn't want to do it. I just got stuck with it."

"You're doing it," her friend said. "That's what matters. And you're standing up for Warner, giving him the divorce. I know that's hurting you, but you're doing the right thing."

"It's about time, huh?" Maddie asked sadly.

"We all have to grow up sometime," Patsy agreed.

"You are sure about that, right?" Maddie queried. "There aren't any exceptions?"

"Nope. No exceptions," Patsy answered. "For women. Some men get to be babies well into their seventies, but not us. Sorry."

"That sucks."

"It won't be that bad," Patsy assured her. "I promise."

"I hope you know what you're talking about," Maddie said. "I can't take too much more of this blinding insight."

"You'll be all right, honey. Recognizing the problem is half the battle," Patsy said soothingly.

"Maybe, but unfortunately, that's not the half that has me worried. It's the half where I have to stop being me and start being this other person who doesn't hide behind her phony marriage, or hop from one country to another always one step ahead of her responsibilities," she admitted. "The woman who actually talks to and listens to her mother."

"It will work itself out, you'll see. In the end, you'll be glad this happened." Patsy's tone was reassuringly convincing.

"I better be," Maddie proclaimed. "Otherwise all this personal growth will be for nothing."

THANKSGIVING

CHAPTER
SIXTEEN

Warner took Bri and Eddy skiing on the Wednesday afternoon before Thanksgiving. They left Samantha at home, because she said she needed the time to shop and prepare the house for the next day. She was planning to cook a big, traditional dinner for him, her kids, her parents, and his parents. Thanksgiving for eight people, and dessert for nine. Maddie was coming over after dinner—by a strange twist of fate. Samantha asked her.

He picked the kids up from school. Sam had given him all their skiing paraphernalia, which he had put in the trunk of his car and was praying that he would actually manage to get the children into. The responsibility made him nervous, but Eddy's enthusiastic greeting and Sabrina's sweet smile made it all worth it. They were let out of school early for the holiday weekend, so they were both in a very good mood, which didn't stop them from squabbling from the moment they got in the car.

"I want a turn," Bri kept saying, in tones that

ranged from wheedling, to whining, to begging. Eddy appeared to be ignoring her.

Neither of them paid the slightest attention to Warner when he asked them what they were arguing about. He finally had to raise his voice. "Guys, guys, what is going on back there?"

"Nothing," both children said innocently.

"What are you arguing about?" Warner asked.

"We're not arguing," they both claimed.

"It sounds like it to me, so whatever you're talking about, stop it," he ordered.

"My Gameboy, you mean?" Eddy asked.

"I want a turn," Bri said.

"Yeah, I guess that's what I mean," Warner said.

"No way, she'll mess up my game," he proclaimed.

"I won't. I'll do what you tell me," the little girl said.

Hoping to avoid another debate, Warner said, "Give her a turn, Eddy."

"It's not fair," he complained.

"Give her a turn, or put it away."

There was a moment of silence, and then Eddy caved. "Do you promise to do exactly what I say?"

"I will," Bri promised, solemnly.

For the next five minutes, they huddled together over the small electronic game, Bri excited about playing her big brother's game, and Eddy equally anxious about it.

"Okay, time's up!" he announced, when he couldn't stand it anymore. Bri obediently surrendered the game, and then watched him play for a while. Their muttered comments and occasional exclamations were completely incomprehensible to Warner. But if they were happy, he was happy.

After fifteen or twenty minutes, Bri's attention wandered from the game. "Uncle Warner, where does snow come from?" she asked.

"The clouds," he answered, praying she wasn't hoping for a more detailed explanation. Luckily, she seemed satisfied.

They listened to rap songs on the radio, interspersed with some oldies on his favorite radio station, which he turned to whenever the music on the rap station got too raunchy. He could do this, Warner thought. He could handle two small children. He was smarter than they were—or at least, more devious than they were. Warner grew more and more self-assured as the afternoon wore on. He even managed to persuade Eddy to wear all his cold-weather gear, despite a slight skirmish over the ski mask.

"It's too warm to wear it. It will itch," the ten-year-old insisted. In the end, he did bend to Warner's will. And just in time. Warner was about to give up.

Sabrina was easier to command. She didn't actually do anything he told her to do, but she didn't argue with him. So she obeyed him, as long as he did all the work. He had never tried to get gloves and mittens on a small, squirming bundle of energy before, and, after he'd finally managed it, he told himself he was going to have to remember to tell Sam how much he admired her. The simplest thing, with these children, was a lot harder to do than she made it look.

He skied with the two of them until it got dark, and a little beyond, then finally got them inside for hot cocoa and french fries. They were excited. They also had that shiny brightness to their eyes, and that jumpy quality to their movement, that told him they were overtired. Sam had said it often enough. When they were exhausted, they acted more energized than ever, but suffered mercurial changes in mood.

"Why did the monkey fall out of the tree?" Eddy kept asking Warner.

"Because he was dead?" Warner answered, after the first time. Bri and Eddy laughed hysterically every time.

He bundled them back into their winter coats and got them and all their gear, and his, into the car, and headed for home. He turned on the mellow, old-time rock that he usually listened to, this time at a lower decibel level meant to lull them to sleep. Bri was out in an instant, but Eddy chattered away beside him. He listened, and nodded, and even occasionally got a word in.

"The first three *Star Wars* were definitely better than episode one or two," he insisted.

"No way. They're pretty good, but Luke and Leia are boring."

"You know that Anakin and Amidala are Luke and Leia's parents, right?"

"Of course, everyone knows *that*," Eddy said.

"Maybe we can go see episode three together, if it ever comes out," Warner suggested.

"Yeah, maybe," Eddy replied, but then he grew quiet.

About halfway home, Warner realized he'd made a fatal mistake. Eddy had mentioned he'd gone to the first two *Star Wars* films with his father. Just the two of them. Warner never should have made that stupid suggestion that he and Eddy plan to go to the next film together. That was the end of the boy's easy conversation. Once Warner thought about it, he knew he had stuck his foot in it right away. What he didn't know was how to fix it.

When they arrived back at home, the boy ran into the house and straight to his room. To his mother's surprise, he got ready for bed without any argument, and didn't even try and talk her into letting him watch a little TV before he got underneath the covers. "That's a first," she remarked.

"I'll explain. Later," Warner said, when she looked at him curiously.

Bri was fast asleep, and he had carried her inside and deposited her in her bed before he got the ski gear out of his trunk to return to Samantha's garage.

"What's up?" she asked, when both kids were changed into their pajamas, tucked into their beds, and the lights were turned off.

"Well, I sort of stuck my foot in it," he started. "I said something like, *By next year, the whole family will all be skiing down the Extreme together, even me.* And then, on the way home, I offered to take him to see *Star Wars,* episode three. That's when Eddy started to act that way."

Sam nodded knowingly. "Eight-year-olds can be moody, can't they?" she asked.

"It's not his fault. I sounded like I was trying to replace his father," Warner said.

"Don't worry about it. By tomorrow morning, he'll have forgotten," she said, placatingly.

"But it's bound to come up again," Warner commented. He was getting a little moody himself.

"Let's not jump to any hasty conclusions. He could have been upset about something else. Something his sister said, or did, while you weren't looking. It could have been anything."

"I don't think so," Warner tried to explain. "I'm pretty sure he resented the implication that—"

Sam cut him off. "I wasn't there, so I don't know what happened," she said stiffly. "But I think we should check out whether there was some other reason for his behavior before we panic."

As far as she was concerned, clearly the matter

was closed. Warner didn't try to argue with her. If she wanted to wait to deal with this problem, they could wait. There would be plenty of time. They had a long road ahead of them. But Warner wished they could have discussed this now, and come up with a plan of action together. He didn't like the idea of waiting for the situation to become even more complicated before dealing with it. That wasn't his way.

Samantha was right about Eddy forgetting to be angry. At Thanksgiving, at the church service, Eddy acted as if nothing momentous had occurred on that dark drive home through the snowy streets. But Warner felt that the boy was a little more circumspect in the way he behaved around him. Eddy made it clear, in subtle ways, that Warner was only a friend of the family. For example, at dinner that afternoon, he insisted on carving the turkey, and at bedtime, he wanted his mother to read to him and tuck him in, instead of letting Warner do it, as he had done for the past month.

Sammy shrugged it off, when Warner brought it up, after the children were asleep. "It's not that surprising, is it?"

"Not at all," Warner agreed. "But what are we going to do about it?"

"About what?" she asked. "It's over now. By next year, he'll be used to his father not being here."

Warner didn't plan on waiting a year for Eddy to accept him. "I really think we should talk to both of the children about this," he suggested. "I think they need to know what's going on. With you and their father, and with you and me."

"Just give it time," she replied. "Let's have a nice relaxing long weekend, and let them adjust. Naturally."

Warner wanted to say that he didn't think they

would just *adjust* to the situation in which they found themselves. The children needed her help. But he couldn't bring himself to say it. For all he knew, maybe she was right. Maybe what Eddy and Bri needed was just their usual routine, as Sammy always said. They knew they had their mother's love. They would come to accept his presence, as long as he was always there for them. He couldn't let it alone completely, though. "Don't you think that we should say something about Radu not being here? Eddy must miss his father even more than usual at this time of year, don't you think?"

"You act as if I hadn't thought about all of this, and I have. But I don't know what to say to them. I don't know why their father isn't here, or why he hasn't called them. What can we say that won't make it worse?" she asked.

"I don't know. Something. Ignoring it doesn't seem healthy to me."

"I'm not ignoring it. I'm trying to make them feel safe, and secure. I'm trying to make them feel as if they haven't lost everything, that their world hasn't changed beyond all recognition. I'm trying—" She broke off, and struggled to regain control of herself. "I'm doing my best to give them what their father tried to take away . . . a normal, happy childhood. Like you had and I had."

"I'm sorry," Warner said. And he meant it. He hadn't realized what Sam had been attempting to do. If she had told him, maybe he could have helped. Obviously, she wasn't ready to lean on him yet. Sometimes he forgot how badly Radu had hurt her. She was so self-contained, so . . . over it. But of course she'd been scarred, deeply. He had to remember that. Those scars might never heal completely.

"Can we just try and be grateful for what we

have? We're here together and we all still love each other. That's what we need to get across to them," Sam pleaded.

"You're right," he said soothingly. "I'm really sorry."

Despite the fact that he did, finally, understand, Warner didn't completely get over his disappointment. Thanksgiving was all about family, and he had been looking forward to this holiday this year with anticipation. He had visions of him and Eddy watching the game together, and of himself at the head of the table, carving the turkey. Suddenly he felt very selfish. If this was going to be his family, he was going to have to learn to put their needs first, ahead of his own.

Warner was starting to get really annoyed. He kept dreaming of Maddie. The dreams started off well enough. He was usually playing with Sabrina and Eddy and then their faces started to change, subtly, into the faces of children he didn't recognize. But they did look familiar. And after a short time, he realized that they were his children. His and Maddie's.

He tried to ignore it, at first. He had dreamed about her, before, and it had gone away. He couldn't control his subconscious mind, and he could rationalize away this minor, unintentional disloyalty to Samantha because it made sense, in a strange sort of way, that he would picture the woman he'd been married to for so long when he imagined himself raising children. But after the fourth or fifth time these unwanted images came to him in his sleep, he started to feel that he had to do something about them. They were starting to make him feel uneasy.

He did not want Maddie in his head like this. She was his good friend, soon to be his ex-wife, but he was in love with Samantha.

Warner obviously couldn't tell Maddie about the dreams, but he could talk to her and get some closure. He laughed as he thought about it. Here he was, for the first time in their long relationship, fantasizing about her in a sexual way. Not that his dreams were, in any way, romantic, but there was only one way that he knew of that they could conceive children together.

When they were first married, and even before, they talked openly about sex. Maddie, being Maddie, had offered to make it a part of their deal. She didn't want him to feel deprived of anything, she said, simply because they were married. And, she pointed out, it would be legal and everything. But he didn't want to complicate their relationship, so they agreed that their sex lives would be kept separate. They were both very busy with school, work, and study, and it wasn't until quite some time after they were married that either of them wanted to become involved with anyone else.

When he did meet a girl he liked, he was studying to get his master's degree in fine art. She was a student in his master's program, and she had met Maddie already, who had explained about their unconventional arrangement. He suspected that it was, in fact, his relationship with Maddie that sparked Alyson's interest in him. Warner was fine with that. Alyson was cute, and talented, and smart. If, when they went to bed together, it was clear that she, at least, felt like they were having an illicit affair, it was all right with him. Anything that made her happy was fine. The relationship didn't last long, though. There wasn't enough drama for her in his prosaic attitude toward cooking dinner for both her and his wife, which he did on a regular basis.

Maddie's first lover, after their marriage, was a jerk named Tom. Maddie met him while Warner was dating Alyson, and he suspected she got involved with the guy because she was jealous—not of Alyson, but of him. She didn't want to be left out. Tom was attractive, he guessed, since Alyson told him so in no uncertain terms. But the guy was an idiot. It came to a head one night, when Tom got drunk and started ranting and raving that Warner and Maddie were cheating on Alyson and himself. He could not be convinced that, as husband and wife, they would forgo sleeping together. That was the end of Maddie and Tom. Alyson followed soon after. Warner thought Alyson and Tom might have ended up marrying each other, but he wasn't sure. He couldn't remember. He hadn't thought of them in years.

The only reason he thought of either of them, now, he realized, was that they were the first two people that Maddie and he dated after their pseudo–wedding. They both learned, from that experience, that it wasn't a very good idea to bring their dates home with them. But they also discovered that they could tell each other about their lovers and remain good friends. If they could do that, then, Warner was sure, they could handle this situation with Samantha. He didn't think it wise to tell Maddie about his recent dreams, especially after the stunt she had pulled a couple of days ago. He would have to get the antipathy between the two women out in the open, though, and deal with it once and for all. Maybe then, he could wake up in the morning without feelings of guilt.

CHAPTER SEVENTEEN

At Thanksgiving, Maddie and her mother finally buried the hatchet completely. By tacit agreement, they didn't speak of Great Aunt Becky or her house. Everyone reminisced about when they were younger, and made toasts about how grateful they were to be together on this holiday for the first time in years. The kids, especially, were happy to have their aunt with them, and Maddie felt a twinge of guilt about not coming home for Thanksgiving more often. She would, in the future, she vowed to herself.

She hadn't been in America for Thanksgiving for a long time, and she was surprised by how much more the holiday meant to her, now that she was in her thirties. She didn't know whether it was because she was older, or because she was seeing the ritual with new eyes, but she was able now to appreciate the nuances she hadn't noticed when she was younger, such as how her father looked at her mother.

After an early meal with her folks, Maddie went to Samantha Wheeler's house to have dessert with

Warner and the Wheeler clan after their very early dinner. Warner played the role of stepfather well, Maddie thought. But something about the setup still didn't feel quite right. She told herself she was imagining things, and tried to forget about it. The company was pleasant, and the pumpkin pie was topped with fresh whipped cream, so she left there feeling sated, if not completely satisfied.

Her last stop that night was at Patsy's house. Patsy's family celebrated late, because the restaurant was open for dinner until eight o'clock.

"I serve the traditional foods that my mother cooks for people who want the big turkey dinner without the work, but I also have a regular dinner menu for my customers who don't celebrate the holiday," she explained. "That's become almost like a tradition, too, for some folks. We get the Nakamuras every year, for example. They want their kids to celebrate the holiday, but they don't want to eat turkey and dressing and yams themselves. They can't get used to stuffing themselves with unfamiliar dishes that are full of fat. This way, they can give their kids, who were born here, the choice of eating what their friends all eat, but they can order a regular dinner. It's fun."

Maddie had to agree. She kept her friend company while she worked. They talked while Patsy cooked, and kept an eye on her staff and her clientele. It was the day for reminiscences. "Remember the year that my mother was too sick to cook and I came to your house for Thanksgiving?" Patsy asked.

Maddie did indeed remember. Patsy was infectious—with her mother's chicken pox—and she passed them on to Maddie, her brother, and her cousin, Damon. "Oh, my God. Teddy wouldn't talk to you for months," she said, laughing.

"That was the last time your cousin Damon *ever* spoke to me, I think," Patsy said, grinning.

"No big loss," Maddie replied, grimacing.

"Are they still harassing you about the house?" Patsy asked, sympathetically.

"They don't need to. The house is harassing me all by itself," Maddie explained.

"Are you still hearing things that aren't there?"

"Yeah, and I don't know what to do. No one can do any work there with it . . . acting up like this."

"I never heard of a house *acting up* before," said her oldest friend. "I'm sorry to say this, but you're beginning to sound a little bit like your mom."

"I know. I can't believe I'm even thinking about this, but . . . ." She took a deep breath. "I think I'm going to have to ask my mother how to get rid of ghosts."

She was going to have to do it. Maddie didn't know anyone else, besides Janet, who might be able to help. She couldn't continue to ignore the whispers, creaks, and laughter, or the strange chill wind that blew through the otherwise warm and homey rooms. She couldn't rent the place out like this. She couldn't even get the workmen to stay during the day, let alone ask someone to pay her to live there.

She had no idea how Janet Delaney would react to her request. Her mother had every right to laugh in her face, although Maddie didn't think she would do that. Janet was not a vengeful woman, and she wasn't petty. But she did have an overriding prejudice against Great-Aunt Becky. She might refuse to go near the house, because of that. Maddie had no choice, though. She had to, at least, ask for her mother's help, and advice. She had run out of options.

She was surprised when Warner agreed to go with her to her mother's house for dinner on the Sunday after Thanksgiving. He had made it quite plain, years earlier, that he wasn't going to interfere with her relationship with Janet. In the beginning, he tried to mediate, but he soon gave up the effort. He said they had to actually want to communicate with each other for him to be able to help. He couldn't force them.

But when she told him why she was going to ask Mom for help, he immediately said, "I'll go with you." He didn't even ask her if she really meant it this time.

"You will?" Maddie asked, dumbfounded.

"Sure," he answered. "It would be great if you could straighten out this mess with your mother. I'll be happy to do anything I can."

Maddie hadn't even told him about her new outlook on life. She didn't think he would believe her if she told him she wanted to change, so she'd been planning to show him, rather than saying anything about it. Maybe he sensed the change in her, though. Or maybe he had some other reason for volunteering to accompany her.

"That's great! Thanks" was all she said, examining his face closely. She couldn't read anything in his expression. For some reason, she was afraid to ask him outright why he was getting involved in this without being asked. She was grateful for his support. As much as she desired a smoother and healthier relationship with Mom, she was not eager to approach her. Maddie didn't have a clue how Janet would react to her request. Her mother had never wavered in her objection to Maddie's inheritance. It couldn't hurt to have Warner there, as a buffer, when she asked Janet Delaney for help with the property she'd inherited.

She was well aware that Warner's presence would not stop Mom from ranting and raving. Having the president there wouldn't stop Janet from speaking her mind. Nevertheless, having Warner go with her would still be a good thing, because, while it wouldn't inhibit her mother, Maddie knew she could count on him to stop *her* from losing her cool.

They agreed that Sunday night, at the weekly family dinner at her parents' house, was probably the best time to bring up the subject.

"There's safety in numbers," she quipped.

"I don't know if your father, or brother, will be all that helpful," Warner commented.

"They haven't exactly said they're on her side," Maddie told him. "They haven't said they were on my side, either, but they sort of implied it."

"We've got a date then," he said.

Maddie nodded. She was going to confront her mother. Respectfully.

She felt optimistic. She didn't have a plan, but she did have a goal. And she had Warner to help her.

When she actually did it, it was less scary than she thought it would be. Everyone was so welcoming to both Warner and herself. Maddie understood that that was because she and Mom had been getting along so well since Thanksgiving, which might change—once she told Janet Delaney what she wanted. She was still hopeful, though. If her reformation had already had this strong an effect after only a few weeks, then maybe her latest idea could work, too. If only the request she was about to make didn't set back the progress that she had already made in repairing the relationship . . . she'd be a happy woman.

"We hear there's a new woman in your life, Warner," Janet mentioned while they were all having a glass of wine before dinner. "We'd love to meet her."

"You have met her already," he informed her. "At church. Samantha Wheeler? Remember?"

"Oh, yes, she seems nice," Mom said, but she didn't sound very enthusiastic.

"You should bring her to dinner one night," Dad said. Perhaps he only said it to make up for his wife's halfhearted response, but Maddie flashed him a grateful smile.

"Thank you," Warner replied. "That would be nice."

"She must be a busy woman," Mom said, eyeing him speculatively. "She's alone with the two children, isn't she?"

"Yes," Warner said baldly.

Janet looked like she was going to say something more on the subject, but apparently she thought better of it, because she just murmured, "Um-hmm," and excused herself.

Maddie followed her into the kitchen. "It smells great in here, Mom. Can I help with anything?"

Her mother looked at her as if she'd suddenly grown a second head on her shoulders. "Sure," she said, after a second. "You can get the rolls into the oven, as soon as I take this casserole out."

"Sure." Maddie waited until the hot dish was safely on the sideboard before she asked, "Why so surprised? I used to help you in the kitchen all the time when I was a little girl."

"I wasn't surprised. I thought you didn't do this kind of thing when Warner was around, that's all," Janet answered.

"Huh?"

"You seem determined to convince Warner that you're not good wife material, that's all," she explained.

Maddie was flabbergasted. "Me? Make Warner think . . . ? But, I, I never tried to convince him I was anything."

"That's why he's moving on, isn't it?" Janet inquired.

"It has nothing to do with me. You know we were never really . . . together."

"I guess I thought that you would come to your senses one of these days, that's all. Now, it's going to be too late."

"Too late for what?" Maddie asked, confused.

"To turn this into a real marriage, like you should have done years ago," her mother replied.

"A real marriage? Why would we, why would I, be interested in doing that to poor Warner? He deserves someone more like . . . like the woman he's dating right now. A nice, healthy, normal woman. Not someone like me."

"And what's wrong with you?"

Maddie stared at her mother in surprise. "You were the one who said he was out of my league," she spluttered.

"Me? I did not. I said you thought he was too good for you. I never agreed with you."

"Well, I don't want to marry Warner, Mom, but thanks for the vote of confidence," Maddie said.

"You already married him," Janet pointed out.

"I know, but it was never real. Now he's in love with someone else." Maddie tried hard to keep the worry out of her voice. She thought she was successful.

"So what's he doing here? With you?" Mom said simply.

Maddie knew it was a rhetorical question, but she did feel a slight temptation to tell her mother of her boneheaded seduction attempt. Luckily, the urge passed as quickly as it came. She hadn't told anyone except Patsy. "He is welcome, isn't he?"

"Always," Mom said. She meant it, Maddie was sure. "I just wish he was here as more than a friend of yours."

"He is. After all these years, he's like part of the family."

"Legally, he is family," Janet commented wryly.

"Not for long now. We're nearly divorced."

Janet tut-tutted and shook her head. "So there's still time," she said.

"Time for what?" Maddie queried, though she was beginning to worry that her mother was going to become obsessed with this new subject.

Keep calm, she said to herself. *One step at a time.* She would deal with Becky's house first. Then, if Mom couldn't seem to handle the change in her situation with Warner, she would take care of that little problem, too. She would not let herself be sidetracked. Maddie had only one objective in mind for this evening, and arguing over Warner wasn't going to help her achieve it. She would not let her mother push her buttons, not this time. She planned to keep a cool head, exercise self-control, and be as patient and persuasive as necessary.

If her mother wouldn't help her, she'd find a priest to sprinkle holy water over Becky's house, or buy a book and send whatever was inhabiting her house away by herself. Janet seemed to know about this stuff, so Maddie wanted to try, at least, to enlist her help before she did anything else.

Maddie was going to wait until after dinner before she brought up the subject of Great-Aunt Becky's house, but after everyone was served, conversation died down, and there was silence as everyone ate their meal. She looked over at Warner, who was tucking into his dinner like everyone else, and finally caught his eye. She looked meaningfully toward Mom, and he raised an eyebrow as if to ask, *Now?* Maddie nodded.

"I wanted to ask for your help with a project, Mom," she began.

"Really?" Janet looked at her curiously. "What kind of a project?"

"Something that I think may be right up your alley," Maddie answered. She took a deep breath. "It's Great-Aunt Becky's house."

"Oh, no," Teddy's wife, Jordana, murmured. Teddy dropped his fork.

"We're trying to have a nice dinner, Maddie. This isn't the time or place," her father said.

"I think the house is haunted, and I wanted you to help me with it," Maddie went on in a rush.

"How can you ask me that, knowing how strongly I feel about that place?" Janet asked, sounding hurt and offended.

"Mom, can you just hear me out?" Maddie pleaded.

"All right, all right. What?" Janet said, her lips tightly pursed.

"I know you don't think I should live there. You've made your feelings very clear. I am trying to understand and respect those feelings, and I need you to do the same for me."

"If you respected her feelings, you wouldn't be talking about this. Not here, and not now," Joseph said.

"I do, Daddy. I swear. I need your help though, Mom. I don't know who else to ask. And I don't want to ask anyone else. I want us to get past this. I loved Great-Aunt Becky. I don't know if I'm going to live there or not, to tell the truth. But I can't just leave her house empty and deserted. Her children don't want it."

"That goes to show you, doesn't it?" Janet asked, snippily. "Even her own children—"

Maddie interrupted her. "That's not the point. I can't turn a deaf ear to her last wish. You know that." Her mother was softening. Maddie could see it. "I need you, Mom. I know you won't believe it, but I think this may even have been one of the reasons that Aunt Becky left the place to me—to bring the two of us closer together. Maybe to make peace with you, finally." Mom started to shake her head, and Maddie hastened to add, "All right, I know, I know. You don't think so."

"No, I don't," Janet said.

"Is there anything I can say or do to convince you to help me?" Maddie asked.

Janet looked down at her plate, speared a forkful of asparagus, and carried it, slowly, to her lips. She chewed, swallowed, then nodded. "You just did it," she said.

She had done it. Maddie couldn't believe it. She had actually persuaded her mother to help her with her house.

"Wow," Maddie said. "Great! Thanks, Mom."

She looked over to find that Warner was smiling broadly at her and Maddie realized she was grinning, too. Glancing around the table, she saw that everyone else was looking relieved. Her family and her friend were as happy as she was that that had gone so well.

"This is delicious," Warner said to her mother, for the second time that evening. There was a chorus of agreement. Also for the second time.

"Wait until you see what I made for dessert," Janet said.

* * *

It was decided that they would wait for the winter solstice to do a proper cleansing ritual in Becky's house, but meanwhile, Janet gave Maddie a regimen to follow—to prepare the way, as it were. She was to salt the corners on the first day of the crescent moon. That was the following Wednesday.

"You're lucky you didn't miss it. You'd have to wait until next month," her mother said when Maddie called her on Monday to check that she remembered the ritual correctly.

"Right, lucky," Maddie echoed, under her breath. She couldn't believe she was doing this.

"What?" Janet asked.

"Nothing. So it's sea salt, right?"

"That's what I use, but I don't think it really matters. You could use any old salt," Janet answered. "The point is that it's a certain chemical combination. Salt is one of those things we tend to take for granted, but it's in the oceans that cover seventy percent of the world's surface, and it is useful to sustain life, and enhance it. It makes sense that it would have a powerful effect on our living space, don't you think?"

"I guess so, I never really thought about it, to tell you the truth," Maddie replied.

"So, hmm, I also think you should burn some fennel, maybe burn a little, to purify the air in the house. You can take a bath with it, too."

"Fennel? What does that do?"

"It smells nice, mostly. And it's supposed to purify, as I said."

"Why is that?" Maddie asked, curious in spite of herself.

"I don't know. There are lots of scents and essences that feel like they cleanse, or smell like they sweeten, the air. I'm not that good at the herbal part of all this. But I looked it up, and fennel is good for Aquarians, which you are, by the way."

"I know my birth sign, Mom. I read the occasional horoscope, too. For fun. I wear amethysts, too."

"That's nice, dear," she said. "Most of them aren't much good, though."

"Oh, yeah?" Maddie said sarcastically. Then she felt bad. "So how did you learn about all this?"

"I picked it up here and there. I never studied it, very carefully, but there are guides that make sense, and articles of course. It can get very scientific, but I'm not good at that stuff. I just remember things that make sense to me. At this time of year it's easier to remember. So many of our traditions are derived from ancient rituals."

"Such as . . . ?" Maddie prompted.

"Well, there's cider—which can be poured onto the roots of evergreens as part of a ritual to honor the health of trees. And there's evergreen itself. Ancient cultures brought evergreen inside at this time of year to lighten the air in homes that were closed up for the winter. Voila! Christmas trees!"

"That makes sense," Maddie said aloud.

"Of course it does. We have these rituals for a reason. We've just forgotten what the reasons are," Janet expounded.

"What else?" Maddie asked, intrigued.

"The yule log, of course. It should be oak if possible. And buy one with some small branches that you can break off, to burn on the solstice."

"Oak?"

"For the ceremony. Also holly branches, and evergreen boughs. It's something I do every year—in with the old, out with the new. I call it Completion."

"Really? I never noticed you burning holly branches," Maddie said, trying not to sound skeptical.

"You didn't see it because you didn't want to see it. You made it very clear that you weren't interested. Even your father, who is very open-minded, generally, doesn't want to know about my witchcraft . . . as he calls it."

"You don't practice witchcraft," Maddie said, but she wasn't certain.

"Of course I don't. I just . . . commune with nature in a very ancient, somewhat female-oriented fashion," Mom answered, reassuringly. "You can decorate the house with the holly branches, and the evergreen. This time of year, they're not hard to find at all."

"Do you think that's because of these ancient customs?" Maddie asked.

"Partly. Remember, humans worshiped the earth, and nature, for two hundred thousand years before patriarchal religions placed man in opposition to nature. And even then the matriarchal religions were replaced pretty gradually," Janet explained.

"I hadn't thought of it that way," Maddie confessed. "You never seemed to doubt religion before."

"I don't. I have faith," her mother responded. "I just have a little room left over to explore other avenues."

"Cool," Maddie pronounced. She was surprised at how much she was enjoying this conversation with Mom. If anyone had told her, a month ago, that she and her mother would be having this discussion, she would have thought they were crazy. Now, she was pleased as punch that it was happening. Who would ever have thought that she and Janet Delaney could talk like this, about stuff like this? And her maddening, irrational, eccentric mother was actually making sense. Maddie was amazed.

CHAPTER EIGHTEEN

The insistent ringing of the telephone woke Warner out of a sound and dreamless sleep. He groaned, and picked up the handset. "Who is it?" he mumbled.

"Me." Maddie sounded wide awake, and disgustingly cheerful. "Have you done *it* yet?"

"Done what?" he asked, a second before he realized what she must have meant.

"It!" she said enthusiastically. She was rooting for him. Heaven help him.

He lay back against his soft down pillows. "Did you call just to ask me that?" Warner asked, grumpily. "It's seven A.M."

"Oh? I thought it was later. I don't usually get up this early on a Saturday, but Mom and I have been talking every morning, and she tends to wake up early, so my internal clock has turned around. And it's a gorgeous day."

"It's supposed to get down to ten degrees below with the windchill factor," Warner told her.

"But the sky is clear, and the fields and trees look so clean and pretty covered in snow."

Warner could picture those fields against his closed eyelids. It was true they were beautiful, but he couldn't imagine Maddie tramping through them at the break of dawn. "You've been outside already?"

"No, I'm looking out of my window. You remember the big bay window in Becky's room?"

"Um-hm," he mumbled.

"I'm all warm and toasty in my flannel pajamas and my comfy robe and slippers, sipping herb tea that I made myself. From herbs!"

He could not handle this much perkiness this early in the morning. "Maddie, I'm going to go back to sleep now. Call me later," Warner said.

"Okay, bye-bye, sleepyhead."

"Bye," he grunted. After he hung up the phone, he lay in bed for a while, trying to recapture whatever dream Maddie's phone call might have interrupted, but it was no use. He was awake.

Warner got up and took a shower, smiling as he thought of Maddie's excitement about brewing a cup of tea. Only she could make such a simple, old-fashioned chore into a culinary triumph.

What next? he thought. He didn't have to wait long to find out. At ten that morning, she called him again.

"So?" she asked.

"So, what?"

"You never answered me. Did you and Samantha *do it* last night?"

"No, and stop asking me that!" She was exasperating. "I probably wouldn't tell you anyway, if we did, because it's none of your business."

"Hey, I'm just curious. Friday night is date night, isn't it?"

"Hmm," he mumbled.

"I went to sleep early, in my great big, empty

bed. Slept like a nun. I just thought maybe one of us should be getting some."

He couldn't help laughing. "I wish I never told you," he said.

"Why?"

He could almost hear her pouting. "Because I should have known you'd obsess over this."

"I'm not obsessing. I mean, I don't stay up all night worrying about it or anything. I just wondered."

"Well, stop wondering."

"I can't. You can't tell a girl that you've been engaging in this incredible foreplay for weeks and weeks and then expect her to just forget about it."

"Maddie, can we talk about something else? Anything else?"

"Sure," she agreed. She was silent for a moment, but it didn't last. "So, what are you going to do today?"

"I don't know. I thought I might hang out around here, paint, or pay a few bills, or something."

"Shovel the walk?"

"Yeah, maybe."

"Want some help?"

"You've got your own sidewalk to take care of now," he reminded her.

"I thought we could maybe help each other out," she said. "I'd shovel snow with you at your place, and then you could come over here."

Her sidewalk was three times the length of his, and she also had a car park at the side of the house large enough to fit four or five cars. "You are a conniving wench," he said.

"If I were conniving, I'd invite you over for hot cocoa and cookies and *then* ask you to help me shovel my walk," she pointed out. "After I had you in my clutches."

"Okay," Warner said. "Come on over."

"Really?" she squeaked.

"Sure," he answered, embarrassed that he hadn't thought to offer to help her before. She wasn't used to being a home owner. She probably hadn't had to shovel snow or mow a lawn since she left high school.

Owning a home was going to be a big adjustment for her. He wanted to support her in it. Maddie had been there to celebrate when he bought his house—cheering him on. She noticed every little touch he added to his home, almost like a real wife. He had taken it for granted. Now he had a chance to return the favor.

He was, however, he decided later that afternoon, going to encourage her to buy a snowblower. He looked out at the path they had cleared, extending from the front door to the sidewalk and around the side of the house to the driveway and the car park. It had taken almost two hours.

"That's better," Maddie said, as she came into the living room after changing out of her sodden clothes. "Are you sure you don't need to borrow something dry to wear?"

"I'm all right," he said. He was tempted to remind her he won the snowball fight, but it wouldn't be—as his grandfather used to say—very sporting of him.

"I put the water on to boil," he offered by way of apology for the pelting he'd given her.

Maddie obviously didn't harbor any resentment. "Thanks," she said cheerfully. "Do you want to stay for dinner? You don't have to cook it or anything," she added quickly.

"There's something going on here," he said suspiciously.

"What?" she asked, guilelessly.

"I don't know. Something's different." Warner realized, as he said it, that, indeed, there was something different about her. He couldn't quite put his finger on what it was, though.

Maddie glanced away, then back at him. She had a pleased expression on her face, like one of his students who had just discovered she got a high grade on a quiz. "You noticed," she said.

"So what's up?" he asked.

"I think I'm finally growing up," Maddie said, uncertain.

He looked around at the house she'd been working so hard on to make into a home, and then at her, standing before him, waiting expectantly for his opinion. They both looked good to him. Really good. "I guess so," he agreed.

She beamed at him. "So you'll stay? For dinner?"

"Sure," he said. Her joy was contagious. "I'd love to."

"You can keep me company while I do all the work," she said, leading the way into the kitchen. "You just sit at the table, and watch."

"I think I'm going to like the new you," he said as she placed a steaming mug of hot chocolate on the table in front of him.

"I'm enjoying some aspects of it," she mentioned. "Especially getting along better with Mom. Her theories aren't nearly as nutty as I thought. They're feminist, even a little radical, which isn't that surprising. But she talks a lot about ancient matriarchal cultures, and nature. It does make sense—now that I've started to really listen to what she's saying."

It was a homey scene, with Maddie bustling about the kitchen while he sat there, drinking hot cocoa. Warner had liked the old Maddie just fine, but he could get used to this pretty easily, he thought.

"So, do you think she really can help you with the house?" he asked.

"She's going to try. She's reading up on it."

"That's a how-to book I'd like to see," he said dryly.

"She's got a lot of interesting books. I don't know which one has the ghosts, or whatever, but she's really well read in the areas she's interested in. I was impressed."

"It doesn't surprise me," Warner said. "Your mom is one smart cookie."

"Yeah," Maddie agreed. "I knew that, but . . . I didn't expect her to be . . . so grounded."

At dinner they talked as if they hadn't seen each other in years: about old times, current events, and a little of their hopes and dreams for the future. Neither of them mentioned Samantha Wheeler. It reminded him of all the other times: college, graduate school, Maddie's visits home over the holidays.

It suddenly struck him how much he was going to miss this. Miss Maddie. For all his talk about how they would always be friends, once they were divorced, and he was with someone else, they probably wouldn't have too many Saturdays like this one. Especially if he got married to another woman. That wasn't a big if. He was going to find someone, and marry her, and start a family. He didn't know where Maddie would fit in.

But Warner had to admit, any other woman he cared about was going to be the *other* woman. Their marriage was a farce, a fake, a trick, but it was still their marriage. They'd been together, legally bound together, for all of their adult lives. He felt a pang of regret at the thought that it would all be over soon. Whatever happened next, Maddie wouldn't be Mrs. Warner Davis anymore. And he wouldn't be her husband. Ever again.

It sent a chill down his spine.

"Shall we have dinner in here?" she asked.

"Sure," Warner answered. It was a very pleasant kitchen.

"Okay."

"I have a question I've been wanting to ask you, but I've been afraid to bring up the subject," Warner said, without thinking.

"What?" Maddie asked. When he hesitated, she added, "We've always been able to talk about anything."

"Yes," he said slowly. "Tonight reminded me of that."

"Me too," she answered, smiling at him. "So, what did you want to ask me?" Maddie prompted.

"Just . . . what would you have done if we had made love that night?"

"What ni—? Oh, yeah. That night," she said, looking away.

"If I understood you, you thought that if we kissed, then we would sleep together, and then I would realize that I wasn't really in love with Sam, right?"

"Something like that," she mumbled, clearly embarrassed.

"Your theory being . . . what? That I wasn't in love with her, I was in lust? And therefore any woman would do to satisfy my . . . needs."

"Okay, I know it was stupid. I'm sorry—" she started.

"No," he interrupted. "I'm curious."

"Warner—"

"What does that say about us?" he pressed. "That we *don't* love each other?"

"We do," she protested automatically. "But only as friends," she added.

"Mm-hmm," Warner murmured, stroking his chin, thoughtfully. "I'm still a bit confused. How did you see that going? I kiss you, or you kiss me, and then what?"

"What difference does it make?" Maddie remarked. "I mean, it didn't work. At all. You weren't even tempted to . . . to . . ."

"Sleep with you?" He finished the sentence for her.

"Right."

"So that proves I'm really in love with Samantha how?" he asked.

"I'm not sure what you're getting at here," Maddie said, looking at him quizzically. "Why else would you say no? There was nothing to stop you, stop us, from making love, except your feelings for her."

"We never slept together before I met Samantha," he said, refuting her argument. "And that didn't mean I wasn't—as you call it—tempted, by the way. It meant we were both happy with our relationship the way it was. Or, at least, that's what I thought it meant."

"I thought we agreed it might wreck our friendship," Maddie answered.

"That was ten years ago. We were young. Neither of us had much experience with sex. And we didn't want to take a chance."

"So," she said, looking at him speculatively, "are you saying we've changed?"

"In the last ten years?" he asked, astonished. "I would definitely say so."

"Does that mean you would have liked to have a different kind of relationship all these years?" she asked.

"No, no, I was happy with our friendship," he answered.

"But you don't think it would have been at risk if we slept together?" Maddie queried, clearly seeking clarification.

"No, I don't," Warner said baldly.

Maddie thought about it for a moment, then asked, "And you were tempted to do that?"

"Well . . ." he drawled, "there have been one or two times when I thought about it."

"I don't believe it," she exclaimed. "When?"

"I don't know," Warner replied. He closed his eyes, in thought. "My birthday, two or three years ago, when you were home for Valentine's Day," he announced.

"I don't remember that," she said, her forehead creased in concentration as she tried to think back to the occasion.

"You didn't have a date, and your birthday was coming up, too."

"February sixteenth, two days after yours. It's not hard to remember the date. But which birthday was it?"

"Twenty-nine, maybe? Or thirty?"

"Oh, yeah! It was your thirtieth. I was going to be twenty-nine. I remember now. That was three years ago. We were both a little freaked out about being alone. I didn't have a date for Valentine's Day, and you were hitting the big three-oh!"

"Yeah, well, that was one time," he said.

"But you and Patsy threw me that birthday party at her restaurant, and I felt better."

"Mm-hmm," Warner murmured.

"Wow! It's too bad I didn't know that you were interested. I definitely would have suggested breaking the no-sex rule that night," Maddie admitted. "Why didn't you say anything?"

"I didn't think *you* were interested," he said, shrugging.

Maddie chuckled.

"What's so funny?" Warner asked.

"It's sort of ironic," she said. "We wasted all these perfectly good opportunities to have sex together."

"All?" he said, teasingly. "That was one."

"Well, I don't know about you, but there were other times when I've been . . . tempted," Maddie confessed.

"I didn't know that," Warner said ruefully. He was suddenly seized with the desire to kiss her. His hands balled into fists at his sides as he withstood the urge to reach out to her.

"And now it's too late," Maddie stated. That kiss she had taunted him into giving her came back to him. He hadn't thought of it much, but he hadn't been able to forget it, either. In the two weeks that had passed since that strange encounter, Warner was reminded, when he saw her and talked to her, of her bizarre attempt to seduce him. Her misguided notion that she should rescue him from himself seemed funny to him, once he got over his annoyance at her meddling.

It didn't seem so funny, or so bizarre, at the moment, though. It seemed sweet and heroic, and maybe a little bit wild, like Maddie herself. All right, so it was unconventional, but that was what he loved about her, wasn't it?

"Are you sure?" he asked musingly.

As the question sank in, Maddie did a double

take. Warner had never seen anyone do that in real life before. Only in the movies. Her eyes opened wide, and then wider. Her jaw dropped and she stood gaping up at him. He reached out and nudged her chin up with his index finger.

Her mouth snapped shut. "Wha—What did you say?" she questioned.

"Why do you think it's too late?" he asked.

"Y—You and Sam?" she suggested.

"You don't sound so sure, right at this moment," he commented.

She was still staring up at him in amazement. "There's the fact that we're about to finalize our divorce, for one thing. And then there's our friendship to consider, which could still be ruined if we broke the rule. Or the fact that you may be in love with Samantha. Take your pick," she offered.

"You're upset," Warner said. "Sorry, I didn't mean to make you feel bad."

"You're messing with my mind, right?" Maddie replied, hopefully.

"No," he answered simply.

"You're not seriously suggesting . . ." Her voice trailed off as she searched his face for some kind of answer. "You don't want to . . . you know . . . now? Do you?"

"I hadn't really thought about it," Warner lied. He realized, now, that he'd been thinking of little else since she kissed him. "Why? Have you changed your mind?"

"Changed my mind?" she echoed. "Of course I changed my mind. It was a stupid plan. You made that very clear."

"I did?"

"Yes, you did. You were obviously completely uninterested in being seduced. You barely even seemed to be affected."

"I didn't?" Warner said. "Oh, that's right." He grinned at her. "But I was affected. I just didn't want you to know that."

"Why are you telling me this now?" Maddie asked.

"I'm not sure," he answered. "I guess I wanted another chance to do this." He leaned down and kissed her. It wasn't like the last time. She was caught off guard, again, but it was a completely different kind of surprise. He wasn't angry with her, now. He wanted her to enjoy this. And he wanted to savor the feel and taste of her himself. That last kiss had been to shut her up. A punishment. This was an exploration.

A very successful one, Warner felt. Maddie's lips, beneath his, were soft, and warm, and they opened to him almost immediately. He delved deeper, his tongue seeking out the heat and sweetness of her mouth, the delicious bouquet that he remembered vaguely from their previous encounter. She intertwined her tongue with his, in a duel for dominance as old as the sexes themselves.

She quivered against him and he ran his hands down her arms to soothe and comfort her, before wrapping them around her back to pull her close into his tight body. She strained away from the contact with his torso, for a moment, though she didn't attempt to end the kiss. He started to pull back, but her arms went around his neck to stop him. Warner took that as a sign to continue. He had never held her like this before. Their previous kisses had been so rushed, so unexpected, but now he felt as if he had all the time in the world, and everything that had happened in the past ten years had been leading up to this moment. Well, almost everything.

"God, you feel good," he said, nuzzling her neck. She was warm, and soft, tiny, but her arms around him were strong. Her grip on him was intense. He pulled her even closer in response. Her body, against his, was pulsing, trembling, and he kept running his hands over her back.

"I can't stop shivering," Maddie said. "It's so odd." Her breath, against his ear, sent a spasm through him.

"Not to me. I'm shaking, too." His mouth was against her ear.

"Maybe we should stop."

"No," he said definitely. "I can't."

"I can't either."

They found each other's mouths, again, and kissed hungrily. Her quaking slowly subsided. He felt the turbulence inside him calm, too. The grip that each of them had on the other relaxed, and they were able to separate, slightly, to peel off his shirt, and hers, so they were skin to skin. Face to face, eyes open. He briefly glanced down at her body, taking in her peaked breasts, and nut-brown abdomen. She examined him, too, not only with her eyes, but with her hands. She skimmed her palms down his torso, as though she couldn't get enough of the feel of him, and then around his back. They dipped down over his backside, tracing the contours there, too.

That one quick glimpse was dangerous. He wanted to see all of her, and he saw an answering hunger in her eyes. But they didn't go further. They closed their eyes, and kissed again, touching those places on each other's bodies that were within easy reach, his shoulders, her neck, nothing below the belt. It wasn't much. It couldn't have lasted more than a few minutes. But it was enough.

He had started something here. Something that was new and yet, not. It had been coming for a while. He could see that now. They might have avoided it altogether, if he hadn't started flirting with her. Hadn't kissed her. Now it was out there. It wasn't going to go away.

"I should go," he announced.

"Okay," Maddie said, in a small voice, picking her shirt up from where it had fallen and slipping it over her head.

"This is getting to be something of a habit for me," Warner said, as he stood up and helped her to her feet.

"What is?" she asked, dazed.

"Fooling around, and then leaving before any actual sex occurs."

"Foreplay, I remember," she said, nodding. "If it's any consolation to you, you are getting really, really good at it." She handed him his shirt.

"It's not," he said wryly as he put on his shirt, and reached for his coat. "A consolation, that is."

"Oh, sorry," she replied. They both turned and started toward the front door. She wasn't really sorry. But, typically, she had to get the last word in. "But it's your own fault. You started this."

"No, you started it," he said childishly. "Two weeks ago." They had reached her front door, but he paused, before opening it. He didn't know what he wanted her to say. Perhaps, "Stay."

Instead, she opened the door for him. "But I quit," Maddie retorted. "So you can't blame me for this."

"I don't," Warner said. "It is my fault."

The lamplight cast a golden glow over her animated face, adding a luster to her shining eyes, and a gleam to her full lips. He was shocked by the force of his feelings. They were completely unexpected. He leaned down and kissed her, once more, gently, quickly. Then he left before he could do any more damage. He had to talk to Sam.

CHAPTER NINETEEN

"I see you bought the holly branches," Mom said approvingly as she entered the foyer and saw the large vases Maddy had filled with holly. Janet Delaney hadn't set foot in Rebecca Tanner's house in almost twenty years, but you wouldn't have known that by looking at her. She acted as though this visit were not at all unusual. Maddie couldn't get over her mother's transformation.

They walked through the house together, but today, the spirits that inhabited these rooms remained silent.

Mom took in the freshly painted walls, and buffed and polished floors, and seemed impressed. "It looks good. You've done a lot of work here, haven't you?"

"Yeah," Maddie replied, trying to sound humble. "I think it's getting there."

"I like it," her mother declared. "It's got a nice feel to it." She stood in the arched entry to the living room at the front of the house and surveyed the warm and cozy room. "I didn't think it would."

"Thanks, Mom," Maddie said, feeling surprisingly proud. Who would ever have guessed she could value her mother's praise so much?

Maddie couldn't believe she had never realized how cool her mother was. The behavior Maddie had always found so annoying and embarrassing actually turned out to be something she could really admire, once she started to understand it. She didn't know what had made her so judgmental, because she was usually one of the most open-minded people she knew. Perhaps that was just the nature of mother-daughter relationships.

Whatever caused them to knock heads all these years, she and her mother were a lot more alike than she had thought. Maddie, too, was intrigued by the glimpses of matriarchal cultures that her work afforded her. She discovered in her study of archeology that a female-oriented hierarchy permeated most ancient societies. The Greeks, for example, had a religion centered around female deities of earth, water, and fire, as well as of the harvest, before the invasion of the mysterious Dorians, who did their best to squash the traditional mother worship. Excavations at Mycenae uncovered numerous terra-cotta figures with potbellies and large breasts—which were originally thought to be fertility symbols, and later believed to be a part of a large cache of goddess figures that had been worshiped by the Myceneans. This second theory was based on more recent discoveries about ancient Greece that led anthropologists and archeologists to the conclusion that those old religions were absorbed into the patriarchal beliefs of the conquerors, and survived to a certain extent. In fact, it seemed that the goddess Ceres, and perhaps her sisters and daughters, became the goddesses of the hearth worshiped in most homes in

Greece and Rome until monotheism replaced pantheism.

Maddie was entranced by the idea of a continuing trend toward mother worship throughout Western civilization. The subject had been virtually ignored in her studies, so each time she uncovered evidence of the religions, it was as if she had connected another thread in a complex puzzle. She showed her mother the pictures in the database she'd compiled in her computer, including drawings of the cache discovered at the cult area at Mycenae.

"I think I read about that, somewhere. I've certainly seen the statuettes in museums and gift shops," Mom said.

"I own a couple of reproductions," she said. She was thrilled that they were, once again, on the same wavelength. It kept happening. And it never ceased to amaze her. "They're packed up in my things somewhere. Did you ever buy any?"

"No, I didn't feel they were part of my culture. I prefer the African figures and masks, and Native American artifacts."

"Right." Maddie had never thought about it, but the stylized clay figures that her mother collected and stored in a cabinet in a corner of the living room were very similar to her own little souvenirs. She had avoided her mother's collection ever since she started to think of Janet as an oddball, when Maddie was twelve or thirteen years old. As a small child, though, Maddie remembered she had loved Mommy's cabinet, with its strange assortment of kachina dolls and eerie African masks, tiny wicker baskets, small clay pots and fragments of dishes, and assorted bits of animal hide and metal and stone. She was going to have to ask her mom to show her her treasures again, one of these days. It was probably quite a respectable collection by now. She suspected it would be unique.

Like Janet, herself.

"The solstice is on the twenty-first," she was saying. "If you don't want to wait, we don't have to."

"No, no, I can wait," Maddie assured her. "I don't think these ghosts, or spirits, or whatever they are, are trying to scare me away or anything. We can coexist. It's just a little unnerving to have them in the house. But ever since you told me that you would help me to get rid of them, I've been more comfortable. It was just feeling that it was all out of my control that made me so tense, I think."

"I know what you mean," Mom said, nodding. "I hate that feeling."

Janet wasn't superstitious after all. At least, not in the way Maddie thought of the word. Her mother was educated and enlightened about a subject that not many people were schooled in. And she was proud of being different. Just like her daughter.

"It's quiet today, but you might still see what I'm talking about, if you hang out for a while. Would you like a cup of tea?" Maddie offered.

"Sure."

Mom followed her into the kitchen. She had painted it a warm, pale apricot, and the old-fashioned, but fully functional, appliances on the counter were bathed in a pinkish glow from the walls. It gave the room a cozy feel. As if they had just stepped back a few decades in time.

"This is nice," Mom said.

"Thank you, Mom."

"It's really special," her mother went on. "You obviously love it."

"Love may be a bit strong," Maddie replied. "I do enjoy seeing a room come together, but it's a lot of work. I hope I can get good tenants who will take care of it for me, rather than wrecking the place."

"So you're definitely not planning to stay?" Mom asked.

"No. You knew that."

"I know, I just thought that you might feel differently, once the house was cleansed. You could continue doing your work from here, couldn't you?"

"I can, but I can go back to Egypt, too. They haven't given away my desk at the university."

"Don't you want to stay, though?" Her mother's tone was a little wistful.

But as glad as Maddie was that their relationship had improved, she wasn't willing to live in the woman's pocket.

"I'm not ready to give up the life I've made for myself in order to settle down here," she tried to explain. "No matter how much I like this house, I can't live in it."

"Can't? Or won't?" Janet pressed.

"Won't, I guess," Maddie conceded. "I just don't think I'm ready for that."

"Why not?"

"Because . . ." Maddie faltered. "Because this town doesn't offer me enough opportunities to do the work I love, for one thing." It was her stock answer over the years when people asked her if she didn't miss home. But that didn't make it any less true.

"I thought you were still translating that carton thing," Mom said.

"Cartonnage," Maddie corrected. "And I am."

"Well, if you can do it here, and communicate with the office over the Internet, why go back? Why don't you telecommute?"

"It's always good to be on-site, if possible. You never know what could come up. And the libraries, and people, there, are incredible. It would be easier."

"Easier to live in a dorm? In a place where you don't know anyone, or speak the language that well?"

"It's not a dorm, it's an apartment, sort of. And part of the fun of living in another country is getting to know the people, their culture, and the language."

"So you want to live there because it will be more fun for you?"

"In a way," Maddie admitted. "Anyway, even if I did stay, it would only be for a while. What about my next assignment? I can't count on finding more positions as flexible as this one."

"At least you would get to stay for a little while. And once you've done it, you might find out you can do it again," Mom said. "You're an expert in your field, right? You might be able to continue to work from home."

"That's just it. This doesn't feel like home to me. Not yet. No offense, Mom."

"If you gave it a chance, it might grow on you," she suggested.

"My life may not make sense to you, but I chose it, and I worked hard to get where I am today. I don't want to throw that away," Maddie told her.

"Where is that exactly?" she asked.

"Traveling all over the world, meeting new people, and taking on new challenges whenever I want. Not to mention getting paid for all of it. That's my dream come true," Maddie answered.

"That was your dream. You have followed it for the last ten years. But isn't it getting a little bit stale at this point? Wouldn't you like to expand on it? You could include your friends, your family, your home. You are one of those rare people who could have their cake and eat it, too, as the saying goes. You're in a great position."

"Maybe in a couple of years, I could try that," Maddie hedged. "Right now, I don't want to be tied down."

"Be careful that you don't confuse freedom and escape," Janet warned.

"What does that mean?" Maddie asked.

"Running to something isn't the same as running away."

"But I'm not running away from anything," Maddie contended.

Mom came right out and asked, "I don't mean to pry, but are you sure you aren't leaving because of the situation with Warner? I may be wrong, but I don't think you were all that anxious to get back to that dusty desk in Cairo, or that awful little man who is supposed to be your assistant. What was his name?"

"Mohammed?"

"That's the one. He sounds like a toad. And with all the problems the Egyptian government is giving you, don't you think it might be wiser to try and work things *out* with Warner?"

"Warner and I don't have anything to work out," Maddie lied. She felt closer to her mother these days, but that was a subject she was not going to get into with the woman. "We're fine."

"Even if that were true," her mother said, doubtfully, holding up her hand to stop Maddie from interrupting, when she would have argued the point, "I'm not saying that it's not, I'm just saying even so, there is always a period of adjustment after a divorce. It can be quite a shock to the system."

"It's not like we were ever really married, Mom, so the divorce isn't going to change anything. Not really."

Her mother wasn't buying that. "Of course it is. That man has always been there for you and you know it. You don't even want this divorce. I can tell."

"Yeah, but . . ."

"But nothing. He's your husband," her mother said wisely. "And soon he won't be. I don't think that's going to be such an easy adjustment for you to make."

"So maybe going away again is the best solution, don't you think?" Maddie said reasonably.

"To a country halfway around the world that won't even give you a visa?"

"I'm sure it will all work out. And Mohammed isn't all that bad, either," Maddie said, trying to reassure her. But she didn't sound very convincing, even to her own ears.

"The cosmos seems to be trying to tell you something, dear. I'd take a listen, if I were you," Mom said.

A month ago, Maddie would have found that statement annoying. Especially coming from her mother. But circumstances had changed. She had changed. Her mother's belief in the stars and the moon and the forces of nature did not seem nearly so ridiculous, now that Maddie knew more about where it came from.

Still, she hadn't completely accepted that her mother was the authority on the subject of astrology that she seemed to think she was. Mom trusted the people she trusted, but Maddie was withholding judgment until she'd seen and heard a little more. She didn't explain all that, but just said dryly, "I'd love to know, what do you think the cosmos is trying to say?"

"Isn't it obvious?" Janet answered, looking at her as if she were a dim-witted child. "You are supposed to stay here, at least for now. Uranus is moving out of Aquarius."

"What exactly does that mean?" Maddie queried.

"After seven years, the planet that has been ruling your stars is moving on. It's going into Pisces starting on New Year's Eve. I could have sworn I told you. I know I told you it's been going back and forth between Aquarius and Pisces all this year. That's probably why you've had all this upheaval in your life lately."

"Is it?" Maddie asked. She couldn't keep the skepticism out of her voice.

Janet sighed. "At about this time last year, Uranus and Saturn both shifted into water signs, breaking the drought—of water, but also of compassion and creativity that we suffered in 2002. And all through 2003, Saturn and Uranus have been partnered up while the world tried to heal. For you, an Aquarian, it was the end of seven years of hectic activity."

"I guess I have been pretty busy since I turned twenty-five," Maddie quipped. "Sorry," she said, as her mother gave her a sharp glance.

"Early this year, Uranus started the shift from Aquarius to Pisces and then, it came back for one last burst from March to September. Since then it's been getting ready to transit Pisces for the next eight years, sort of like it did from January to March of this year. Do you remember how you were feeling then? Sort of up in the air?"

"How do you know that?" Maddie asked. She didn't remember exactly, but she had a vague feeling that her mother was right.

"Your letters. I could tell from the letters you wrote. And it wasn't entirely unexpected, anyway. Let me show you." She opened her purse, which she had been wearing slung over her shoulder, and pulled out her calendar. "It's all in the stars, honey." She had found the page she wanted. "See, here. Aquarius." Maddie looked over her shoulder as she read, " 'Crises encourage the development of skills you otherwise would not have considered.' "

Maddie's mouth dropped open. "I can't believe it actually says that."

"It's all here, in black and white. And listen to this. 'A change made in August or September releases you from some limiting circumstance and is ultimately for the best.' That was when Great-Aunt Rebecca died."

Maddie read the words in her mother's spiral-bound calendar with a mixture of wonder and disbelief. "This is wild," she finally said. She looked away from the book, back at her mother. "But it's all pretty general. It could mean anything."

"It sounds familiar though, doesn't it?" Mom said shrewdly. "And this is the best part, right here." She pointed her index finger at a sentence at the bottom of the page. " 'Some unexplained facet of your nature may burst out, surprising everyone this year, especially if you have something you've been hiding.' "

That was enough for Maddie. "Okay, okay. It does seem like the book is accurate." The prediction about the unexplained facet of her personality seemed particularly eerie, after her recent realizations about herself and her relationships. "But I'm not hiding anything," she averred.

"Aren't you?" her mother asked.

"No," Maddie said definitely. "You know me. I couldn't keep a secret to save my life."

"Maybe it's something you don't know about yourself, yet," Mom said knowingly. "Anyway, we'll find out soon enough. New Year's Eve is only a few weeks away."

Maddie thought she would probably be leaving about that time if everything worked out with the house and her visa and all. A month from now, she'd be back in her office in Cairo. Uranus would move on to Pisces. And Warner and she would be friends again, if they didn't let things go too far between them.

She told Mom that she wasn't good at keeping secrets, but there was one secret she was determined that she would never tell anyone. She was in love with her almost ex.

A signature would make their divorce final, and she had never dreaded any single act as much as she did signing those papers, but she couldn't tell her mother about that. Because Mom would never let her walk away from Warner without a fight.

Janet Delaney was not a woman who would stand quietly on the sidelines. She would want—she would insist!—her daughter to tell Warner about her feelings. If Maddie refused, she would probably tell the man herself. Even though she was a pragmatist, Mom was still a hopeless romantic when it came to stuff like this. For years, she pushed Maddie to try and make the marriage something more than a convenient arrangement. She even pestered Warner about it a little, in the beginning. But Maddie always thought Mom's hopeful attitude was just the product of wishful thinking.

If she had known that Warner might have entertained the notion, Maddie would have considered altering their original agreement. There had definitely been times when she sort of wished the no-sex rule was suspended for at least a night or two. However, it never occurred to her that Warner might have wished the same thing.

She had discovered, too late, that their marriage had had possibilities she never even dreamed of. Unfortunately, the revelation came at precisely the wrong moment, when those possibilities no longer existed. That was why Warner's confession not only surprised her, but also made her feel terribly sad. Maddie didn't want to say good-bye to him, knowing what she now knew, but there was nothing else she could do.

He said he loved her, and she had no problem believing him, but when he kissed her, he obviously wasn't serious. She had never seen him like that before. It was as if the man she had known for so long had been replaced by a stranger. The only explanation she could come up with for his odd behavior was that he was confused.

Confused, quite possibly terrified, and truly in love for the first time in his life.

It had to be scary to be on the brink of getting exactly what you always thought you wanted. It certainly would be for her.

Once their divorce was final and she wasn't here to muddy the waters, he would come to his senses and marry Sam, just like he had planned. Then, after everything settled down, Maddie would come back and salvage what she could of their friendship. It wouldn't be the same, of course. But it would be enough. Because she wanted him to be happy. And this, as far as she could tell, was what he wanted.

Maddie was pretty sure that she could live with that. She could be content with just being his friend. Just as long as she didn't lose Warner altogether.

"Let's get started with the yule log," Janet suggested.

"It's out on the porch," Maddie told her. "It was a little bit big." They went out to look at it together, and found they could lift it if they worked together, but Janet didn't think it would fit in the fireplace. They measured both the log and the fireplace, and it seemed Mom was right. Maddie had to cut the darn thing almost in half, which was no easy task, especially for someone who hadn't handled an ax or a saw in years. But she managed.

Once they got the yule log inside, her mother prepared the fire. "Before we light this, let's go and give thanks to the trees."

"The trees?" Maddie repeated.

"Oxygen-giving, life-sustaining, fire-feeding friends of humanity," Janet said, nodding.

"Okay, why not?" Maddie said. "How do we give thanks to the trees?"

"You've got cider, right?" Mom said. "Pour us out two glasses, and we'll take it outside. I've got a recitation in here, somewhere." She started to root around in her bag.

"I'll get the cider," Maddie said.

Armed with her mother's prayer, and the cider, they went out to the biggest pine tree they could find in close proximity to her house. " 'Great Mother, Divine Aspect of All Being, accept our offering,' " Mom read. " 'On the shortest day of the year, we welcome the longest night. This is the night of the dark moon. We are in the womb of the Goddess, the place of dreams and infinite possibilities. This night, we look deep in the still places of our minds, hoping to see visions of the future.

" 'Together, we cast a sacred circle around You, givers of air, fire, and water. From this night on, the days grow longer, and the sun touches the world and the creative force within You and within us. Help us to find oneness. Thank You for Your gifts, Your presence, Your power. May harmony and balance be restored to Earth. Blessed Be.' "

"Blessed be," Maddie repeated, weakly. This was not what she had expected. It was more formal, more real, than she had anticipated. Her mother was like a priestess, or something. But when she stopped chanting, she was just Mom. She circled the tree, in her faux leopard coat, pouring out her libation, and Maddie followed suit. It was freezing, but they stood there for a moment, listening to the wind, as if they expected someone to answer.

"Come on, honey. Let's go inside," Mom said.

Maddie, cowed, turned and led the way. She couldn't quite get her mind around what had just happened. Her mother seemed so powerful, so self-assured, while she read that invocation. It didn't seem silly at all. It felt natural, and right, and her mother seemed so wise and wonderful at that moment. Perhaps she wasn't crazy after all. Mom actually appeared to know what she was doing.

Maddie listened with newfound respect to her mother's instructions for the rest of the afternoon. There were moments, of course, when she felt ridiculous. Trying to draw her vision of the future, for example, when she couldn't draw a realistic-looking apple, made her feel like an idiot. In the end, though, she felt strangely empowered. And closer to her mother than she had felt since she was a very little girl. Maybe Mom and she could have the kind of relationship she'd always wished for. It didn't seem impossible anymore. Nothing did.

"That's it," Mom said. "We've done everything I can think of. How do you feel?"

Maddie didn't know how to answer that. "I'm . . . happy," she replied. "How do you feel?"

"Pretty darn good," Mom said smiling. "Exorcizing ghosts is sort of fun."

"Yeah," Maddie agreed. "Thanks. I couldn't have done it without you."

CHAPTER TWENTY

Wife. It suited Maddie more than Warner thought it would. Now that he realized how deeply his feelings for her ran, he couldn't help wondering if maybe they could turn their pseudo-marriage into something real and lasting. They were, after all, ahead of most couples already. They knew how much they cared about each other. They also knew they could share everything they thought, or felt, or believed, and, no matter what happened, they would go on loving each other. They always had.

Most people, Warner thought, might have difficulty maintaining a friendship that included a fake marriage, let alone one that spanned ten years and the Atlantic, the Mediterranean, and who knew how many of the world's other oceans? But not Maddie and himself. They had stayed together despite everything. And it wasn't just distance that separated them. They were also very different people.

Luckily, they appreciated each other's unique qualities. She had always admired the parts of him that other people thought were strange. Maddie was the only woman he had ever known who not only applauded his abilities in the kitchen, but thought they were an added attraction. Other women he dated didn't seem to know what to make of the fact that he loved to cook and bake, or that he spent so much time and energy decorating his house. Maddie called it nesting, and said it was one of the things that made him so sexy.

As for him, he loved everything about her. He couldn't get over how smart she was, and thought it was strange that some men found that threatening. He loved her mind, and the way it worked. He liked it that she was so quirky and that she was busy, right now, celebrating the winter solstice with her equally eccentric mother. Maybe it was a day more strictly suited to last-minute Christmas shopping, or preparing for Kwanza, but he thought it was adorable that Maddie and her mother were going to dance around a pine tree and burn up her Christmas decorations, or some such nonsense. He wished he could be there.

They did have a few obstacles to overcome, of course. He didn't expect this woman to make it easy for him. Maddie was terribly afraid of commitment. She always had been. Warner didn't know why, though he suspected it might have had something to do with her fear of being ordinary. Whatever. He would dedicate himself to helping her to get over it. In fact, he was counting on it. Warner had every intention of convincing Maddie to stay with him, forever. He wanted her to come and live with him, in his house, and be the mother of his children.

There was no one else for him.

Maddie had been right all along about him and Samantha. They were definitely not meant to be together. He had been fooling himself.

The question was, did Samantha know, or had she been fooling herself, too? Had she always thought that they would eventually go their separate ways—he to some other woman, and she to wait for Radu to come home, or perhaps to slowly realize that he was never coming back? Warner didn't know how to ask. He didn't even know how to start.

Luckily, in the end, it wasn't as difficult as he had expected. He went to see her that afternoon, after work. The kids were out in the yard, playing in the snow, when he pulled the car up in front of the house. As he walked by, they tried to get him to join them, and he felt a tug at his heartstrings as he thought of all the times they had played together in the last six months. Warner was going to miss that. A lot. He felt a pang of regret at the thought that breaking up with their mother meant saying good-bye, as well, to the possibility of ever being their dad. But it was for the best.

He couldn't bring himself to just walk in through the front door, but it felt too weird to knock. He walked slowly around the side of the house and tapped on the glass panes of the kitchen door, waiting for her to look out at him and smile before he came in.

Sammy was making soup and sandwiches, dinner for the children. "Would you like some cream of tomato soup?" she asked him.

"Sure," Warner accepted, taking off his coat, hat, and scarf, and hanging them up on the highest of the pegs beside the kitchen door, the one that only he could reach.

"What's up, babe?" Samantha asked. She didn't seem surprised to see him. Then again, why should she? He'd spent as much time here, in the last few months, as he did at home. "You look like you've got news," she prompted him. Perhaps she sensed that this wasn't an ordinary visit. She looked at him curiously.

Warner didn't know if she always looked at him that way or not. He couldn't remember. It made him feel callous and coldhearted, especially given the news he had come to impart. "I've been thinking," he started slowly, and stopped.

"That can be dangerous," Samantha joked when he didn't go on.

"Yeah," he agreed glumly.

"What is the nature of these deep thoughts?" she prompted him airily.

"I—umm—I've been thinking about us," he hemmed and hawed. "You and me."

"Oh, yeah?" She looked amused. She had no idea what was coming. Warner felt awful. "And have you reached a conclusion?" she asked.

"I have, sort of. I don't think that we, I mean I, I mean it, this thing, will work out," he said.

"Oh?" She stopped stirring her soup and turned to face him, her expression unreadable. "What brought this on?"

"I, umm, realized that I, that is, we . . ." He couldn't finish.

"You what?" she questioned.

"I'm in love with my wife," he confessed finally.

"Your—" She stood staring at him, astonished. "Maddie? That's what this is all about?"

"Yes," he said, embarrassed.

Samantha still stood there, unmoving, as if it required all of her concentration to absorb this information. Then, she surprised him by smiling.

It wasn't a big smile, or a particularly cheerful one, for that matter. It was more of a quirk of the lips, accompanied by a nod of confirmation, as if Sammy had been debating a different response, and decided that this was more appropriate. At least, that was how it looked to him.

"So, all right," she said, and turned back to the stove, where the soup was boiling.

He was surprised that she was so calm. "I never meant to hurt you," Warner said despite the fact that she didn't seem too devastated by his revelation.

"I think I knew, before you did," Sam said. "I knew there was something standing between us. I thought it might be Radu. But this makes more sense. I mean, after all, he's been gone all along. The only thing that's changed, recently, is Maddie's coming home."

He started to apologize. "I didn't mean to—"

She cut him off. "I know. At least we found out in time."

"Yeah," he agreed, surprised that she was so unaffected. He didn't think it was for show. It could have been the shock that made her seem so cold, or she might have been numb, but he didn't think that was it. The truth was, he realized, Sam was no more in love with him than he had been with her. He couldn't help feeling that they'd had a very narrow escape.

He was thankful that she had stopped him from having that chat he'd been so eager to have with the kids. If he had done that, he didn't think he could easily have gone back to being Uncle Warner again. Not that her children needed him, not as a parent, anyway. She could handle that just fine. But he was so glad he wouldn't be disappointing them.

He would miss their Friday nights together.

"You're still welcome on Friday night," Sam said, as if she had read his mind.

"I was just thinking I was going to miss that," he said. "How did you know?"

"I know you," Sam said simply. "And that makes it all worthwhile, don't you think?" She smiled, and he knew that they would be fine.

"Absolutely," Warner said with conviction.

"Go play with the kids," she ordered. "Tell them that dinner will be ready in fifteen minutes."

He got down his coat from its—his—peg, and he put it on as she continued to prepare the kids' meal.

Before going outside, he moved over behind her, and leaned down to kiss her cheek. "I love you, you know," Warner said.

"Me too," Sam answered.

"I brought the mistletoe," Warner announced when Maddie opened her door to him later that evening. He held the sprig of dark green leaves with its frilled white edge over her head and reached for her arm.

Maddie stepped back out of his reach and called over her shoulder, "It's Warner, Mom."

Janet Delaney emerged from the back of the house and took in the scene as she entered the foyer. "We're about done here," she informed him, as he lowered the mistletoe he'd been holding up in the air.

"No rush," Warner said. "I thought maybe I could help."

"Thank you, sweetie, but I don't think so. We've done pretty much everything I can think of already."

"Did you meet *them*?" he asked, as casually as he could manage.

"Nothing audible, but I could feel their presence," Maddie's mother said.

"So they're not gone?"

"Not yet," she told him. "But I think they will leave. Soon. They might have some unfinished business keeping them here a little longer."

"Mom says it can take time for them to get the message," Maddie added.

"Oh?" Warner managed, just barely, to keep any sarcasm from his tone, despite his skepticism. Janet had always dabbled in this occult nonsense, but Maddie used to be as cynical as anyone else about her mother's eccentric behavior. More.

Clearly, though, that had changed. Warner could accept that. Maddie could become just as kooky as her mother. He'd get used to it. All Warner wanted was for her to let him be a part of it. Like Joe Delaney, he could support his wife whether he believed in the same things she did or not. Her newly discovered interest in the paranormal only made her more adorable to him than ever.

Now, all he had to do was convince her of that.

"I'll hang up the mistletoe, then. Okay?"

"Sure," Janet said, smiling. Maddie didn't say anything, but when he asked her for a hammer and a nail, she brought him the toolbox.

"Would you like something to drink?" she asked. "I've got some great fresh cider."

"That sounds good," he agreed, pulling a chair below the archway between the foyer and the front hall so he could climb on it to put up the fragrant mistletoe. Maddie gave him one last nervous glance and went down the hallway to the kitchen. *Go ahead, run,* he thought, though he didn't say it aloud, since her mother was standing a few feet away. *I'll be here when you get back.* She might not know it yet, but he had no intention of leaving this house without her giving him a kiss under the mistletoe that he was hanging over the archway.

Janet stayed and watched him as he worked.

The cutting was suspended over the center of the arch by the time Maddie came back, and he climbed off of the chair.

"Care to try it out?" he asked the daughter. She shook her head and handed him the glass of cider she brought for him.

"That's bad luck," the mother said, and stepped up to give him a kiss on the cheek.

"That's what I thought," Warner said, lying through his teeth. He gave Janet a grateful look.

She responded by asking him, "Are we going to see you on Christmas, dear?"

"That depends on Maddie," he answered.

"You do know you don't have to wait for an invitation from her, don't you? You are always welcome."

"I think Warner probably has plans, Mom," Maddie said.

"Oh, yes, your young lady. How is she?"

"Samantha?" he supplied. "She's fine." He didn't know why he didn't just tell Maddie about the situation with Sam. But he couldn't talk about that in front of her mother. There was just too much to say.

Maddie led them both into the living room. "Sit down, sit down. I'll get us something to nibble on," she said. "An appetizer."

Janet refused politely. "I've got to go feed your father."

"I'm not hungry," Warner said. "Thanks."

"Can't I get you anything?" Maddie asked. She sounded somewhat desperate.

"You're a little tense," he commented. "Did everything go well with your ceremony?"

"Fine, fine," Janet said soothingly. "Maddie, settle down somewhere, will you? You're making me nervous."

"Sorry." Maddie subsided into an overstuffed chair next to the couch.

Janet focused her attention on him. "I think it went very well. The house feels peaceful now, don't you think?"

"Umm." Warner didn't know quite how to respond. "Sure," he finally said, lamely. The house didn't feel any different to him, but he hadn't heard any voices or laughter this time, which was definitely an improvement.

"I think we rid it of all the restless spirits that were ready to move on. I didn't meet them, so I don't know what they were like, but from Maddie's description of them, I don't think they were malicious, or mean. They sound like they just need a little help to move on to the next plane of existence," she said happily. "Hopefully, they got it."

"That's great," Warner replied, with all the enthusiasm he could muster.

"I hope it worked" was all Maddie said.

"I've got a good feeling," Janet declared. "I guess we'll know if I'm right soon enough."

"Uh-huh," Warner mumbled. The silence that followed was only slightly less awkward and he didn't know how to break it.

"I guess I'll go," Janet said, rising.

"Okay, Mom," Maddie chirped, jumping up out of her chair.

"Stay," her mother commanded. "I know the way out. You have a guest."

"I don't mind," Warner offered. He wouldn't object to walking both women all the way to the front door. Maddie would almost certainly have to pass under the mistletoe.

"No, you two relax. I can let myself out," she insisted. "It was nice to see you, Warner," she added.

"It was my pleasure, as always," he replied.

Forlorn, Maddie watched her mother leave the room. "Good night," she said, softly. After Janet left, she wouldn't look at him. "I, um, didn't expect to see you here tonight," Maddie said, awkwardly.

This was sort of fun. He had never been able to throw Maddie off balance like this before. He hoped that this display of nervousness meant what he thought it did. He hoped it meant she couldn't stop thinking about the kisses they'd exchanged, either. "I thought I'd drop by and see how it went today," he explained, watching her. She didn't answer. After a minute, he mentioned, "It seems like you and your mom are good."

"I guess," she replied, shifting in her seat.

"Why are you so edgy?"

"I'm not," Maddie protested.

"It's not just me, your mom noticed it, too," he persisted.

"It was sort of a strange day. I guess that I might be reacting to that," she said.

"What did you guys do here?" he asked.

"Well, we purified the house with herbs, which we boiled, and burned, and threw in the fireplace, with the yule log. Actually, before that, I had to cut the yule log so it would fit in the fireplace. I've got the blisters to prove it."

"Let me see," Warner said.

She held out her hand and he scooted forward in his seat to see it. Maddie didn't object, or even seem to notice, when he took her hand in his. She jumped when he kissed the reddened pads of her fingers, though.

"That will make it feel better," he said, at her look of surprise. She opened her mouth to say something, but he jumped in before she could speak. "So what else did you and your mother do to the house?" he asked quickly.

The diversion worked. "We burned holly, and pine, and recited some stuff, like poetry." At his look of disbelief, she nodded. "And a list of our achievements from the past year and our goals for the future, specifically this next year."

"New Year's resolutions? I expected something a bit less, I don't know, traditional," he commented. "Or maybe something more ancient, or primitive, like chanting."

"Me too," Maddie said. "Mom did chant, a little, but it was all pretty New Age."

"Were you disappointed?" he asked.

"I will be, if the ghosts don't go away," she answered. "If they do, then it was definitely worth it."

"It doesn't sound like it was that bad," he said mildly.

"It wasn't," Maddie immediately agreed. "I didn't mean to make it sound horrible or anything like that. I liked it. I'm just not used to talking with my mother quite that openly. It was pretty emotional. We both said we wanted to get to know each other better as one of our goals in '04. I meant it. And she did, too. She almost cried."

"What about you?"

"I got a little choked up, I admit."

"How do you feel now?" he probed.

"Drained. Exhausted, actually. All that soul searching takes it out of you."

"I meant how do you feel about the purification ritual? Do you think it was effective?"

"How should I know? I've never done anything like that before."

"Your mom seemed happy," he pointed out.

"Yeah." She smiled. "I guess a little discomfort is worth it, since I got to do some serious female bonding."

"I thought females didn't need to bond," he said facetiously.

"Females, no. Mothers and daughters, definitely. Even Samantha . . ." Maddie's voice trailed off.

"What?" he prompted.

"It's going to come out wrong," Maddie said.

"No, it's okay. What about Sam?" he asked.

"She told me she and her mom have problems, too. Not that there's anything wrong with that. It's normal, that's what I'm trying to say. That's what she was trying to say."

"I've seen them together and they seem to get along fine. Sammy and her mother."

"She said the same thing. They get along, as long as they don't spend too much time together."

"Sounds like an interesting conversation. Wish I was there," he teased.

"It was," Maddie said defensively. "Interesting, I mean."

Warner found this intriguing. "So what else did she say?"

"Just that I shouldn't worry about it."

"She did, did she? Hmmm," he said thoughtfully.

Maddie squirmed a bit in her seat. She looked rather uncomfortable at the direction that this conversation was taking. "I don't think I ever got the chance to tell you how nice I think she is. Samantha."

That was the understatement of the year.

"Why now?" he asked.

"It was one of my resolutions, if you want to call them that. I'm going to be more supportive of you. And her. You two, together." She faltered.

"A little late," he mused aloud.

"Better late than never?" she suggested, trying,

and failing, to sound as if she didn't feel guilty and ashamed at the way she had behaved.

Warner knew he should just tell her he had broken up with Samantha, but he didn't. He supposed that he was embarrassed about having been so wrong. And he was also worried about what Maddie might say. He wasn't ready to hear her say, "I told you so." Worse yet, she might feel sorry for him.

Anyway, she ought to feel guilty. She might not know it yet, but she had achieved her goal. She broke them up. Perhaps not in the way she planned, or expected, but . . . it was partially her fault. "So how do you plan to support us?" he asked. He wouldn't have been human if he hadn't felt the need to rub it in a little, he thought, justifying his behavior to himself.

"I thought we could start with a nice family dinner. Here. With you and Sam and the kids."

"I don't suppose you'll want to kiss me under the mistletoe in front of her," he said regretfully.

"No," Maddie agreed. "Not a good idea."

"Then I want my kiss now," he said, rising.

"Get your butt back down on that chair, mister. There will be no kissing here tonight," she said sternly.

He stood next to her, instead. "Is that another resolution?" he asked.

"Not really," she answered. "It's a new rule. I just made it up."

"Do you really think you can enforce it?" he asked.

"Warner, if I didn't know any better, I'd say you were flirting with me."

"Maybe I am. It's harmless, right?" He leaned over to kiss her, and Maddie shrank back into the thick cushions of the chair. She didn't get very far before his mouth found hers. For someone who had just instituted a no-kissing rule, she didn't hold much back. In a minute, she was up, out of the chair, eagerly kissing him back. Suddenly, she pulled away. "This isn't right. I— You and Sam—"

"Sammy and I decided you were right about us not being right . . . for each other."

"You did?"

"Aren't you going to say I told you so?"

"Me?" Maddie said, feigning shock and indignation. "I wouldn't do that." Smiling joyfully, she pulled his head back down to hers.

"So what are your other resolutions?" he asked, grinning.

"I forget," she murmured against his mouth.

They stopped talking then. They made their way upstairs, stopping every few feet to kiss and caress each other. They both started to shed their clothes the moment they got through the bedroom door. They unbuttoned her blouse, together, still kissing, then had to separate so he could pull his shirt off over his head. It went flying as she unhooked her bra, and let it slide down her arms to the floor. He toed off one shoe, then hopped on one foot as he pulled off the other without ever taking his eyes off the slide of her slacks down her legs. His hands captured her attention as he unzipped his pants, and she put her hands on his shoulders as he stooped to take them off, then pulled him, with her, onto the bed.

She was beautiful, as he might have expected, and she seemed to enjoy looking at him as well. They had known each other for so long, been so close, that there was no shyness, no coy looks between them. They took each other in, greedily getting their fill, with eyes, and mouths, and hands, too, as they lay next to each other, touching, and tasting and kissing and stroking whichever parts of each other came within reach. He caught her, for a moment, hands stretched out to the side, his legs between hers, her wrists imprisoned in his grasp, until she was still, looking up at him, a dazed and bewildered expression on her face as she tried to tug her hands free. She smiled and reached up to catch his top lip between hers and suck it into her mouth. Distracted, he let her hands go, and she used them to push him over and roll atop him, to straddle him and hold him still, in turn.

Laughing, they grappled with each other, the back of his hand sliding across her breast and making her gasp, her leg sliding between his thighs and making him jump. Then, slowly, they settled on their sides, facing each other, arms around each other's waists, and slid into each other, joining together, and becoming serious, at the same time. They looked into each other's eyes, as they moved their hips into each other, and away, her hands on his shoulders, his hands lower, at her waist, until he couldn't stand not to put his lips on hers, his tongue in her mouth, and slide deep inside her, eyes closed, so he could feel every inch of the warm, silky body touching his. She moved with him, her nails digging into his back as she reached her climax and strained against him, drawing his soul out of his body to float free.

They lay, entwined in each other's arms, gasping for breath. Warner, at least, was unable to move, other than to kiss the top of her head, which rested on his chest.

"I'd say that was . . ." she panted, "almost worth waiting for."

"I'd say we wasted ten years," he retorted.

"We're here, now," she said. "Be positive. Look at that moon." Warner angled his head toward the window to see the shining white circle of light.

"Is it full?" he asked.

"No, I asked Mom today. She said two more days till the last full moon of the year." Maddie yawned.

"She would know."

"All of a sudden, it seems like she knows everything," she said sleepily.

"Oh, yeah? Like what?" he asked, curious.

She didn't answer, and he let her sleep, wondering if her mother had predicted this. There was time. He would ask her in the morning.

CHRISTMAS

CHAPTER
TWENTY-ONE

Her parents had thrown a party every Christmas Eve for as long as Maddie could remember. Friends, family, neighbors, everyone was invited. It was an open house that started after dinner and continued on, through Midnight Mass, which her parents always attended while their friends continued eating and drinking and carousing at the party until the Delaneys returned to open gifts and make merry until the wee hours of the morning.

The party changed with the passing of the years. When Maddie and her brother were very small, it was primarily a party for the grown-ups, but as they grew older, adolescents and then teenagers took over the house for the night while the adults faded into the background. Those same teenagers, and their parents, still attended the annual Christmas party now, many with their own small children in tow. They and her parents' older guests seemed more like contemporaries these days. The generation gap had been bridged.

Through all the changes, the tenor of the party never altered. It was a night for merriment and food and wine and, above all, family and community. Many of the same people attended a night or two of the family's slightly more mellow Kwanza celebration, which started on the night after Christmas and went on for the next six days. They were part of a close-knit group that had come together before she was born. But the annual Christmas party was open to anyone—the more the merrier. It shifted and grew, changed and yet remained the same. It was a touchstone Maddie had always counted on, one night of the year on which, no matter what else was going on with the family, the Delaney house was a cheerful, magical place to be.

This Christmas Eve was no exception. The house was full. The lights twinkled on the tree, and candles flickered in the windowsill and on the mantel. Kids ran about underfoot, and their parents and grandparents got louder and louder as the level of punch in Janet Delaney's huge crystal punch bowl got lower. Patsy and Maddie escaped to her old room, which was the guest room these days, in which the bits and pieces of her parents' unfinished projects were scattered about.

"I'm leaving as soon as I rent out Great-Aunt Becky's house," Maddie announced.

"What's the rush?" Patsy asked.

"It's time that I got my life back on track, that's all," Maddie answered.

"I don't want you to go. It's been nice having you around the last few months," her old friend said, sadly.

"Warner says he wants me to stay. He's trying to talk me out of going."

"That's only natural. We've gotten sort of used to having you around again."

"It has been fun," Maddie said. "I think I might try to find work closer to home in a year or two."

"Why not just stay here now?" Patsy asked.

"Right now it's too complicated. I think I'd better wait until things calm down."

"What things?" her friend asked curiously.

"Warner has changed his mind about the divorce," Maddie said, in a voice barely above a whisper. "He broke up with Samantha."

"So what's wrong with that? That's what you wanted, right? No Sam, and no divorce."

"True," Maddie said slowly. "But maybe it would be best if we got the divorce anyway. I mean, we got it started and everything."

"What changed *your* mind?"

"Warner did. Ever since he broke up with Samantha, he's been . . . acting strange."

"Strange how?"

"He wants us to stay married. Be married for real, I mean," she said. "He says he loves me."

"Oh, that," Patsy said, with an airy wave of her hand. "It's about time."

"What? Are you nuts?" Maddie exclaimed.

"He's been in love with you for years. And you love him, too. It's obvious."

"Not to me, it's not. We're friends. Good friends."

"There's no reason you can't fall in love with a friend. Even a good friend," Patsy said, tongue in cheek. "Just tell him you love him, too. Or," she said as Maddie shook her head, "don't."

"It's not that simple and you know it. What if he's on the rebound? Or worse, what if he's wrong about us? What if we do this, we get together, and then we break up?" Maddie wailed.

"So, you break up. It's not the end of the world. It happens all the time."

"It would be the end of our friendship!"

"You're just scared, admit it, Mad."

"I admit it. I'm more than scared. I'm terrified.

I'm not trying to hide it. I've been saying it all along. That's why I'm getting out of here."

"That sounds like the old Maddie—the one who's always on the run. I thought you were turning over a new leaf?"

"I am. I'm trying. But this isn't what I had in mind. I thought I'd kind of ease into it gradually. I didn't expect a marriage proposal from my own husband."

"I still don't see what you're so freaked out about."

"I guess it's because I can't stay, but I don't really want to go."

"Talk to Warner. Tell him how you feel."

"I can't do that," Maddie said sadly.

"Why on earth not?"

"Because I don't know how I feel," she tried to explain.

"Oh," Patsy said, clearly at a loss. "All I can tell you is you'd better figure it out. And fast."

"Thanks for all your help," Maddie said sarcastically.

"Hey, what are friends for?" Patsy joked. "Come on. We need more to drink. And I want to see if Warner's here yet. I can't wait to see this."

"Patsy Jones, you are a witch."

"Have I told you, you're sounding more and more like your mother every day?" she retorted.

"That's only because I can't say the b-word in this house on Christmas Eve," Maddie countered.

They went back out into the living room and headed for the serving table to refill their wineglasses. Warner hadn't arrived yet, so Patsy joined her husband. Maddie mingled with the crowd, trying not to think about what Warner might say or do when he got there. Ever since the winter solstice, when they had watched the moon rise from her bedroom window, she had been avoiding this showdown. He left early that Monday morning to get to school. He couldn't cancel class, he'd explained, much as he wanted to stay and talk, because his students' final projects were due. She said good-bye, grateful for the reprieve. Maddie didn't know what to say to him.

She had thought of nothing else for the last four days, but she was no closer to an answer now than she had been then. She didn't want things between them to change. She was thrilled by his touch, and she would have had no qualms about becoming his lover, except that that was not what he wanted. It wouldn't be enough for him and they both knew it. She, on the other hand, didn't think she had any more to give.

She loved him. She might even be in love with him. But she wasn't sure. And their friendship was too precious to her to risk it on the possibility that they could have more. She didn't need more. She didn't want more. She had been happy with the way things were. Maybe it wasn't perfect the way it was, that was made clear to her when she thought Warner was going to marry Samantha, but as much as she hadn't wanted that, she wasn't at all sure about this, either. Who was to say that he wasn't just bouncing back, like a rubber ball, to the other extreme? What if it wasn't her he was in love with, but the idea of being in love, getting married, having 2.5 kids, and living happily ever after in his cute little house?

That was all he had ever wanted. And she didn't think his desire for that dream would sustain them if things went wrong: if her work took her away too often, or if she couldn't have children, or if any of a hundred other things happened. They needed more than a pipe dream if they were going to have a lasting marriage.

Her attention was caught by the sight of her father, talking to his friend Vince, standing by the Christmas tree. She watched him as he quickly scanned the room, and found what he was looking for—her mother. He refocused his attention on Vince, but not before Maddie realized that that was what she was afraid was lacking in her relationship with Warner. They were each so independent. So different. They would need much more of what her parents had, love, and tolerance, and respect for each other as individuals, in order to stay together.

It might seem as though they already had that, and she had to admit that they had something close to it, but that might have been because they were friends. What if it didn't last? Making a bigger commitment, trying to live up to their vows, that could ruin everything. Her father seemed to love her mother unconditionally, but Warner disapproved of her, most of the time. Although . . . lately it seemed she caught him staring at her with that half smile on his lips quite often. She found the expression disconcerting, and so hadn't thought about what it might mean, until now. But perhaps it meant that, now that he was in love with her, he would be less critical. Maybe . . .

She was so deep in thought, she didn't hear her mother speak to her.

"Where were you?" Mom asked, after she got her attention.

"Just thinking."

"Did you say hello to Mrs. Althurst? She was asking for you."

"Yes, I saw her, and I said hi."

"She told me that you went to see her back in September and you were acting a little strange. She's been worried about you ever since. And something about being sorry she couldn't come to your party?"

"Oh, right." Maddie had forgotten all about her party. It felt like years ago, rather than a couple of months, since she'd been so paranoid that everyone around her was suddenly going to die. It seemed funny now, and she smiled at the memory. She must have seemed very strange indeed, going around to see everyone she knew over the age of fifty and inviting them to a party. "I was a little freaked out by Becky's death at the time, remember?" she asked her mother. "I invited everyone I ever spoke to, I think."

"Oh, yes," Mom said, nodding. "Thank God you got over that one pretty quickly."

"I wanted to be sure I told all the people that I cared about how I felt about them," Maddie said defensively.

"I remember," Warner said, appearing at her side suddenly.

"Hello, dear," her mother greeted him. "Merry Christmas."

"Merry Christmas, Janet. I brought the mistletoe," he said.

"That's nice, dear," Mom said absently, scooping up a plate that she seemed to have suddenly noticed was empty. "I've got to get more sandwiches. Excuse me."

She hurried off and Maddie was left alone with him. Technically, she corrected herself, she wasn't exactly alone with him. They were in a roomful of people, but she felt as if they were cut off from the others, occupying a bubble of space no one else could enter.

"It worked last time," he said.

"What did?" she asked.

"The mistletoe. I thought I'd give it another

shot. If it does the trick again, I plan to lay in a life-time, year-round supply."

"What are you talking about?" she asked, distracted by his nearness, the cool whiff of snow coming off his clothes and skin, and the underlying clean, male scent that was so familiar to her.

"The other night," he said baldly.

"We can't talk about that here," she warned, with a quick glance around at the party guests who filled the room.

"I'm not about to pass up this opportunity," Warner replied. "No one is paying the least bit of attention to us, anyway."

That wasn't strictly true. Patsy and her husband were watching them with great interest, Maddie noticed. It didn't seem the time to bring it to Warner's attention, though. He was intent on hashing out their dilemma, onlookers or no.

"Why have you been avoiding me?" he asked.

"I was confused. I still am. Maybe we should talk about this later, when I figure out what to say."

"When do you think that might be?" he asked. "Next year?"

"That's only a week away," Maddie pointed out.

"A week is a long time," he said grimly. "Especially when you're waiting to find out if the woman you love feels the same way about you."

"You know I love you, Warner," Maddie said. "That's not the point."

"It is to me," he countered. "But okay, what is the point in your opinion?"

"It's us . . . it's this." She waved her arms wildly, then realizing how that must look, she folded them, sedately, across her chest. Quietly, she continued, "I've been thinking that we're about to jump into something that neither of us is ready for."

"I'm ready. So are you. We're both well over twenty-one, Mad."

"Yes, but a month ago, you were planning to *marry* someone else."

"I have never loved anybody but you, Maddie. That was a mistake."

"So how do you know you're not making another one now?"

"Because I feel it," he said definitely. "Don't you? And don't try to lie to me, you know you're no good at it. Just admit that we belong together."

"Maybe we do, but . . ."

"Maybe is good enough for me. Just tell me you're not going to leave now, when we're just beginning to realize how we really feel about each other."

"It might be better if we cooled it, for now. If this thing between us is real, it will last; if not, then no harm done. And if it does last, I can always come back."

"I don't want to wait," he said forcefully. "I want us to spend time together, and get a new start as husband and wife. We've been in this limbo long enough already."

"All right, let's get out of it. Why don't we go ahead with the divorce and start fresh? Then we can start dating . . . or whatever. That way, there wouldn't be so much pressure."

"If we did that, the divorce wouldn't be any more real than our marriage was."

"We could just try it and see how it goes," she suggested hopefully.

"A divorce doesn't usually work that way," Warner said grimly.

"Our marriage wasn't conventional, who says our divorce would have to be?"

"What if it works out, like I know it will? Do we get married again?"

"Why not?" she asked.

"It just doesn't make sense, that's why not," he argued. "Besides, I love you, Maddie, and I want to stay married to you. For real this time. Please give us a chance."

"I will," she said. "I want to. You know that. I'm not saying we shouldn't talk about it, or even sleep together. But marriage is such a big step . . ."

"The beauty of this is that we are already married, and committed to each other. I don't know why that scares you so much. That part, at least, isn't new. Not that I wouldn't marry you again, in a second. I'd love to."

"Once was enough!" Maddie said quickly. "And I think the fact that we're having this conversation proves it."

"Once was good. Twice would be even better. But we can worry about renewing our vows after we get this settled. Right now, I need to know what you're planning on doing next. I thought we had something special that night. Something that was important enough to stay and fight for."

"It was great, but didn't you . . . ." She leaned in closer. "Didn't you think it was a little bit strange? I mean, after all these years."

"Honestly?" he asked. She nodded. "It felt perfectly natural to me to wake up in your bed," he answered.

"Well, it felt weird to me."

"Is that why you ran away?"

"Partly," she admitted.

"I never would have slept with you if I thought it would scare you so much. I thought it would make us closer."

"Since when?" Maddie asked.

"Since I realized that I was in love with you," Warner said.

"And when, exactly, was that?" she inquired. "When we were rolling around in my bed?"

"I think I've been in love with you since the beginning," he said. "But I didn't realize it until after you tried to seduce me."

"I sure couldn't tell that I had that effect on you," she said.

"Maybe I should have told you how I felt before I acted on it, but I was so happy. Happier than I've ever been in my life. And you were so cute, trying to be supportive of my relationship with Samantha when you were obviously dying of envy. I couldn't resist rattling your cage. Just a little."

"A little?" Maddie said indignantly. "That whole show of hanging up the mistletoe *in front of my mother?*"

"Your mother always said we should stop messing around. She knew."

"Huh! That was her scheming to get more grandchildren."

"So let's give her some."

She bristled. "Do you think that's funny? What is wrong with you, Warner? I told you I am not ready for this. It's just too much for me. I'm really sorry." It broke her heart, but she had to make him understand that she was not going to suddenly change her mind, and her entire life, at his whim.

"I think you underestimate yourself. And I'm not ready to give up on making this marriage work," he said. "I loved watching the moon rise with you and I'm not going to just go away and forget about it because you are afraid. I will never let you go, Maddie. I love you."

"It's time to go to Mass," Patsy said, popping up at Warner's side. "Are you two coming?"

"Umm, sure," Maddie replied. Anything was better than this.

Warner appeared to share her feelings. "Okay," he said.

He sat next to her in church. At first, she was careful not to let any part of her body touch his, but her anger and frustration slowly faded away as the candles flickered and the choir sang.

On the walk home, when Warner laced his fingers through hers, it felt good. She was sandwiched between him and her father and mother. Teddy and Jordana and the kids were a little ways ahead, talking and laughing. Maddie supposed that that was how Warner pictured them looking someday. She couldn't imagine it. On the other hand, this was nice, too. Her parents were quiet, content, possibly thinking of church, or anticipating their arrival at their house where all their friends were waiting for them. Not a bad life. Not at all.

If Warner would be happy with that, she thought she could be, too. She did love him, despite everything she had said and in spite of her fears about their future.

He was right. She was in love with him, too. She just didn't trust it. Yet.

Back at her parents' house, they exchanged a few gifts with friends and with each other at the urging of the children. Warner pulled a small velvet box from his pocket, and, despite everything that had happened, she wasn't surprised. Maddie took it with trembling hands. It contained two simple gold bands, one larger than the other. Wedding rings for Christmas. It was the kind of romantic gesture she would expect from Warner. It was also the kind of hokey sentimentality she spent her whole life trying to avoid.

"Whenever you're ready," he said softly, for her ears alone. "I'll be waiting."

That did it. Just when she thought he was being an insensitive jerk, he had to go and say something like that. Something that made her feel like she'd be nuts to turn him down.

She couldn't hide his gift from her niece, who was eagerly awaiting a glimpse. To be honest, she didn't want to try. The rings were beautiful.

Everyone wanted to see, and they all oohed and aahed as Lorraine paraded around the circle with the box.

"Beautiful," Jordana said.

"Does this mean what I think it means?" Patsy asked.

"I agreed *not* to divorce him, if that's what you mean," Maddie told her, which earned a burst of laughter from those gathered around them. Warner's answering smile was guarded. She hadn't really answered the question, and he knew it.

Maddie couldn't figure out how she felt. The emotion that dominated was a strange mix of happiness and sorrow. She didn't think she was supposed to feel like crying at this moment. She escaped out onto the porch, eventually, when she thought that no one would notice. She was wrong about that, though. Her father followed her.

"I wanted to congratulate you," he said. "But I don't think I'm supposed to do that. The groom gets all the congratulations. The bride gets good wishes."

"Do you suppose that's because once he's bagged her, supposedly he's done his part? The rest is up to her?"

"I doubt it," Dad said. "Marriage is a partnership. It won't last unless both of you work at it."

"Mmm," Maddie murmured. She thought about that for a moment. "Can I ask you something, Daddy?"

"Sure, anything, sweetheart."

"Do you and Mom both work at it? Because, to me, it looks like you're the one who makes all the compromises. You live the way she wants to. You go where she wants to go. You hardly ever seem to ask for, or get, anything you want."

"Like what?" he asked, looking surprised.

"Peace," Maddie said. "She gets you all caught up in her stuff, which I don't think you're that interested in, and then you have to clean up the mess."

"Is that what you think?" he asked.

"That's how it looks."

"Look closer, Maddie, honey. If it seems like I'm the one who does the giving, and she's the one who does the taking, which is what it sounds to me that you're saying, then you're not seeing us at all. Your mom has given me everything I want out of life. To you that may not seem like much, but that's because you're so much more like she is. You are curious about everything, and you want to see it all, and do it all, like Janet. We go where she wants, on vacations, because if she left it up to me, we'd never leave. But I like going with her. She makes everything exciting, and fun. Your mother is never boring, never dull. And so my life is never dull."

"That doesn't tire you out?"

"Yeah, sure, but in a good way. I love it. Don't you know that?"

"I guess I didn't. But I do now. Thanks, Dad."

And later, when she said good-bye to Warner on the porch, held in his strong, warm arms, Maddie was finally sure she had made the right decision.

"I love you," he murmured into her hair.

"I love you, too," she said, and meant it. She was in love with him, and she wanted to be with him forever. But she was deathly afraid that when he let her go, and walked away, her doubts would all come rushing back. What was she doing, taking a chance on hurting him so badly? He was her best friend.

"Warner—" she started to say.

"Don't be scared," he said soothingly. "Everything will be all right. I promise."

Maddie felt a weight lift from her heart. They were in this together, the way they always had been. Which meant that it would all work out, because they would take care of each other. He would always be there to comfort her when she was afraid. She would never leave him. That was what marriage was supposed to be about, and they had had that all along.

NEW YEAR'S DAY

CHAPTER TWENTY-TWO

Warner woke up early on New Year's Day filled with a sense of purpose. He slid out of bed, careful not to disturb his wife, who was snoring gently on the right side of the bed. His side, until a week ago.

He dressed, quickly and quietly, and let himself out of the room, and then out of the house, carefully closing the door behind him so that it didn't make a sound. The revving of the car's engine seemed incredibly loud in the early morning stillness, causing his heart to race right along with it. He sped over to Maddie's house and, with hands that weren't quite steady, let himself in the back door with the key she had given him. Once inside, he leaned back against the door and took a deep breath.

"Relax," he said to himself. He wasn't doing anything wrong. He wasn't even likely to get caught. Maddie probably wouldn't stir for hours. They had been out until the wee hours of the morning the night before.

Their New Year's Eve celebration had been like

a dream. They had a romantic dinner, and danced, and drank champagne, and at midnight, they shared a magical kiss. To anyone watching, they probably looked like a million other young couples, but Warner felt that kiss held the promise that he and Maddie hadn't made yet. Not in words.

When they got home, he listened to his answering machine while Maddie went on up to the bedroom, their bedroom, which she had been moving into all week, slowly but surely. Warner knew she didn't feel as comfortable as he did with the change in their relationship. She still looked slightly surprised, if happy, to find him there when she woke up in the morning. It was as if she half expected him to suddenly change his mind and decide this new arrangement wasn't going to work out after all.

There were five messages on his answering machine. Three from friends wishing him a happy new year and two from Janet.

"Where are your rings, dear? I keep seeing your hands, and they aren't there" was all she said in the first message, then abruptly hung up. The second, half an hour later, was longer and even more eerie, though she started it by claiming, "I didn't mean to make you nervous or anything with my earlier message. I kept getting that niggling feeling that something was wrong, and suddenly I realized it was because of your wedding rings. Warner, and Maddie, if you're listening, it's time you put them on now."

Warner had wondered what happened to the rings. Maddie had taken them with her on Christmas Eve and he hadn't seen them since. But they had to be somewhere here, in her house. Maddie had brought a number of her things over to his house, unpacked them, and actually put them away. Warner, thrilled, had helped her. So he knew the rings weren't there. He had searched her purse and coat pockets the night before, after listening to Janet's messages.

Knowing Maddie, he they could be anywhere. He tried to be methodical in his search. He started with the obvious places: a jewelry box, a larger box of knickknacks and keepsakes, and the drawers of the vanity table, in her bedroom. After he had thoroughly searched that room, he couldn't help getting a little bit nervous, but he couldn't give up. Not yet.

They weren't in the refrigerator, which he knew to be one of her favorite hiding places. He did find a number of important-looking documents, and her grandmother's pearls, there, in a cereal box. He checked the bottom of the laundry basket, too, where he found a waterproof makeup bag containing a ruby ring and a largish collection of amethyst and silver earrings, necklaces, and bracelets. The girl was strange, but he believed he knew her well enough to solve this mystery, if he kept at it.

Janet called when he'd been searching for a little over an hour. "Hi, Warner," she said, as soon as he picked up the receiver. "Check in Becky's hidey-hole. It's behind a loose stone in the fireplace, third from the top on the right."

"Thanks," he said, but he was talking to dead air. She had already hung up the telephone. One of these days, he was going to have to ask Janet how she did that.

Sure enough, the velvet box was hidden in the small dry space, just as his mother-in-law had foreseen. The rings were still inside. He rushed home to find that, thankfully, Maddie hadn't awakened during his absence.

He brought her breakfast in bed, a ritual they

had discovered they both enjoyed. They ate there together, wearing matching oversize T-shirts from the collection he kept for coaching Little League.

"Your mother is coming today, right?" Maddie asked, biting her lip nervously.

"Yes, and will you please stop worrying about it? She'll be fine."

"I'm sure *she* will. I'm the one who needs protection," Maddie claimed.

Warner had to admit that a week wasn't a very long period of adjustment, but since he slid into his role as her husband with ease, it seemed funny to him that it was such a leap for her to think of herself as his wife. They had been such good friends, for so long, that they had an advantage over most newlyweds. The really hard parts were behind them; they didn't have to worry about such things as getting to know each other's friends, or whether the two families would mesh. Ted and Jordan already treated him like a brother, their kids accepted them as an uncle, and her parents . . . well, that had never been a problem. He and Joseph and, especially, Janet, had a strong relationship already. His mother, however, was another story. She never had understood either his marriage, or his moving to Richland Township, and she and Maddie had always circled around each other, and him, like she-wolves, guarding their cubs. It was a territorial thing, he guessed.

Mama Davis had been much more pleased to hear about the divorce than she was to hear that they were going to try and make their marriage work. "It's not like there's anything she can do to us. We're adults. And we have been married for the last ten years," he said.

"I don't think your mother is going to see it that way," Maddie warned. "She never liked me."

"I like you. That's all that matters," he said, and leaned over to kiss her. He took the small black velvet box from the drawer in the side table where he'd hidden it before waking her up. "I thought we might want to wear these, as a kind of protective shield," he suggested.

"Really?" she asked doubtfully. "Don't you think she might find that a bit threatening?"

"It's a wedding ring, not a gun," he said, keeping his tone light.

She took the box from his hand as tentatively as if it were a firearm, and opened it slowly. She started down at the golden bands, as if in a trance.

"What are you thinking?" Warner asked, when he could no longer stand the suspense.

"I don't know. I guess I just don't think it's me," she said, closing the box again and handing it back to him. Warner felt a sharp pang of disappointment, but was careful not to let his feelings show.

For all her insight into her daughter's psyche, Janet Delaney was not always right about Maddie, apparently.

"Would you like to exchange them? For something less traditional, maybe?" he asked.

"No, it's not that. They're perfect," Maddie replied. "But I feel like we're still breaking the rules, you know?"

"Not really," he answered.

"I mean, it's fun. Like having a love affair, but one with my own husband. I'm enjoying it."

Warner wished he could say the same thing, but he had had enough of that feeling during the years of his fake marriage. The allure of that particular game had worn off, for him, a long, long time ago. He wanted normalcy, some semblance of a conventional marriage. "You are having a love affair with your husband," he pointed out.

"You know what I mean," Maddie said. "It's that delicious, slightly naughty feeling you get when you know you're allowed to do something, strictly speaking, but it's a little risque." She slid down on the bed, and stretched like a cat. "Like wearing really provocative underwear." She smiled flirtatiously. "Or eating dessert first."

He could live with being dessert, Warner thought. For a while, anyway. "It was just an idea," he said, dropping the rings, still tucked in their little box, back in the drawer of the side table.

Something in his tone of voice must have caught her attention, because she examined his face carefully, then asked him, "Are you all right?"

"Sure. Fine," he answered.

"Okay, give me the darn thing," Maddie said.

"I don't want you to feel like you have to wear it for me—" he began.

She cut him off. "Just give it to me," she commanded.

He fished the box out of the drawer and handed it to her.

She untied his ring, and handed it to him; then she took out her own and held it in the palm of her hand. "Funny that you happened to have this here now," she said suspiciously.

"Your mom mentioned that today might be a good day to leave it lying around somewhere," he told her.

"Hmm," she murmured, slipping it over the tip of her finger and off again. "How did you find it?" Warner shrugged. He couldn't tell her he spent an hour searching every nook and cranny of her house. "I thought I hid it pretty well," she said.

"You did," he confessed under her penetrating, questioning gaze. "Your mother told me where to look."

"It figures." She grinned, ruefully, as she slipped the ring on her finger at last. It had all been worth it, to see his ring on her finger. It felt as though the final piece had fallen into place. Their marriage was finally real. And so was their future, together.

"It's hard to keep a secret from your mother, especially when she's got psychic abilities," Maddie said.

"Even when she doesn't," Warner agreed, as he slipped his ring on, too. He knew his mother wouldn't believe in the rings the way he did. The symbolism wouldn't be lost on her, but she had never trusted Maddie. He just hoped she wouldn't say anything to his skittish wife that would make her run away again. He'd just managed to get her ensconced in his house, and his life, and he really didn't want her haring off before he'd even had a chance to convince her that their marriage wasn't going to be the ordeal she seemed to imagine it would be.

"Don't worry, Warner," Maddie said, running her hand across his forehead. She frequently did that. Smoothing the worry lines away, she called it. "We'll get through this just fine."

"I know," he said, smiling down at her. "I have faith."

Dear Readers,

I hope you enjoyed meeting Maddie and Warner, her mother, his girlfriend, her arch enemy, and his two favorite kids. The story that brought them all together was fun to write. I am left with only one regret, which is that I couldn't figure out how to give Sabrina a daddy for Christmas. That was the original plan, but as you may or may not know, the story doesn't always come out the way that the author hopes it will. Things come up. The characters take over. Authors end up doing things they never thought they'd do, such as trying to boil fennel. In my next book, hopefully, the research will not require going anywhere near the stove, since I am hopeless in the kitchen.

Cross your fingers for me and keep an eye out for that next book.

Sincerely,
Roberta Gayle

ABOUT THE AUTHOR

Author Roberta Gayle has written five contemporary romances, including *Coming Home; Nothing but the Truth; Mad About You; Something Old, Something New;* and *Worth Waiting For;* and two novellas that were published in the anthologies *Seasons Greetings* and *Bouquet.* She began her career as an author by writing two historical romances, *Sunshine and Shadows* and *Moonrise,* and someday she'd love to return to that genre. Meanwhile, her latest novel, *The Holiday Wife,* is a romp in which the old-fashioned concept of the marriage of convenience is given a modern spin and mixed liberally with age-old questions about popular subjects such as why mothers drive their daughters crazy, and how do the stars really affect our lives down here on planet Earth.